W9-AJO-487

A YEAR OR SO WITH EDGAR

For David McDermott

George V. Higgins

ALSO BY THE AUTHOR:

The Friends of Eddie Coyle
The Digger's Game
Cogan's Trade
A City on a Hill
The Friends of Richard Nixon
The Judgment of Deke Hunter
Dreamland

A Year or So with Edgar

GEORGE V. HIGGINS

HARPER & ROW, PUBLISHERS
New York, Hagerstown,
San Francisco, London

Portions of this work originally appeared in the *Washingtonian* magazine.

A YEAR OR SO WITH EDGAR. Copyright © 1979 by George V. Higgins. All rights reserved. Printed in the United States of America. No part of this book may be used or reproduced in any manner whatsoever without written permission except in the case of brief quotations embodied in critical articles and reviews. For information address Harper & Row, Publishers, Inc., 10 East 53rd Street, New York, N.Y. 10022. Published simultaneously in Canada by Fitzhenry & Whiteside Limited, Toronto.

FIRST EDITION

Designed by Eve Kirch

Library of Congress Cataloging in Publication Data

Higgins, George V   1939–
  A year or so with Edgar.
  I. Title
PZ4.H6365Ye 1979 [PS3558.I356]   813'.5'4   78–20206
ISBN 0–06–011873–3

79 80 81 82 83 84 10 9 8 7 6 5 4 3 2 1

For Loretter

Prologue

Three days after I finished this book, I rewarded myself with an afternoon of golf. I enjoy golf, although I do not play it very well (low 90s); I console myself with the opinion once voiced by a sycophantic assistant pro at Congressional, to which I belong: he said that I would shoot in the low 80s if I could only manage to play more often. And if, of course, I took many more expensive lessons from him. Unable to do the first, and unwilling to do the second, I replied that golf was usually a way for me to relax and occasionally a way for me to discuss business with a good client, utterly free of telephone intrusions from other clients who are human hatcheries for emergencies.

On this particular Thursday afternoon, though, golf served as a mere palliative. It was the only way that I could bring myself to confer with Duncan Brann. I loathed Duncan Brann, and I found it difficult to conceal my relief when he suffered a fatal heart attack, leaving the family-controlled Brann Marine Fabricators Corporation to his congenial son, Joe. My firm held onto the corporation's legal business in Washington. I was no longer obliged to nod appreciatively as Duncan, with the features of a carpenter ant and the expression of one feasting on the main beam of an old and valuable home, reported his latest excesses with Las Vegas ladies whom he was pleased to call "showgirls" (he did concede that he always tipped them, usually one hundred dollars). Duncan's adventures in marathon sex never seemed real to him until he had regaled me with their details—I am by no means sure that they were real to anyone else, even then—and Brann Marine always had urgent legal matters for immediate discussion whenever Duncan returned from the desert, full of tales about "snatch" and "pussy." All bullshit.

The only way I could endure these recitations by the old man—when he died, he was fifty-five, seven years older than I am now, but he seemed old to me from the day that the senior partner in the firm, Ed Bradley, handed him on to me, the newest partner—was to do something else while I listened. Preferably something done outdoors, so that when Duncan completed his confidences, in a very loud voice, I would not be confronted with a secretary blushing crimson outside my office. That was golf.

Duncan belonged to Larkspur, out in Fairfax, Virginia. Larkspur is not an especially exclusive club, but neither is it the sort of place where a rational human being would expect to encounter a Duncan Brann. Duncan should have been out on the public links, early Saturday morning, loading his golf bag with six-packs of National Bohemian taken from the cooler in the trunk of his white Coupe de Ville, joking with two truckers and a postal supervisor about arriving on the first tee before the "niggers," as he always referred to blacks, got home from stealing chickens. But he was a member at Larkspur because it was a major investment of another of our clients, which had gotten into considerable financial difficulty as a result of utter mismanagement in 1972 and had admitted several Duncan types, at outrageous fees, to stay afloat. The only defect in the strategy, the client said ruefully, was that after it succeeded, the Duncans remained.

Duncan, as usual, had played quite well that day. Then the sky darkened as though some merciful God had pulled a window shade on the sun. We trotted from the fifteenth tee quickly enough to reach the clubhouse just slightly drenched, Duncan only three strokes back. He was a terrible man, a lecher and a bore, but he was, for all of his obesity, a pretty-fair country golfer. He asked me once: "How come you don't just let me beat you? Once. I'd settle for fuckin' once." And I said: "Because you'd hate me if I did that, Duncan, and I'd lose your business, as well as the match." I said it heartily. "I won't mind if you beat me, Duncan, but I've more respect for you than to take a dive for you." I did not say that I have more respect for myself as well. I may lose, but I don't toady.

At the clubhouse, Duncan invited me for the usual drink. And, I presumed, the usual horror show—once, in the lounge, having more adventures to recount than he had been able to finish in the regulation eighteen holes, he wound up with this flourish: "Tell me, Quinn, you know how come we act this way? The damned fool things we do for pussy, a lousy fuckin' goddamned piece of ass? Whaddaya think it is we're tryin' tah find in there with our little flashlights, huh? Think we grow up, thinkin' we must've left somethin' behind, and we spend our whole life huntin' for it? That it, Quinn? You think? Huntin' in cunt?" I was glad, that rainy Thursday, to have two excuses for him, in addition to the tried and tested one I always used, about having to get home to work on papers.

"Can't do it, Dunc," I said. "I want to get a shower and some dry clothes. . . ."

"I'll wait around," Duncan said anxiously. Duncan always offered to wait around while I showered. Duncan did not stink, so I assumed he showered at home. The only explanation I could ever muster for his refusal to shower at his club did not involve the fear of picking up athlete's foot, which he had mentioned; I think Duncan had what he feared was abnormally small equipment and did not wish to display it in derogation of his stories about the showgirls.

"Ah, thanks, Duncan," I said, "but I've got something else to do when I come out.

"Back to the office," Duncan said resentfully, as he always did.

"Ultimately," I said. "But the fact of the matter is, one of my college classmates's got a son entering George Washington Law School this fall. The kid's down here to visit a girlfriend, or something, and the guy asked me to see the kid and give him some advice about Washington law firms. That sort of thing. The kid's staying out here, so rather than drag him all the way into the city, I told him I'd see him after our game. *Then,*" I said, "I've got to go back to the office." I could not resist that and felt mean after I had done it. "I'll be lucky if I get home before midnight." The apology was an outright lie. I had no home to go to, and it would be a long time before I obtained another one, if I could manage it at all; the yawp of loneliness which filled me I took to be the penance for my falsehood.

Duncan was appeased. I could always appease Duncan. Ed Bradley knew I could. That was why I got Duncan. He liked his lawyers to be busy and also to be compassionate toward the offspring of their friends. It was Duncan who had compelled the manager at Larkspur to hire Terry O'Keefe, the son of the night watchman at our old offices at 1175 Connecticut Avenue, as a full-time bartender. Without that job, there would have been no American University education for young Terry. "I'll see ya," Duncan said. "Hey, I'll call ya when I get back from my next trip, okay?" He winked at me. "I'd ask ya to come along," he said, "but I know that the better half wouldn't stand for it, and if you're pussy-whipped, you're pussy-whipped. You're still my favorite lawyer." He slapped me on the shoulder, and I made at least a feeble grin.

There was no need for anyone to fear fungal infection in the Larkspur men's locker room. It was clean, with new, waterproof blue tweed carpeting, and perhaps because others interrupted in their play by the rain had chosen Duncan's route to the lounge in order to put something wet on the inside as well as the outside, I had it all to myself as I showered. Apparently the two men who selected the next row of lockers, as I sat drying my feet in the guest row, assumed that they enjoyed similar privacy. They made no inquiry as to whether anyone else was around, and since I have picked up a good deal of useful information by listening to conversations not meant for my ears, I made no effort to alert them.

". . . told me about her," the first man said. "Must've been, oh, five, six years ago. Pointed her out to me at this reception they had down at the Pan American Union. Forget what the hell it was for. Didn't even remember seeing her, till last night, far as that goes."

I thought I recognized the voice. It had a peculiar timbre, the sort of voice which you would remember if you heard it from a total stranger conversing with another stranger in an elevator. The inflection was odd, too. It was nothing foreign or of regional dialect; while the man did not sound like John Wayne, or Bing Crosby, or Jimmy Stewart, he did have a distinctive voice. One which an enemy would find easy to imitate and mock.

" 'Arthur Gill introduced us,' she said, 'awhile ago, I'm afraid.' " The speaker adopted what he evidently considered to be a British accent.

The name Gill was enough for me to recognize the speaker as a man whom I never met, and never wanted to. He served as a minor partner in Temple, Gill & Massey when my firm had offices on the same floor at 1175 Connecticut. The fellow's bowels and bladder seemed to be synchronized with those of another fellow in his firm, as well as with my own. Whenever

5

I went to the men's room to relieve either of mine, they seemed to be in there, relieving theirs, chatting as they squatted in their stalls.

Sometimes it was about how much they had won or lost, betting on the Redskins. On other occasions their subject was a new female employee, who evidently appealed to both of them. I knew, six or seven years ago, a great deal about how each of them got along with his wife. How many children they had. What they believed best suited to extirpate the crabgrass in their lawns out in suburban Virginia. I heard about their drinking bouts, mutual and separate, and I knew, without desiring to know, which Washington *Post* features they found agreeable, and which offensive. I forgot all that information, quite cheerfully, the instant we moved Bradley, Bellow, Knight & Quinn to 1665 M Street, taking a whole floor in a new building to double the size of the firm. But I remembered that voice.

That recollection did not surprise me. What did surprise me was my virtual certitude of the identity of the woman he was describing.

"Well," the first man said, "the minute she mentioned Gill, the old fucker, and I heard that accent, I knew right off who she was. 'The best blow job in Washington,' Arthur told me. 'Loves it. Absolutely loves it. Got the whole shebang in her mouth one night, and I never felt a tooth. Thought my own brains were coming out when I shot my wad, but never a nip. Swallows it, too. Never gags on it, like the others do that say they like to swallow it and then get stuck with it in their mouths, and all of a sudden they gotta go pee-pee, so they can spit it inna the flush. Offered to fuck her one night, sort of Services Rendered kind of thing, you know? Wouldn't let me.' "

"Arthur Gill is an asshole," the second man said.

I agreed, silently, with that. Arthur Gill is an asshole. He has been for years. I did not recognize the second speaker's voice. I continued to dust my feet with powder and dress

6

myself. And I waited for the latest news of that meek, no, demure, lovely little British girl, whom Edgar Lannin, my old friend, had shown off to me, back years ago when his marriage was coming apart, and he wanted me to see that he'd be better off when it collapsed.

"This is Linda Morse," Edgar had said proudly to me, his sport jacket rumpled, his eyes bleary, his face filled with exploded veins. "Works at the British Embassy. Linda, this here's Peter J. Quinn. Oldest and dearest friend." At the time I had thought: Oh, my God. This kid can't be more'n twenty-three; Edgar's pushing forty, robbing cradles like Leopold and Loeb.

I said to Edgar, when I saw him next: "Hey, old pal, old buddy, why don't you leave the kids alone, huh? Pick on somebody your own size." Edgar told me Linda Morse was twenty-four, able to choose her own escorts. He also told me, as I recall, to go and fuck myself. "Or Jeanne, if she doesn't have a headache."

Edgar was drinking too much in those days. I went home that night, filled with righteousness, a solid family man, providing for my brood while wayward Edgar defiled his manhood, pursuing young cupcakes.

"Arthur Gill may be an asshole," the first man said, "but Arthur Gill knows ginch like K. C. Jones knows basketball. The Bullets may not win the championship, but it's not because K. C. don't know the game. Arthur may not score every time that he goes out, but the guy's pushing seventy, and he still knows where to get a piece of ass on short notice. So I said to this broad. . . ."

"How old is she?" the second man said.

"Getting along," the first man said. "She's gotta be thirty, thirty-five. She's no rookie. She's got the hair all Farah Fawcett-Majors, and the boobs in one of those French bras so that the nipples stick out through her tank-top just like they do on the kids and you're supposed to think she hasn't started to sag yet. But they do, and she's got a few miles on her.

"Look, that's what Arthur told me, and if Arthur told me,

he told a lot of other guys, too. Arthur was never a man, keep a good thing to himself. Especially since he's worried about his prostate now."

"Should think he would be," the second man said.

"Well," the first man said, "I dunno if Arthur was right, back when he introduced us, but I can tell you something: if he wasn't, he can sure spot a comer. You wanna get your brains blown out some night, get ahold of Linda Morse. She will make you feel things you never would expect in an Algerian whorehouse."

"What's she do?" the second man said.

"Already told you," the first man said, "she gives you. . . ."

"No, no," the second man said, somewhat irritably. "I mean. . . ."

"She says she's an interior decorating consultant," the first man said. "But she lives at the Watergate, condo, and you wanna get ahold of her, try the doorman there. But don't tell her you'd like to come up and see her sometime, because I think what the explanation for this thing is is this: some guy that's out of town a lot is keeping her, and what she does to guys like me and you is just a little free-lancing. Keeping her tongue in, you know? Tell her your wife's out of town and you need a companion for some goddamned embassy thing, or any other goddamned thing you can come up with, and offer her fifty bucks. For the evening."

"I can't take no hooker to no embassy," the second man said.

I had finished dressing by now, having stalled my appointment with Don Talbot's kid as long as I could. I dread those interviews. I always expect the worst, the snotty, preppy progeny of good, tough people, who endowed their offspring with all the material rewards of their own hard-won success and somehow let the kids conclude that they deserved it, by the grace of God. The confidence of those kids is insufferable. To be patronized by a kid who has gotten away with sneering at his father's back for years is an experience to be welcomed in the same mood as a root canal.

"Asshole," the first man said. "Her old man's got a tap on that line. You ask her if she'll blow you, he's gonna hear it and get mad. You pick her up. You say you had a lousy day at the office, and how about just havin' a nice dinner at Paul Young's, or something. You get there, you buy the dinner, it costs you ninety bucks, and you leave three fifties onna table. Excuse yourself, go to the men's room. You come back, one of those fifties is gone. You look at the table. You throw a twenty on the pile. You leave and get blown."

"I can't afford a hundred-and-seventy-dollar blow job," the second man whined as I passed the lockers where they sat. They did not look up at me.

"You're not paying a hundred and seventy," the first man was explaining. "The blow job is fifty. What's the matter, you don't like a nice dinner?"

To reach the lounge and terrace of the Larkspur Country Club, you pass the ballroom where the children of privilege are bored at Saturday dances, alternating with the Saturday dances when their parents arrive half drunk in outlandish outfits. The shine on the floor reminds you of that on a Cadillac limousine in livery service: the gloss is high, but the effect is forced, and you feel confident that the upholstery on the French Provincial chairs, lined up against the walls and drapes, would prove upon examination to be tacky, with dim stains.

I went into the dimness of the paneled bar. Terry was polishing glasses to be filled for the relaxation of the people sitting under the awning on the patio, watching the heavy rain etch the soil on the eighteenth fairway, where a slothful ground crew had failed to keep the grass hardy. I said hello to the kid.

"Mister Quinn," he said.

"How's it going, Terry?"

"I had worse days," he said. There was a copy of Faulkner's

Light in August open on the service bar beside him. "I'll have better. This summer school thing's a bitch."

"Should've taken it off," I said. "You could use a little break now and then, you know."

"Mister Quinn," he said, "if I did, my dad'd get them to put me on the morning cleaning crew, little extra money. All I want to do is finish up as fast as I can. Get out, and make a living for myself."

"I thought you wanted medical school," I said. "Your marks okay?"

"Mister Quinn," Terry said, "I haven't been off the Dean's List since I got in there. But I don't know what the hell I want. It was my father, wanted medical school, but he never even got college. So I have to get college, because he didn't. And then I'm supposed to get medical school, because he didn't. Yeah, fine. Great. But what about me? Where do I come in? I'm twenty-one years old. I'll be thirty before I can practice medicine. And then suppose I don't like it? What do I do when I'm thirty-two, and I got a family, and I'm a doctor, but I don't wanna be a doctor? What do I do then? Hand the degrees to my father, and let him be the doctor while I go do the night watchman thing? I'm getting captured, and I'm not even in the Army."

"Terry," I said, "I'd like a Beck's Beer."

Terry cracked the beer and handed it to me.

"Mister Brann's bill. Is there a kid named Jerry Talbot here?"

"Asking for you?" Terry said.

"Yeah," I said.

Terry's expression was pleasant enough. "He's out on the patio in his crocodile shirt from Britches and his nice white pants and loafers from someplace else," Terry said. "He told me to put his Kirs on your bill. Should I put them on Mister Brann's, too?"

"Yup," I said. "And do something else for me, okay, Terry?"

"What's that, Mister Quinn?" he said, using the innocent face.

"When you start getting discouraged," I said, "try not to. And if that doesn't work, don't blame me for your troubles, all right?"

"I don't intend to have any, Mister Quinn," Terry said. "I'm gonna start off, doing what I like, and if that doesn't work, I still won't have any troubles, because I'll be doing what I like anyway."

Jerry Talbot had a pair of wraparound sunglasses perched atop his sun-bleached light brown hair. He had the smooth, even features of a child of good-looking parents, and he wore them in what he thought was a successful attempt to mask what he believed to be a fearsome, feral cunning. He was wrong on both counts. But he was only twenty-two and could perhaps be expected to acquire a few redeeming marks of distress on his features, and a little confidence in his animal craftiness, before he was turned loose upon the world to accomplish real damage. "Jerry Talbot?" I said, wanting to say: "John Dean?"

Jerry arranged his face in what was intended to be an expression of eager and deferential expectation. But his eyes examined me the way that a pawnbroker peers at a cheap diamond from behind his loupe. He was appraising my life expectancy; utility to him, the possible downside risk of offending me; the best available means of cozying up to me; and the likely amount of effort involved as compared to the expenditure of the same amount of effort devoted to the cozening of somebody else.

"Mister Quinn," Jerry said, "I certainly appreciate you taking the time out of your busy schedule to talk to me like this. I would've been happy to come in to see you at your office."

It was about seven or eight years ago, when the first grown children of my classmates—those who had married early; I married late, as did Edgar—began to call for my estimable guidance. It was then still considered an honor to have been

11

Special Counsel to the President. Not only by me, but by them and their parents. I was honored by their honor. I made hour after hour available in my actually quite-busy schedule to address their career problems, direct them to government agencies, and even tell them why it was that they could not afford to live in Georgetown, the way Jack Kennedy had. To tell the truth, I rather enjoyed it. It was kind of fun.

Then it began to dawn on my partners that I was not billing very much for the hours I spent with my adopted nieces and nephews, mostly nephews. And it registered on me that I was not cagily placing future allies in critical positions on congressional committee staffs and in federal regulatory agencies, where they would be receptive to their old friend's pleadings for surcease of his clients. No, I was nurturing, I believe the phrase was, a generation of vipers, with memories so short that they would bite me and my clients as readily as they would bite anybody else. Just so long as there was somebody to bite.

I got a kid a job—*I got the kid the job*—on the Federal Trade Commission which positioned him to harpoon a product upon which one of my clients had spent almost twelve million dollars. When I went up to see him, it was as though I had been the job supplicant, and he the interviewer. Where it had been "Mister Quinn" before, it was now "Peter," and he was quite determined in his decision to hurl that harpoon. "In the public interest," of course. Which was bullshit—it was in the elective interest of the Congressman whom he'd been cultivating for a committee General Counsel's slot. And that was why he sank my client. It was also when I began to learn that the Borgia-Medici skills did not die out with my generation, but had possibly been improved in the next.

I therefore began to treat those impositions on my time for what they were: ritualistic dances, the same as all the rest. The first purpose was to vindicate some classmate's—college or law school—claim that he could deliver to his kid the full attention of a former White House Counsel. After all, there's no need in pissing off old Joe in Schenectady, refusing his kid an interview and embarrassing Joe to the point at which he sends his local tire company to Covington & Burling the next time they need Washington counsel.

The second purpose was to get a look at the kid. We always need bright associates, and so do our friends on the Hill. It does not one bit of harm to do everybody some good. When I can, I do.

The third was to divert and confuse the little shits, so that they would stay out of my hair, at least, if not out of that of everyone else. Graven in the stone of the National Archives, as I noticed the first morning I cabbed up to the Hill from the basement office where I started at the White House, is what is either a grave admonition or a sizable encouragement: *The Past Is Prologue.*

I looked at Jerry Talbot, and I could see in his eyes that he would never be an ally or a threat. He was just a little shit. "Jerry," I said, "your father's an old friend of mine. How is Don anyway?" I sat down.

"Dad's fine," Jerry said. "Really enjoying himself. Now that we're mostly grown. . . ."

"How many Talbots are there?" I said. "Little Talbots, I mean." Goosing him. It showed in his eyes. He didn't like it.

"Five," Jerry Talbot said. "I'm the oldest." Then he blurted: "Twenty-two." He was immediately sorry.

"Twenty-*two,*" I said. "My God, I must be getting old. Here's my classmate's kid, twenty-two years old." I chuckled. "Time passes so quickly when you're having fun. Well, tell me, Jerry, what can I do for my old classmate's twenty-two-year-old son?"

By now he was so uncomfortable that it would have required saintly patience not to have taken satisfaction from it. I lacked that patience. "Well, sir," he said, "I don't know how much Dad told you, but. . . ."

"Oh, hell, Jerry," I said, expansively, "don't call me sir.

Makes me feel old. Call me Pete. All my friends call me Pete. Like Pete Rose, you know?"

Nobody calls me Pete. Never has a friend of mine called me Pete. I do not object to being called Pete. I just don't look or act like a Pete. I look and act like a Peter. Many times I have wished to be a Pete. I'm just not.

Jerry Talbot looked blank. He did not know who Pete Rose was. I was kind. I explained. "Cincinnati Reds?" I said helpfully. "Pete, Pete. Third baseman. *Very* good third baseman."

"Oh," Jerry Talbot said. "Yeah. Well, uh, Pete, uh, I dunno, really, what Dad told you."

"Not a helluva lot, Jair," I said. "Old Don said you were fixin' to go to law school, lookin' for a few pointers, things like that, and would I talk to you? So, here I am. Whatcha want?"

"Well, uh, Pete," Jerry said, "I was wondering what you could tell me about . . . see, well, about Washington politics and stuff. I guess. Really."

"Dirty business, Jair," I said. I shook my head, solemnly. "If I was you, I wouldn't want no part of it. Make an old man out of you, about fifteen minutes. I'd stay out of it, I was you. Your old man's doing pretty well, I understand."

I had heard nothing from or about Don Talbot in at least fifteen years, and that was one of those idiotic items in the Fordham alumni magazine. I didn't have the foggiest idea of what he was doing or where he was doing it. "If I were you, Jair, I'd get my law degree and go home and go into the family business."

"Gee, uh, Pete," Jerry said, "uh, Dad's with the corporate counsel office of General Tire. I, ah, I don't think he can do much for me, what I want to do."

"What is it you want to do?" I said.

That put Jerry on firmer ground. "Communications law," he said. He liked the sound of it. "Communications law," he said. "In Washington."

"Communications law," I said. "Washington. Why Washington?"

"Well, you see, sir," Jerry said, leaning forward, now anxious to please, "my, uh, my girl. . . ."

Years ago, when I was badgering Congressmen to vote for various presidential programs which carried with them no assurances of federal judgeships, wetlands reclamations, acreage allotments, and farm-pond subsidies for each and every person registered to vote in their districts, I encountered an old rattlesnake from Georgia who kept a spittoon by his desk and used it frequently. But he did not use that old spittoon as often as he used the device of interruption, to discombobulate young White House assistant counsel earnestly engaged in pressing some point having to do with what was right and just. Edgar, then in excellent fettle, recommended to me that I give careful heed to when it is that rattlers go foraging, which is at night, and also to whatever happened to a certain project to construct a new post office in the rattler's district.

I caught the rattler hunting one night in a rather sleazy nightclub. The next day, when I visited him in his office, I mentioned both the nightclub and the young lady in his company. I also mentioned the President's dismay at the discovery that the new post office had not gone through and the President's full commitment to seeing that it did. Which turned the trick. I never forgot the spittoon, and I never forgot interruption as a technique of debate either. Rude it may be, but it works. "Your girl?" I said. "You want advice from me about your girl?"

"No, no, ah, Pete," Jerry said. "My girl, we want to get married, and she wants to live down here. I wanted to talk to you about communications law."

"Shee-it," I said. "You should've asked me about girls. I know way more about girls'n I do about communications law, and I dunno shit about girls."

"Oh," he said.

"You know anything about communications law?" I said. "Television, radio, that kind of stuff?"

"Uh, well, no, Pete," Jerry Talbot said. "See, I mean, I'm just starting law school and everything, and uh. . . ."

"Yeah, yeah," I said. "You know anything about communications?"

"Well," Jerry said, "I was hoping you could tell me."

"Tell you what?" I said. "I'm a lawyer. You want a communicator. You know any communicators?"

"Uh," he said, "well. . . ."

"Reporters," I said. "Broadcasters. Station owners. That kind of people. Know any of them?"

"No," he said.

"Neither do I," I said. "Except one, which your dad also knows. Edgar Lannin. Lannin doesn't know shit about the law, but he communicates like the devil. I *know* he'd be glad to see you. He's another classmate of Don's."

"What's he do?" Jerry said.

"Well," I said, "just about anything he wants, near as I can see. He's the Washington bureau chief for the Boston *Republican*. But he's also on television more'n Jimmy Carter, these days, and with much better results, as near as I can tell. There's no holding the guy."

"Where can I find him?" Jerry said.

"Have you ever seen a Washington, D.C., phone book?" I said.

"Sure," Jerry said.

"Look him up under Boston *Republican,*" I suggested. "And if that doesn't work, try Mrs. Vernon Capeless, eighteen-thirty-one Wisconsin Avenue Northwest. I understand she often knows where he is."

"Can I write that down?" Jerry said.

"Fine by me," I said. Jerry fished a ballpoint pen out of the little leather handbag I was astounded to see him carrying. He wrote it all down. Painstakingly. I was sure it was the

16

worst afternoon he had had in a long time. I was glad of it, too.

"Can I," Jerry said, "can I mention your name?"

"Suit yourself," I said. "Your dad knows him."

"But you know him better?" he said.

"Son," I said, suddenly sick of the games, "I have either known Edgar Lannin for thirty-two years, or else I have finally gotten to know Edgar Lannin in the past year. I dunno which it is, but it sure God has been interesting. I can tell you this, though: Edgar Lannin sure knows me."

And that, I think, is where I may as well begin.

One

I have known Edgar Lannin for two-thirds of my life. In my mind that comes to a little less that twenty years, because in my mind I'm just shy of thirty. I have a very stubborn mind. It is not one whit deterred by facts from what it knows to be the truth. The truth is that I am approaching my thirtieth birthday, and I have known Edgar almost twenty years. The fact is that I am approaching my forty-ninth birthday, as my driver's license and my passport conclusively establish, and I have known Edgar for some thirty-two years. Our friendship is older than we are.

When I met him, one of a herd of callow kids with short haircuts, obligatory new sport jackets, clumsily tied neckties, and well-polished shoes, Edgar was also entering the freshman class at Fordham. Then we were both very much men of the world, dutifully attending compulsory chapel; obediently filing in for hour after hour of simpleminded catechism classes denominated "Theology"; daily fulfilling the prediction made by some old Jesuit, long dead, to the seminarian who had struggled with Logic, Ethics, Metaphysics that if he did but persist, he would become a Jesuit himself, positioned to torment legion after legion of young men in captive audience with the same dull stuff; laboring desperately to master Greek, Latin, French, Spanish, and German (none of which I truly ever managed, all of which I have put resolutely from my mind); and attending "voluntary" weekly meetings of the Sodality of Our Lady except during the week we spent on compulsory retreat, confined to quarters in New York, where even pups our age could legally buy booze. Fordham played football then, and we dated girls from Catholic schools who left room for the Blessed Virgin when riding with us in cars and giggled "No" (and meant it) when we tried to feel them up through their clothes. "We really had a good time," Edgar said once. I agreed. "You know why we had such a good time?" Edgar said. "Because we didn't know a goddamned thing."

But we thought we did, and there was no one around to contradict us. Most of them were greener than we were. Oh, a lot of them came from New York and were street-smart in matters that had long eluded this virgin from the Midwest and the virgin down from Boston, but as uncertain as we were, Edgar and I, we knew enough to feign knowledge and affect boredom when they began to boast of their various expertises. By the end of October the natives had become convinced that Edgar and I were the real lions, simply because we were from Somewhere Else. Just by keeping our own counsel, we became respectable, and this despite the fact that we both suffered the misfortune of being smart. It was not accounted an asset to be smart in college then, Fordham or anywhere else, but we overcame that handicap along with our provincial origins and ended up with many friends.

We did that mostly by sarcasm. My parents had sharp tongues, and therefore, in self-defense, I developed one myself. But even having grown up in one long vocal skirmish, I was unprepared for Edgar. Edgar excelled at giving guff. He still does. He always has. Even when he was sinking into the trough of depression several years ago—to the point at which I decided that seeing him was just no longer sensible—he retained that vicious gift for shrinking another man down to pocket size while the victim looked on. Of course, he was filled with that lethal combination of self-pity and self-loathing when he fled from Washington, one step ahead of the ward where they treat the DTs, and that caused him to devote most of his sneering to himself, which was distressing to watch. Something like attending the suicide of an Olympic pistol champion. But in college, when he was on top of the world, that streak of meanness took effect on others, keeping them at bay until they decided to be friendly. I was his best audience and his most capable ally on the flanks. It was probably because we both were lonely.

Edgar went back to Boston after we graduated. I matriculated at Columbia Law School. Edgar went to work for the Boston *Republican* and loved it. I studied *Rylands* v. *Fletcher; Palsgraff* v. *Long Island RR;* the Rule Against Perpetuities; and the Rule in Shelley's Case. I hated it. Of *Rylands* I recall that somebody did something and inadvertently caused water to flow onto someone else's property. *Long Island* had something to do with a firecracker in a package. I had little interest then in what it was that Shelley did to cause such a commotion, and I have less now. As for Perpetuities, it has something to do with lives in being plus twenty-one years, but what that was, I do not know. I got it all down, and I vomited it all up, and I got good marks and made Law Review, but that was as far as my commitment went.

That was because I knew what kind of lawyer I wanted to be, and neither Mrs. Palsgraff, Mr. Fletcher, Shelley, or any railroad could conceivably have been of any service to me whatsoever in my chosen field of law. I wanted to be a rich lawyer, and I was not interested in the slightest in visiting Korea as an active combatant, so I studied hard in law school to stay in there and to get rich when I got out. I do not apologize for this ambition: I think any intelligent young man does very well to take action appropriate to preventing somebody from blowing his ass off, particularly when, if successful, that action will enable him to live well for the rest of his life.

I do confess that my cynical dedication to my studies made of me a little prick. I didn't have much fun, and neither did I give much. It is difficult enough to make friends in law school anyway, because each class is a gang of cutthroats, the prosperity of one being the adversity of the next. If Doakes outstudies you and finishes first, you will get his leavings on the job market. What you get may be better than what he took, but what he takes may be precisely what you wanted. If you took one hundred young and healthy sharks, and put them in a tank, and starved them for three years against the promise that you would present the largest of the survivors with the largest, tastiest tender tuna he had ever seen, you would not have more than three sharks in that pool when your promise came due, and two of them would be fairly gaunt and quite relieved when the big one got his fish. That is the way law school worked, at least then, and that is the way I worked.

That servitude effectively divorced me from Edgar. I was reluctant to admit that I no longer had the time to hell around with him, because that would have sounded like the truth. The truth was that I no longer had time for him, and I did not like that truth either. On the other hand, Edgar showed no inclination to press the matter, probably because he got a good look at me at our first encounter after graduation from Fordham—though considering his condition when he arrived for that reunion, I don't know how he could've gotten a good look at anything.

It was billed as a Christmas party, at the Biltmore. It was actually an adventure in anxiety. Several had been drafted and were awaiting orders. Those who had taken jobs were still nervous about their abilities and wondered if they should've put the whole thing off with a little dose of graduate school. Those who had "gone on" were defensive about their obvious refusal to tackle the real world. Those who were dating steadily brought their dates, while those who were married right after graduation brought their wives—we were all very young then; now when I attend a party, those who are married generally bring their steady dates, while those who are dating steadily bring the strongest of the primary challengers. Everybody was too animated, and therefore, almost all of the males had too much to drink and became tipsy as the evening wore on.

Edgar did not come and get tipsy. When Edgar arrived, he was shitfaced. He had been out baiting bears or something with some other reporters he had met on some big story or other, and he was about as nervous as a corpse. He slurred his words, told dirty jokes, told my date she had nice tits, embraced me fondly, declared the place was full of jerks, and left. I am mortified to say that I can recall telling my date, whose name I cannot remember, that Edgar was "the kind of friend that one outgrows." He lacked substance, I said. Balance. He was not aware that life was in earnest. Some damned thing. I was absolutely full of crap, in my three-piece suit. She agreed with me, of course. I think she was a graduate of Marquette, doing something in Marketing in New York, but there were so many of them, just like her, that I cannot be sure. They all lived with three other "girls" in a two-bedroom apartment and quarreled about who ate whose grapefruit. Whoever she was, she was as big a fool as I.

In time I escaped from Columbia with my degree and passed the bar, a new associate at Warren, Coblenz (there were about seventy other partners in the firm when I got there—the seniors, some forty years or so before, had decreed that no further names be added to the official name of the office, to everyone's relief, particularly those who answered the main number on the switchboard). That was exactly what I wanted. One of the things I wanted.

Let me explain. Warren, Coblenz deals in serious money. They always have, and they always will. If somebody from Warren, Coblenz is representing somebody in the deal, somebody in the deal has a lot of heavy bread and is worried. Men and companies hire Warren, Coblenz because they have fortunes to be held hostage and are willing to dribble away paltry sums in six figures to protect the main cache. A new associate at Warren, Coblenz, if suitably behaved, in time becomes a junior partner. After that, if he is diligent in his tasks, deferential to his masters, makes no waves, and otherwise deports himself with dignity befitting a man enfeebled by having lived threescore and ten at high speed, he becomes a senior partner, an adviser to Presidents, a consultant to the World Bank, an Ambassador Without Portfolio, and a member of the Board of Directors of Transamerica. Minions attend to his drudgeries, and lackeys make his reservations on intercontinental jets, first class, of course. Tailors wait willingly without his office until his barber whisks off the cloth and dusts his neck with talc. His secretary's secretary's secretary remembers to send four dozen yellow roses to his wife on their anniversary, with instructions to leave them and card with fond note in the keeping of the doorman at the Pierre condominiums, and his Mercedes limo idles at the curb until his personal jeweler has displayed a sapphire necklace which he deems acceptable to his mistress. If you can stand it till you're fifty, you're on the threshold of immoderate gratification. Assuming, of course, that after twenty-six years of wretched groveling you can still remember what gratification is.

Do not misunderstand. I sniveled with the best of them. I kowtowed and I "yess-massuhed" every chance I got. I wasn't that much different from the way I was in law school. I got the hang of it right off. I wore the wing-tip shoes and well-pressed pants. I kept my hair cut short. I arrived before eight in the morning, and I was still furiously—and visibly, of course—at work until after eight-thirty every night. I had chicken salad sandwiches at my desk for lunch. I drank iced tea with those sandwiches. Winter, summer, spring, and fall, I drank iced tea with lunch. When I was invited out to lunch with partners, at some place like Caravelle, I declined sweet vermouth on the rocks and drank iced tea. I hate iced tea. I worked at least a half a day on Saturdays, when I wore a tweed sport coat with leather buttons, an Oxford cloth shirt with a rep stripe tie, gray flannel bags, and penny loafers. When I knew an influential partner would be working on the Sabbath, I worked on the Sabbath as well. I submitted billable hours up the yin-yang. I kissed ass assiduously. I did not make saucy remarks. I said "yes, sir," and "no, sir." I was a common whore and one of the best hookers that firm ever saw. I may lack integrity, but when it comes to a piece of work, I can do anything I set my mind to.

That purposefulness paid off. Among the senior partners was one Michael Riverton. First house-Catholic to make senior partner (this is not the slam at Warren, Coblenz that it may seem to be—for all its faults, the outfit is determinedly Affirmative Action oriented, and has been for years. It was not race, or religion or any other accident of birth that deferred Catholicity from inclusion among the seniors until Mike came along. Mike simply had more staying power than any of his Catholic predecessors. Or less pride). Mike was gray all over. His hair was gray. His face was gray. His suits were gray, and he had a small, gray, wistful smile that made one think he must be close to sixty-five, when he was only fifty-three. Mike had Made It. The cost of Making It had come right out of his marrow, but he had Made It. He took two briefcases home each night to Briarcliff, and he brought them back in the morning. That was not unusual. In fact, the security guard at the lobby desk after 6 P.M. would have been suspicious of any Warren, Coblenz lawyer who left the building without at least one briefcase. What was unusual was that Mike read everything in those briefcases before he came back in the morning, and annotated it in pencil.

Mike was a decent man. Having made his mark, as the firm's saying went, in antitrust, he undertook to pass on what he took to be his own good fortune. He adopted protégés and treated them well. He attempted to save them some of the agony he had endured, while providing to them some of the amenities he had lacked. Those amenities included weekend invitations to his summer house at Hempstead, where lemonade was served—Mike's uncle was a hopeless drunk in Chicago—and polite conversations were conducted. I had an arm's length friendship with another junior partner named Shapiro at Warren, Coblenz. At the Coke machine one day he obtained change of a quarter from me—Cokes were still a nickel then—and said that he had heard that I had been out to Hempstead. "Nice time?" he said. "Moderate," I said. "Nice people." "Uh-huh," Shapiro said, "but not as nice as you are, for a senior partner with three unmarried daughters, youngest three years out of Marymount College, all in need of good Catholic boys for husbands. Play your cards right, you could do pretty well in this place." Shapiro, later to appear in more congenial surroundings as Assistant General Counsel to the Senate Rackets Committee, was an evil-minded man.

When I was by the calendar twenty-seven, I married Jeanne Marie Riverton in an 11 A.M. ceremony at Our Lady of the Angels Church in Briarcliff, New York. The reception was held at the Briarcliff Country Club. Mike Riverton spared no expense, and I used no judgment. Mike laid out about twelve bucks a head for prime ribs to feed a bunch of people too drunk to appreciate them because of the plenteous booze they had gobbled from the open bar. He paid extra for the band, which included a fellow who played the piano but doubled on the accordion and sang the songs about the bride cutting the cake and feeding the groom. My first error was in asking Shapiro to be my best man, which created consternation in the Rectory of Our Lady of the Angels and resultant discomfort in the Riverton home, Shapiro being a pagan and all—he offered to wear a yarmulke, if that would help; I told him the Oxford jacket would be sufficient. My second error was in asking Edgar to serve as an usher. He became annoyed at once that I had not invited him to be best man. Flustered, I said that I was afraid that if I did, he would show up drunk, or else not show up at all, and that he would goose all the bridesmaids, the bride, and perhaps the groom as well, if he did show up. Edgar got rather stiff at this rebuke. He agreed, sullenly, to be an usher. He showed up for the wedding rehearsal drunk. At the dinner afterward, he honed a fine edge on his condition with approximately fifteen Ballantine Ales. He offered two toasts which scandalized the parents of the participants in the ceremony and failed as well to please the star, Jeanne Marie Riverton. That out of the way, he goosed each of the bridesmaids, found one—a classmate of Jeanne's from college—who did not take it amiss, made arrangements to leave separately with her, returned to the restaurant to make his farewells to the other guests, kissed me wetly on the right cheek, goosed Jeanne, and vanished into the night with whatever her name was. Jeanne said she did not like Edgar.

On the morning of the wedding, Edgar drove into the parking lot of the motel in his rented Ford Falcon in the same clothes he had worn in his disgraces of the night before. With him was the bridesmaid—her name may have been Diane—in the same clothes she had worn the night before. Diane looked woozy. Edgar looked dissipated. I raised hell, noting that he was a bit late for an eleven o'clock wedding, straggling in unshaven and unwashed at nine-forty-five. Diane, if her name was Diane, wove back and forth and looked bleary. She kept mumbling about her dress and shoes, which I took as reference to her costume as a bridesmaid.

Edgar explained. He explained with dignity. "Diane and I," he said, "have been out all night. We are tired. We are willing to endure this foolishness because of our fondness for you and whoever the hell the bride is, but we do so in a state of great fatigue, and you had done well, sir, to leave us alone."

"And why is that, may I ask?" said Shapiro, who was resplendent in his togs and therefore did not know enough to stand mute when Edgar started talking.

26

"Because we got as drunk as goats, Counselor," Edgar said, "befitting this joyous occasion. Then we went to the Hot Pillow Motel, registered as man and wife (Mister and Missus James Meredith, if I recall correctly. Which is unlikely), paid in advance because we had no luggage, and spent the early-morning hours fucking each other's brains out. In addition to other perversions."

Diane nodded solemnly and burped. "This is true," she said.

A cab brought Diane's uniform to the motel. Four Bloody Marys brought Edgar around—after about a pint of Visine for each eye, he looked almost human and could stand erect without weaving. Diane had two Bloody Marys after a cold shower and looked marvelous. We were young then and had wonderful powers of recuperation.

Diane looked a bit dazed at the altar, but Edgar was a paragon of charm at the ceremony. Shapiro received several hard looks from the monsignor, but Jeanne looked gorgeous, and I could have stood almost anything for her. My life was falling into place. When we turned to leave the altar, I was not surprised to see that Eleanor Riverton was crying. I was somewhat taken aback to see that Mike was wiping his eyes, too. It was in all a touching occasion.

Until Edgar spotted the accordion at the reception. Seated at the head table, of course, he took full advantage of the limitless champagne. By the time Shapiro had meanly wished Monsignor and all the celebrants "Shalom" at the end of his toast to me and Jeanne, Edgar was gassed again. The prime ribs were served after the fruit cup, and the rosé wine poured. The bandleader arose from the piano bench and strapped on his accordion. Edgar jumped to his feet, red in the face. Shaking his fist at the bewildered musician, he shouted: "If you play 'Lady of Spain' on that fucking thing, I will personally kill you."

Edgar's voice carries. The conversation of eight hundred people sweltering in a room without air conditioning in June died out like the faint breeze that had tantalized the wedding party as we emerged from the church. The monsignor's mouth, abundantly open to say a grace that easily doubled in length the Gettysburg Address, dropped open again, but nothing came out. Jeanne hissed like a snake. I said that I could not make Edgar sit down. That was the truth. Edgar had an audience.

He spread his arms like Elmer Gantry. He raised his eyes toward heaven. He lowered his eyes. He furrowed his brows. He said: "Ladies and Gentlemen. Fellow Bacchanalians. I thank you for your attention. Here is the truth, as received from Mount Sinai: No Good Ever Came Out of an Occasion at Which an Accordion Was Employed. Mister Piano Player: Sit down and play your goddamned piano. Throw that squeeze box in the river, or stick to Polish weddings. I have spoken."

Edgar sat down and drained his sixth or seventh goblet of champagne. Diane giggled. The piano player went back to the piano. The wedding guests stared for at least two minutes. Slowly they regained their senses and returned to their fruit cups. Jeanne said, in an icy whisper: "Well?" I said: "Well what?" She said: "Are you going to do something about him?" I said: "I don't have any morphine on me. Just keep feeding him drinks and he'll pass out." She said: "And take Diane with him." I said: "I don't wear Diane's pants. If Diane's pants come off, I didn't take them off." She said: "Eat your fruit cup." The wedding pictures were lovely. We looked absolutely blissful, especially in the picture with the wedding party.

For the next year we lived in a comfortable small apartment on the East Side. If Edgar came to New York, I did not see him. For some reason or other, he seemed to be under the impression that he would not be welcome at our house. Or if welcome, not comfortable.

I did not miss him. I was busy. I was working my ass off at the firm. I was also working my ass off at home. I assembled Danish Modern. I had dinner out when Jeanne called from the New York Board of Trade to say that she was bushed. We did Theater and we did Metropolitan Museum of Fine

Arts. We did Guggenheim and we did Village. We painted walls white and we framed our own bullfight posters. We shopped for thick area rugs and we flew to Puerto Rico for tennis vacations. We drank jug wine and we ate cheese. We read the *Village Voice* and the New York *Herald Tribune.* We were indulgent toward friends who brought pot to smoke at our house, although we did not like it. I went to work every morning at seven-thirty, latest, and never got home— seldom got home—before eight at night. We spent Thanksgiving and Christmas with her parents in Briarcliff and sent warm letters to mine. We were perfect.

One night she said: "I think we should get a dog." "Dog?" I said. "I want a dog," she said. "What kind of dog?" I said. *"A* collie," she said. "I think: a collie." "The fuck're you gonna do with a collie in this place, shitting on the white rug all day while we're both working?" I said. "I want a dog," she said.

I know it's incredible, but it is true. I never knew I thought it until I said it. I said: "You want a dog? Fine. I want a new life."

"A new life," she said.

It had taken her awhile to react, which was understandable enough. I had used the interval to reflect on what I had said. I had decided I had said exactly what I meant. "A new life," I said. "I don't like this one."

"Like what?" she said.

"Lemme think," I said. "I know. Anything else. I hate this shit. I don't want to become Plastic Man, and I'm getting there."

"I suppose you want children," she said.

At the time I thought I did. And that was how we mature, responsible adults, by candid and complete discussion, decided that we would get the hell out of New York and start a family in Washington. I did not consult Edgar about this decision. I did not consult Edgar about anything then. If I intended to sleep in the same bed with Jeanne, let alone generate babies

29

in Jeanne's belly, it was unwise to do so much as mention Edgar. As far as I was concerned, Edgar was gone. Then, at least, I hoped he would stay gone. Edgar was a pain in the ass.

Two

Edgar tracked me down. I was not dismayed, but I was surprised. Not at his enterprise. Edgar has always been able to find what he wants to find. At his interest. I thought Edgar and I were finished.

"Rotten motherfucker," Edgar said. "Smart-ass candy-coated knee-jerk liberal. The hell is this crap about Assistant General Counsel to the high mucky-muck of the whatchama-callit? I thought you were gonna be a high-powered New York lawyer. What the hell did you do? Go straight?"

In a manner of speaking, I had. Mike Riverton, along with everyone else at Warren, Coblenz, had Contacts. Contacts included the junior Senator from the Sovereign State of Missouri, who was then by way of angling to become Secretary of Commerce and appreciated a recommendation of a young lawyer—lawyers are young much later than other, more pedestrian folk; lawyers are still young when they are in their mid-forties, bedraggled though they may be—who Could Be Trusted to handle delicate matters for campaign committees. I told Mike that Jeanne and I wanted to start a family, which was true.

I told him that the hours I was obliged to keep at Warren, Coblenz made me uneasy about doing that, since they would certainly throw the entire burden of child raising onto Jeanne. I told him we had been talking about my shifting into government, so that we might have time to raise a family in which the children would have both a father and a mother.

It was all true, but it was not all of the truth, and it was probably just about the most cynical speech I had ever made. I had not spent nearly six years at Warren, Coblenz without learning something. One of the things I had learned was how to neutralize a potential opponent by tempting him with rewards that would fall to him by supporting you. Another thing was timing: the neutralizing must be done before he mounts the opposition, lest his collapse be made difficult by his desire to save face. We needed Mike's blessing for the adventure, and I got it because I knew my man.

I knew Mike felt guilty about the time he had spent rising to senior partner. He told me many times that his daughters had been born one morning and entered college by nightfall, as far as he had been concerned. I played on that.

I knew Mike was a rampaging, hell-bent-for-leather Roman Catholic. He went to Mass every Sunday, and he received Communion. Twice each year he made the nine First Fridays, if he could find a year with eighteen months in it. He was a daily communicant during Lent. He was fearful about what would happen when Pope Pius died (and what Pope John did more than justified his apprehensions). Mike and Eleanor wanted grandchildren, and they said so, often, recounting the beauty and intelligence of grandchildren they had seen in the homes of their friends. They stayed away from questions that would have given them more information than they wanted about the Pill. But they made it very clear that sex was for the procreation of children and that they wished to know when it was that we planned on procreating. Jeanne, after all, was their only married daughter, and Mike told us jokingly that he did not think Eleanor could survive the birth of a grandchild to one of her unmarried daughters (the likelihood of this occurring was nil, unless some randy angel got the wrong address on an Immaculate Conception errand; Jeanne's sisters were about as attractive to men as a couple of stevedores might have been).

Mike vibrated softly to my pitch, like the strings of an antique violin. He beamed. He smiled. He clapped me on the back. He took me to lunch at the Grill at the Waldorf. He ordered up a martini for me and proved reckless enough to drink a celebratory manhattan of his own. He said that he would see what he could do with Dennis Gordon's office, and he insisted that Jeanne and I accept an interest-free loan of twenty thousand dollars to get us started on owning our own home (that little house in Georgetown, ten years later, fetched us a profit of more than forty thousand dollars; since Mike, then dead three years of cardiac arrest—he would have had it now, if he had not then, considering what has happened to Jeanne and me—had given us the money with strict orders never to mention it to Eleanor, I kept it all). He also offered advice.

"I'll get to Dennis this afternoon," Mike said. "But Dennis isn't going to be able to do anything right off. It'll be at least a month or two before something decent opens up, and you'll want to tie up the loose ends here anyway. If I were you, I'd get involved in politics for a while. Something on a state committee. Maybe, you want to, I could speak to Murray Klein. Murray's very active in the Humphrey thing, and that man's going to be the next President of the United States."

I said I thought Kennedy would get it. "Kennedy," Mike said. "Well, I'd like that, of course. About time we had one of our own in there. His old man was smart enough when he was here, that's for sure. But he's young, Peter, awful young. And there are stories about him. Women. He's an awful chaser, from what I hear, and you can't do that if you're going to run for President of the United States. Besides, we've already got your Jewish friend Shapiro working with Matty Troy's

group on that one. If Kennedy wins, we're covered there anyway. But the firm doesn't have anybody with Humphrey, and
I think that's a big mistake."

"I can't stand Humphrey," I said. "He talks too much."

"Peter," Mike said, "if he's going to win, and I think he
is, what matters is not whether you like him—it's whether
the firm has somebody around him who knows who to talk
to."

I put Mike off on that. Before he had a chance to find out
that I'd been traveling around with Shapiro under cover of
darkness, building the Kennedy organization, Senator Gordon's office came through with a nice little slot on the House
Small Business Subcommittee. It gave me plenty of time to
cultivate people on the staff of the junior Senator from Massachusetts, and I used it to advantage.

That was how Edgar found me, about a year after we moved
to Washington. He had some secondary role in the *Republican*'s
coverage of the Kennedy campaign, and he was often in Washington from 1960 until he moved to its bureau in 1964. He
called me from time to time, but by then I was out of town
a lot, on leave from the subcommittee to work on Gordon's
responsibilities for the Kennedy effort in Missouri. And when
I was around, I did not return Edgar's calls.

In other words, I had my life, and I did not want Edgar
in it. We went to Mass at Holy Trinity on Sundays, and we
attended small dinner parties in Georgetown, at which curry
was served. On Sundays we went to the Angler's Inn out on
the old Canal Road; we drank white wine years before anyone
drank white wine. On Sundays in September, Jeanne went
out to Middleburg and took riding lessons with Frippy Melanson, who lived next door to us.

Frippy's husband's name was Jack, and he was heavy at
Justice in the new administration. He had been equally weighty,
at around twenty-seven, at the Yale Law School. Jack was
in Civil Rights. Pretty soon I was, too, leaving the subcommittee behind. It amuses me now to recollect how much we knew

of civil rights, Mississippi, and the will of God in those years. I don't know anywhere near as much about those subjects now.

Remaining in dutiful service as my point man, Jack left Justice a year later, moving to the White House. There he put in more than an occasional word for me; that was how I went to work in the office of General Counsel to the Secretary of Defense. I have heard a lot of mean things said about Robert McNamara, but none of the young men who worked in his band, so far as I know, ever agreed with them. Less than six years after I arrived in Washington, I was Special Counsel to the President. In theory I was brought in to advise on matters of national defense. In fact I was prevented by the rush of liaison work on the Hill from ever doing much of it. I also started to see Edgar again, but not because I chose to.

Edgar in those days had a curious assignment with the *Republican.* He ran the bureau, which was small, and he also covered the news. But twice a week he furnished two columns of opinion the way that the Manhattan Project turned out a couple firecrackers to divert and amuse the Japanese at Hiroshima and Nagasaki. When he had filled his allotted space in the *Republican,* he accepted numerous free-lance offers which came his way from national magazines aware that he was from Boston, had covered the Kennedys, and was somewhat less than enchanted by Lyndon Baines Johnson. A word or two from Edgar, published in *The New Republic,* incited a mood in Lyndon that made strong men run for cover.

Jack Melanson, promoted to Undersecretary of the Treasury, took some of the resultant heat. Disliking it, he showed the poor judgment to suggest to the President that I might be able to do something to blunt the sharpness of Edgar's attacks. The President, as I received the quote, replied that I had better goddamned right well fucking try to do something about Edgar.

I cannot claim that my White House experience refined my language. What it did, actually, was unrefine my language to the point of coarseness it had reached in college, before I got some class and went to work in New York. White House lawyering is frustrating work. Dwight David Eisenhower complained that nobody in government paid any attention to him. Ike was President. All I could do was represent that I spoke for the President. This ofttimes brought hollow laughter from the fellow on the other end of the line. At first puzzled, I learned by the effect of one of my explosions to be a little less polite. When in receipt of a response to my claim of speaking for the President I received from some indolent bureaucrat the insolent reply "Who gives a shit?" I replied in measured tones: "This afternoon, not much of anybody. Tomorrow morning, one more person than there is today. Because I am going in to see the President at five-fifteen, and I am going to take your fucking head off at the fucking goddamned knees, and you will be out in the fucking street with your files in the rubbish before they can get out the first edition of the *Post* tonight. Tomorrow you will care, and maybe then you will spread the word. You're gonna have the time, shithead, because I have had a ration of you that'd choke a fuckin' elephant, and when that goddamned elephant shits, my friend, he's gonna shit on you." The change in the gentleman's attitude was remarkable.

On the assumption that the President's selection of vocabulary manifested an emotional investment at least equal to my own in the use of such language, I did damned right try to do something about Edgar. It fucking near cost me my liver. I would have made the sacrifice. Anything would have been preferable to going home.

The boys were infants and in full cry. While Mike and Eleanor were devoted grandparents, they were devoted in Briarcliff, and we were by way of going nuts in Washington. Jeanne was more fun than a barrel of nails once the kids came along, and I was only too happy to spend two or three nights a week stroking Edgar at Nick and Dottie's, or some other place where a liquor license was in hand and the servants and other patrons did not intrude upon the conversations. Not that it did any good: Edgar told me, up front and head on, that he thought Johnson was being an asshole on the war, and that he intended to keep saying so in the newspaper. But for me, whose day began at 7 A.M. and did not end until midnight, it was a lot simpler baby-sitting Edgar than it was baby-sitting the President. And vastly more enjoyable, too. Actually, perhaps it did do some good: my bad companionship kept him away from the typewriter as effectively as his kept me away from Jeanne.

Three

To borrow a phrase somewhat tattered from overuse by several clients of the firm who later found themselves in serious difficulties with various other parties (one of them was an Ed Bradley client, who had a memorable evening with a Fourteenth Street hooker and a police officer named Munoz): it all started out innocently enough. Back on one of those wretched, drippy, muggy-gray days that we can get in Washington in April, last year, my secretary, a decent woman named Pauline Battle, chimed the intercom to inquire, somewhat uncertainly, whether I desired to accept a local call from someone identifying himself as Edgar Lannin. "He sounds a little drunk to me," Pauline said. "I wasn't sure if you knew him." Pauline unfortunately forgets to put calls on hold sometimes when using the intercom.

"If he sounds a little drunk," I said, "I know him. Put him through. It's got to be the same one."

"I am not a little drunk," Edgar said. "I have never been a little drunk in my life. I go a good one-ninety-five in my underwear. Never drunk, seldom sober, that's my motto."

"Bright college days," I said. "The hell are you, Edgar?"

"A bit worse for wear," Edgar said, "but nowhere near as bad as I was when I left."

"You're back," I said. Edgar had left some several months before, returning to Boston for what he described as "Rest and Recuperation."

"Lemme check," Edgar said. "Yes, I seem to be back. But only temporarily. Yup, I'm here all right. That is, I am here, and I seem to be all right."

"What're you doing here?" I said.

"Among other things," Edgar said, "I seem to have a little problem involving the law, and I thought perhaps we might have a bite to eat and chat about it. I think I am by way of looking into securing new counsel. I thought I would solicit your advice."

"You couldn't've picked a better night," I said. "Jeanne and the kids're attending some confounded celebration at the Cathedral School."

"The Cathedral School," Edgar said. "My, my, Mister Quinn, have we turned Episcopalian?"

"No," I said, "we have not. The kids next door to us were born that way, and they invited ours."

"I feel much better," Edgar said. "Thought you'd turned from a Hoper into an actual, goddamned Protestant in our old age. Have dinner with me, the Jockey Club?"

"When?" I said. I had had a good day. It was almost six o'clock. I was ready to leave.

"Now," Edgar said.

"What I never understood, all the time I was here—" Edgar said, spreading his hands over the red tablecloth at the old Jockey Club, to demonstrate that he had been baffled and was still not entirely certain that he had figured anything out, "and keep in mind, I was here a long time, until I was either gonna leave or my liver was gonna give out, which was when I did—but what I never understood was what you Washington lawyers *did.*

39

"Now I've been at this business a helluva long time," he said reflectively, looking at the cloth, "and I am not an unintelligent man. I never said I was any kind of a genius, but I can find my way around Horace James Circle in West Roxbury, Massachusetts, and escape from the Santa Ana Freeway in LA without getting killed. I know a restaurant in Cincinnati where you can get a drink even if you're not wearing a leisure suit. I am what you call your basic man of the world, and I would never eat a hot dog in the airport at Saint Louis, no matter how hungry I was.

"In other words," he said, "you can't fool me, boy. I have seen the elephant and heard the owl, as old Ulysses S. said, and I take no crap from anybody. But I watched you devils for years, and I never came close to understanding what it was you did.

"You must," he said. "They must do *something*. I mean, besides what you can see them doing. They walk into offices looking grim, and they walk out of offices looking grim. Sometimes they walk into offices looking happy and come out looking grim, or the other way around, and sometimes they do the same sort of thing with congressional committees, and then afterwards they won't tell you anything.

"I have been thinking about that," he said. "Not ever since, because there is this thing with the mortgage and the car payments and the alimony and support, but every now and then. When I haven't had something more entertaining on my mind. It's only taken me the better part of three years, away from the bastards, to figure out what it is the bastards do.

"I cannot brag about this. Close to three years is a long time for a self-confessed journalist to take, to figure something out. It's nowhere near as long as it took the whole pack of us to figure out what Tricky Dick was really up to. And we didn't really do it then. But it's still a pretty long time. I admit I am embarrassed. But at least I know. That is, I think I know and that is about as close as I am gonna get in this lifetime.

"What a Washington lawyer does," Edgar said, "is this: a Washington lawyer does not tell you anything. *Anything.* And he charges somebody a lot of money for it. For not telling.

"Now that," he said, "is why people in my line of work have so much trouble understanding people in your line of work. Because what we do is tell everything we know as soon as we know it and sometimes even before we know it. When a reporter goes and starts asking questions to a Washington lawyer—by the time the reporter gets here, he's probably pretty good, or he wouldn't be here in the first place, and he knows all these lawyers that he met in Des Moines, there, that're always snuggling up to the newspapers and buying guys drinks so their latest miracle'll get good play in the A.M.s, and it always does because we're easy—what he thinks he has got by the tail is the same sort of animal he had penned up in the County Courthouse in Abilene. The hell they call them mouthpieces for, huh? They talk all the time.

"This," he said, "is like the parson asking the *fille de joie* what a nice girl like her's doing in a place like this. It is like some goddamned birdwatcher from Gloucester, where the most exotic thing he ever saw was a scarlet tanager, giving you a detailed summary of the flight patterns of penguins. You Washington guys, the last thing you want is your name in the papers. And you go to great lengths to keep it out. When a lawyer in this town gets his name in the paper, it means he made a mistake and he has to do the honorable thing and shoot himself.

"Lemme tell you something," he said, "all right? Cats don't know anything about dogs, and dogs're equally as ignorant about cats. Reporters don't know anything more about lawyers here than dogs do about cats. One of them runs, and the other one runs after the one that starts running. That is the limit of our usual acquaintance with each other and pretty much satisfies our mutual curiosity. It is very seldom that your average dog will actually catch a cat, and even more unusual that he would have the foggiest idea of what to do

41

with the animal after he bagged it. You gonna eat a cat? You really do like Chinese food? Your regular dog has more sense. He's in it for the sport.

"So is your Washington lawyer," he said. "Your Boston lawyer is a lawyer who practices law in Boston. He has his office, and his associates, and his secretarial help, and maybe an investigator or so, and if he is so disreputable that he goes to court now and then, he goes to court now and then. Your New York lawyer does not go to court—he thinks court is vulgar. Your Philadelphia lawyer only takes airplanes to Chicago and other places—he doesn't know whether court is vulgar. He thinks: having an opinion of whether court is vulgar is vulgar. Your San Francisco lawyer represents Transamerica and eats at L'Etoile, and your lawyer in Los Angeles has something to do with the Industry. Which means he doesn't know any more about movies than you do, but does have a drink now and then in the Polo Lounge.

"Your Washington lawyer is different," he said. "For him, life is pinball, and he's the man who is expert with the flippers. He may be a deaf, dumb, blind kid, but he sure plays a mean pinball.

"What the guys in other towns do is try to keep their clients out of court, keep their tails out of the cracks, and generally play CYA, which is Cover Your Ass. What your genuine Washington lawyer does is acknowledge that his clients have tails, and then he does the best he goddamn can to fill in all the cracks. While stopping Congress and the agencies from making new cracks.

"The way he does this," Edgar said, "has absolutely nothing to do with practicing law. Washington lawyers practice law the same way Universal Abrasives manufactures toilet paper—they don't. They do something else. The first thing somebody wants to know about a lawyer in Miami is whether the guy is a good lawyer, and how come you think so? The first thing anybody wants to know about a lawyer in Washington is when he was Special Counsel to the President, you should excuse the phrase, and was that President a member of the same party as the President we got in there now? And then whether he got indicted lately for anything serious.

"You guys," he said, "are as cozy as a mink-lined jockstrap, and way more comfortable when you're the client and you got them between you and a chilly SEC investigator. You play shortstop the way Marty Marion did it for the old Cardinals: they're always stooping down and picking up pebbles. It looks like you're wasting everybody's time until the next ground ball goes out to them, and they scoop it up so clean it seems like it was never on the ground. Lawyers in the other towns try to keep their clients out of trouble, and get them out with minimal damage if they get in it anyway. Lawyers in Washington try to make it impossible for their clients to get into trouble, no matter how ingenious or disobedient they may be. If there ain't no law, my son, there ain't no way that you can break it, no matter how big a jerk you may be.

"Now if you look closely at one of your fellow swimming birds," Edgar said, "you will gradually come to see that the most important thing he does is Nothing. But he does Nothing in a very stylish way, and he did not climb out of his crib knowing it. He learned it somewhere along the line.

"That is usually going to turn out to be a fairly long line," he said. "You will generally find that the magician was not born here. Instead he comes from Worcester, Massachusetts, or some godforsaken place in Texas or Nebraska. Which he himself has also forsaken. Obviously he is here because he did not like Worcester. Also because he got into a high-powered law school, or a low-powered law school, and survived the experience still smart enough so he didn't have to go back to North Carolina when he got out.

"A Washington lawyer who tells you he's from Spokane is like Lana Turner telling you she's from Schwab's Drugstore: it's true, but if you believe it, you're a fool, and his tailor is so good he cut the suit so that you can't even see the outline of the dorsal fin.

"Let me tell you something: when you come out from having breakfast at the Metropolitan Club with one of those guys, and it's such a nice day, what with the cherry blossoms and all, that you both decide to walk, and his chauffeur fires up the limo and follows you along the curb, all the way to where the lawyer's going, you did not just finish breakfast with a naturalist, all right? You have been woofing down the sausages and eggs with a very formidable customer, whose Mummy did not bail him from the hospital, where he was born, in no limo, and who has told you not one thing more than he has decided it is in the best interest of his client for you to know. If he buys you steak tartare at Paul Young's in the evening, and you order it medium rare, he will have your fillings before the sherbet comes, and your reputation with his stewed prunes the next morning.

"The first thing to remember is that Washington is a small town. There are those of the opinion that it is a small southern town. I brook no bickering. Grace Metalious made a dime or two off of the goings-on in a small town. Morgantown, West Virginia, has the coal mines, and Washington, D.C., has the other thing.

"There is a difference, but it is not important. The similarity is that everybody in Washington does more or less the same thing. Just like LA. The people who don't have anything to do with the Industry spend all their time trying to get something to do with the Industry. The people who have something to do with the Industry spend all their time backchatting with each other, except for when they're backstabbing each other. The people who watch the Industry, which is the newspapermen, become part of the Industry within a week of the time they start watching it.

"The product of the Industry, in Washington, is laws. Therefore, lawyers occupy the same place in Washington that directors and producers occupy in Hollywood. The difference is that almost nobody in LA is trying to stop the product from being manufactured.

"In Washington, at least half the people on the production line are devoting all their energies to stopping it. You have two kinds of people on the line here: foremen and saboteurs. They are, for long periods of time—the average useful lifetime—the same people. When the Democrats throw the Republicans out, the Democratic saboteurs become foremen and the Republican foremen become saboteurs. Eight years later they switch places again. Washington is probably the only town in the world with two Mafias—the In Mafia and the Out Mafia—and it works in exactly the same way. You reward your friends, and you punish your enemies. The stakes're about the same, too: life and death. It doesn't look like life and death, but that is exactly the way it is, and all these fellows down here know it. Which may be why most of them look so grim most of the time: because their clients know it, too, and're about as merciful as Genghis Khan when they don't get what they want.

"I dunnno where Northwest Orient Airlines's got its company headquarters," he said. "I could find out, if I wanted, because I can still go out and get a story now and then, like I did when I was running the bureau three years ago. If the desk starts getting grouchy about my philosophizing and it becomes clear I'd better go out and do some actual work until they calm down, I go out and do it. But things're pretty calm right now, except in the saloon Ham Jordan happens to pick for his nightcap and grabs somebody's boob or something. I spend most of my time making everybody's life miserable for them just from what I read in the morning papers. Columns're easy. So, not being really interested in where Northwest Orient's got its main office, I am not going to look it up.

"What I am reasonably sure of," he said, "is that Northwest Orient does not have its real headquarters in Washington. Neither do Braniff, Pan American, American, Delta, all the rest of them; they all work out of Somewhere Else. Same thing with Merck Pharmaceuticals, Atlantic Richfield Oil, the Prudential Insurance Company, General Motors, Bavarian Motor

Works, and Metro-Goldwyn-Mayer. But I would be willing to bet you the next round that every single one of those outfits has got itself at least a rifle squad of Washington lawyers, and most of them have got them in battalion strength.

"Now, when you think about it," he said, "that is a situation which you very seldom see in any other town. Oh, you will get your F. Lee Bailey flying around the country, your Percy Foreman and your Louis Nizer, and your occasional Edward Bennett Williams working out of here. But they are unusual.

"Lawyering is a generally local sport, like boccie or touch football; it is very unusual for a lawyer to have a regional practice, let alone a national rep, because mostly courts are local, statewide at the most, and that includes the federal courts, and the local lawyers and the local judges don't feature outsiders coming in and creaming off the heavy sugar.

"When you hear President Carter talking about regionalism, you should think about the strong possibility that Pennsylvania licenses lawyers by counties, because the boys in Harrisburg don't feature competition from the lads in Philadelphia. And they are equally upset when some alien being shows up with a case in Bucks County, but with New Jersey tags on his Continental. This, of course, is something the New Jersey carnivore can readily understand, because his learned brothers in New Jersey've done everything but electrify the border fences to keep Philadelphia lawyers out of Secaucus and New York lawyers out of Newark.

"If you get in the shit in Ketchikan, Alaska," he said, "and you know what is good for you, you will scout up a lawyer right there in Ketchikan. If you are really determined to bring in a hotshot from Chicago, you'd better be smart enough to get one that's cute enough to make sure local counsel stays in on the case, and the cash, and sits right beside him in the courtroom.

"If you want to see something funny sometime, go watch a trial in Edgartown, when the local guy in the rumpled tweed is defending the local medic against a malpractice suit brought by a New York stockbroker who didn't like the way his hang-nail got treated and brought in the guy who does his legal work on Park Avenue to get him justice. The visitors never know that they've been cut until they turn their heads and they fall off.

"Now," he said, "it is exactly the same way here, in Our Nation's Capital, except that you very seldom get a local plaintiff. When Colt Firearms gets alarmed about federal gun control legislation, they get alarmed in New Haven, not in their main offices on L Street. But what they are concerned about is what is happening in the committee hearings up on Independence and Constitution.

"They are not dense. They know very right well that somebody down in the bowels of the Rayburn Building, somebody they never heard of, can make a nasty exit wound in the whole industry, and will probably do it, too, unless somebody else they never heard of, laboring unseen in a windowless office in a law firm on M Street—like you, my friend Peter—thinks up a way to stop him. Which will keep the Thirty-eights moving out of Colt Firearms in New Haven. Which in turn will keep those diligent gunsmiths in roast beef and mashed potato, with lots of butter.

"Let me put it to you this way," he said. "Can you even imagine the bonanza it must have been for Washington lawyers when old Jimmy came headlong out of Plains and scared the living shit out of the whole restaurant trade with that little gem about knocking out the three-martini, deductible lunch?

"Who the hell is gonna leave a hundred-twenty with the cashier at the Four Seasons in New York if he can't take it off the corporate income with a little piece of paper when he gets back to the office? I'll tell you who's willing to spend his own money in the amounts that those guys charge: somebody who's tried every other blessed thing that he can think of, short of a mink cape and a diamond necklace, to get that little cutie into bed, and none of them worked, and he's getting nervous.

47

"I kind of think," he said, "that there are not so many of those guys left around. Not enough to support a big restaurant, for sure. Because the little cuties've gotten considerably more cooperative in that line since you and I were lusting for them in our hearts, but just about nowhere else. Romance in the high-ticket restaurant business went out with the panty girdle, is what I think, and the majority of the folks who destroy their silk cravats with béarnaise sauce're doing it on some business account. If that cash ain't overhead no more, but income, it's going to be as scarce as unicorns, and there isn't a maître d' in the world that doesn't know it.

"What he is ignorant of," the man said, "as he stands haughtily in the foyer of Le St. Germain in LA, is the names of those members of the Senate and the House—and more particularly, of those members of their staffs—whose weight, cholesterol, and glyceride levels will drop precipitously within a week of the date when the law takes effect that will force them to take themselves to lunch and dinner. Because then they will be munching at the Blue Mirror, on hot dogs, and will soon run out of matches from Cantina d'Italia, where they serve fine veal in various disguises.

"You see what Jimmy Carter did? In one fell swoop, he united the owners of Jack's in San Francisco and Paul at the Sans Souci. He brought them together. He made them care about each other. Until he gave that little saber just the slightest rattle, the folks at Scandia in LA were pretty much casual about whether the parking lot at Anthony's Pier Four in Boston was crowded. After it, their mutuality of interest became surpassingly apparent.

"I know a guy," Edgar said, "who has a covetous streak. Name's Herbie. He has a modest swimming pool—he wants a tennis court. He has a Jaguar XJS. He skis two weeks each year at Vail—he wants a condominium at Snowmass or Steamboat Springs. He flies by charter to New York—he wants his own Learjet. He has a law degree, and he has an office on Connecticut Avenue—after Carter went after the restaurants, there was only one thing in the world that he wanted, because he figured it would get him all the others, and he told me what it was.

" 'I got a client,' Herbie said, 'that's a small textile manufacturer, and never mind where. What he does is make the cloth they use in high-priced men's suits. He knows all the guys who make cloth for medium-priced men's suits and all the guys who make cloth for low-priced men's suits. He also knows a great many of the guys who make the cloth that goes into the clothing that women are wearing to work. And he thinks I am a great lawyer that could turn the Potomac into Beaujolais.

" 'What I want is for the President to have Jody Powell say that he's thinking about proposing to make the cost of business suits deductible from your taxes. If I could have that happen, when I die I would not object to going to hell, because I already would've spent a whole lifetime in heaven and would probably be bored with it.

" 'Because, if *El Presidente* would be kind enough to do that,' Herbie said, 'my client would spend that night sluicing his bowels with Dom Pérignon and planning his villa in the south of France. Then the next morning, when his liver was in arrest and his temples were pounding, he would hear Congressman Balk and Senator Block denouncing the very notion of deducting those business suits, and otherwise raising the devil with Tom Pettit, NBC, Washington. And my client would call all his buddies and set up a conference call so they could weep salt tears together.

" 'Then, at the end of it,' Herbie said, 'he would suggest that they all get organized and hire me, and they would agree. And he would call, still sobbing a little. And I would say: " ' "My friend, you have got a very serious matter here. But I became very close to Congressman Balk's closest adviser, when I was Assistant Counsel to the Armageddon Committee five years ago. Only last year I was instrumental in changing a key vote that sent a hundred million dollars in sewer projects to Senator Block's state. I think I may be able to help there. Now my partner, as you may know, was Deputy Assistant Subaltern Counsel at Treasury for several years, so I'm sure we'll be able to help there."

" 'I would even keep a straight face,' Herbie said. 'Then, when I was through, I would pay off my bookie and go into Dave's office and say: "Screw the new Jags, my friend. Whaddaya think of Ferrari Boxers? Eighty-seven grand, legalized and certificated for import to America? Want two, one for rainy days?" '

"That," Edgar said, "is what I mean. Another thing that made it difficult for me to understand what you lawyers *do*. In my line of work, the windfall is when Time, Inc., buys the Washington *Star* from Allbritton. If I work for the *Star*, what I got from that happy event is reasonable assurance that the managing editor and I will not be applying for welfare for a few more years, or going over to see the *Post* and telling Ben I didn't have anything to do with the *Ear* printing all that stuff about him and Sally, and are there maybe any openings coming up on the rewrite desk? I will not starve, but neither will I get rich, as the Holy Scriptures say, and if it was a windfall, Joe Allbritton gets the apples.

"You lawyers," Edgar said, "get the windfalls, and the goddamnedest thing can bring them. A criminal lawyer in Philadelphia knows today that he will get fatter than a goat in the next year or so. Because when they threw Marston out as U.S. Attorney, they obviously had to pick a guy to replace him who will have to indict every son of a bitch in sight, or they'll lynch him and finish Carter in the process. Your criminal lawyer may have starved last year and fallen six months in arrears on his subscription to *Law Week*, but as soon as they get the motor going in the grand jury, he'll be discussing very serious matters every day. But what he gets will be peanuts, you should pardon the expression, compared to what his counterpart down here, in the lobbying line, expects to get when the stuff hits the fan, because his market is so small.

50

"You see what I mean," Edgar said. "If the prosecutor in Philadelphia proposes to get you altered at a trial in a court of law, you will go to your criminal lawyer in Philadelphia and say to him: 'How much will it cost me to have you prevent him from cutting my balls off?' And he will tell you, and you will be happy to pay him, because even the thought of what they want to do to you makes you tingle, and money is no object.

"Then your criminal lawyer will go out and order up a big steak dinner, with a shrimp cocktail first, an espresso after, and the next day he will pay *Law Week* and tell his partner they can hire their secretary back again and stop doing their own typing. But if they propose to make business suits deductible, Herbie will be taking calls from Laramie and Kansas City and telling those guys that make suits that it's a very serious matter, but maybe they should all plan to meet at Bagatelle, because he does have some ideas. Pointing out at the same time, of course, that the cost of the trip from Laramie, and the room at the Madison, and the little bottles from the top drawer of the bureau in the Madison, and the lunch at the Bag, too, are all deductible business expenses.

"My friend will charge those birds three times what the guy in Philly will nail the poor hood who just wants to stay out of Leavenworth and make a living in the contracting business, like he always did. And Herbie will have ten or twenty many times as many guys to charge, as the guy in Philly has. Who will all retain him to represent their corporations, which deduct his outrageous fees. Which means the government does not collect fifty-two cents in taxes for every dollar that they pay him, and his clients will think they got a bargain.

"Herbie," Edgar said, "will think he got a goddamned Ferrari. Every time he starts to wonder if he did, all he will have to do is go down to the parking lot and look at it. He will say to himself: 'Of course, of course. It was cloudy this morning, and I brought the blue one.' And let me tell you something," Edgar said, "Herbie will probably bill the guy in Laramie for the time it took him to check.

"Now," Edgar said, "if I can have some espresso, now that we got all that out of the way, we can maybe get down to business. I honestly did not know what it was that you guys did. Now I think I do. I still don't understand it, but I think I know what it is. What it is is this: it is finagling. That is what your Washington lawyer does.

"That is what your Washington lawyer does," Edgar said, "if you have the good judgment to get yourself a good Washington lawyer. I did not have the good judgment to get myself a good Washington lawyer. I was under the impression that because I was getting divorced, and showing the poor judgment to get divorced while I was living down here, what I needed was a Washington divorce lawyer, which is a cheap sleaze. Well, not that I needed a Washington divorce lawyer, but I did not think that I could afford a good Washington lawyer. What I did not know is that a good Washington lawyer is much less expensive, in the long run, than a Washington divorce lawyer, even though he costs more in the short run. Because everybody down here is so goddamned used to finagling that when there isn't any finagling going on, people get very uncomfortable and tend to penalize the guy that didn't have the brains to go finagling. You follow me?"

"I follow you," I said. "I don't like it, and I don't agree with you, but I follow you."

"Good," Edgar said. "Now, what I did was get an asshole. He had a law degree, to be sure, and he specialized in divorce work, to be sure, but with all of them accoutrements, the guy that I got was an asshole. You follow me."

"I follow you," I said.

"You have met," Edgar said, "the Wicked Witch of the East."

"I thought it was the Wicked Witch of the West," I said.

"The movie was wrong," Edgar said. "Mary Claire comes from Teaneck, New Jersey, and that is not West unless you live in Provincetown, Massachusetts, in which case you are probably queer and not to be trusted anyway.

"The Wicked Witch," Edgar said, "enjoys fucking up my life. Gives her something to do. Couple rainy days, she stays home, but instead of tatting doilies, she finds something wrong with the support agreements and the alimony agreements and all those other dumb things. Which is another way of saying that the asshole which I had before screwed up on the agreements, or else she could not do these terrible things to me.

"Now," Edgar said, "classmate, bosom buddy, all that sentimental stuff, here is what I think: the asshole probably hasn't got time for my mundane matters anymore, if indeed he ever did. This is because he knows what I paid her, and he knows what I paid her lawyer, and he knows what I paid him, and he knows how much I had. The bunch of them should've gone into partnership and bought out King Saud.

"What I am," Edgar said, "is this, and he knows it: I am a little goddamned short. I don't have any trouble with Congress, the IRS, or the White House, at least that I know about so far. But I, too, even as thee, am forty-eight years old, or crawling up on it. I got kids thundering around the house I used to live in, carrying college applications and stuff. If I don't right now, I am gonna. And I did give her the goddamned house and all. Now I think maybe it'd be nice if somebody got the goddamned decree modified so maybe I wouldn't have to deduct seventy-eight percent of my take-home pay before I know what I've got left to maybe spring for a TV dinner for myself. So, what I want to know is three things, and you just give me the answers in order and save everybody a lot of time, which I cannot afford. All right?

"First thing: can I deduct this dinner? I mean, you had the prime rib and all, and it may not have been absolutely necessary to go for the Nuits-Saint-Georges when the Cabernet Sauvignon would've done just as well, but that's all right. Can I?"

I said: "Yes."

"All right," Edgar said, "then I will pay for it. Otherwise, you would get stuck, because I know you would find a way to deduct it. But I would like to take you to dinner.

"Second thing: can you handle the modification thing, so maybe the old bitch finally has to go to work, like the rest of the big kids?"

"Yes," I said.

He inhaled deeply. "This is the part I hate," he said. "Still and all, I got to ask: how much is it gonna cost?"

"Well," I said thoughtfully, "we're old friends, Edgar, and after thirty years, all I can say is that I'm glad you've gotten things pretty well straightened out for yourself. If you have. After all, we were roommates at Fordham. The only time you ever rejected my advice was when you decided not to go to law school. As much, much more than a new client, you're an old friend. And I agree with you. You're under an extremely onerous burden, and clearly, something has to be done about it. On the other hand. . . ."

"Yeah?" he said.

"Well," I said, "you do have a very serious matter here, and while I don't doubt that I can help. . . ."

At first I thought he was going to cry, and so I immediately reassured him. Then I thought that he was going to hit me. We got that misunderstanding straightened out. Then we went to court. We drew the justice whom I shall call Judge Walrus. Judge Walrus believes that Charlotte and Emily Brontë were liberated women, much to their detriment. Judge Walrus has a Holy Cross degree and a permanent affliction of the brain. Judge Walrus does not believe that the mothers of small children, weighing about one hundred pounds each, should be allowed to leave them unattended at school, or that such ladies should go to work.

Unfortunately for Edgar, Mary Claire's lawyer was as conversant with the views of Judge Walrus on the Sanctity of Marriage and the Family as was I. Therefore, Mary Claire's lawyer brought a counteraction for a Cost of Living Increase.

Mary Claire's lawyer won. When that news came down, Edgar really did cry.

I lacked the gall to send Edgar a bill. But, it seemed at the time, there was a bright spot in the whole period: another client of the firm's, in Syracuse, was extremely pleased to learn that I had been of some help in drafting new pollution regulations which left him with a virtual monopoly on the manufacture of marine heads. Joe Brann told him that, because Joe Brann was looking to the future, when Duncan would retire, or something, and thought to arrange for himself a bit of a layoff on Brann Marine Fabricators' legal bill. Joe was voluble in my praise. The boating industry began to place calls to our office, about representation on the Hill. Ed Bradley assured the other partners, senior to me, that I deserved substantial credit for the new business, and they gave it to me. Nobody so much as inquired about the hours, unbilled, I have devoted to Edgar's little problem. Right after its melancholy conclusion, I embarked for three weeks' vacation in the villa I had rented on Majorca. It was not my fault that Jeanne did not come with me. I invited her several times, but she kept talking about who would take care of the boys.

Jeanne having declined, I saw no reason to go by myself. I can't cook worth a damn. Maggie Capeless could give Escoffier a run for his money, and she was on vacation, too.

Four

I saw Edgar again in May, when I was in Boston. There had been a little trouble with a piece of clean-water legislation proposed by the Massachusetts legislature. My clients in Syracuse asked me to connect with their local counsel in Boston. I was only too happy to comply. I took the risk—and lost—that Boston counsel would be some jerk I could not stand. But shaping up the little fool—to the point at which he understood that saying something dumb on Beacon Hill could cause a monumental screw-up on Capitol Hill with some federal legislation we were fighting—took but the afternoon. I was able to call Franklin Melcher for dinner.

I have known Franklin since law school. I did not like Franklin in law school, and if the truth be known, I do not like him all that much now. Actually, that is wrong: I like Franklin pretty well now, but the reason for his rise in my esteem came after our evening in May, when he displayed a side of his character that I had never seen before.

It was in law school the conventional wisdom that Franklin Melcher did not shit. This was a deduction from the manifest

56

fact that his ass was made of iron and could not possibly undergo the requisite expansions and contractions. Franklin Melcher, with his hair cut short and his pince-nez on his nose, could endure longer hours on hard law library chairs than anyone else in our class. He knew the tax regs inside out and the most recent decisions of the National Labor Relations Board before they were published in the *Federal Register*. He knew the Rule Against Perpetuities. He seemed to have a fair grasp of the Federal Rules of Civil Procedure, even though he had not the slightest interest in ever entering a courtroom.

Franklin was a law buff, an odd trait for a law student; he actually loved what the rest of us found utterly boring. It was only meager consolation for us to hear one of our most pedestrian professors declare that the A students became law professors, the B students became partners in major firms, and the C students made all the money. Franklin was a terrifying machine to behold for anyone who harbored an occasional urge to take a night off, see a movie, and have a few beers. When he was named editor of the Law Review, the news spread as would have word that the sun had risen in the east that morning; from the second week of first year, no one had expected anything else.

Franklin was a prick on Law Review. I was case-note editor, flogging second-year students into prose mistakable for English, explaining cases deemed of great consequence to the legions of practicing lawyers who dwelt upon our every syllable. It was rather humiliating, later on, to discover that virtually no lawyers in the real world read any Law Reviews at all—the only lawyers who read Law Reviews are the lawyers who were on Law Review in law school and miss it. They work for lawyers who were not on Law Review and can afford to hire other lawyers to read and digest Law Reviews for them. Franklin made a hard job tougher. He was, as Jeanne observed, picky, picky, picky. He was also utterly without humor. He was a very disagreeable man to deal with.

After graduation, Franklin took his high grades and his

Law Review certificate and his wing-tip shoes back home to Boston. There he became an earnest associate in an earnest firm with several names and a penthouse office in a bank building. He gravitated toward corporate financial law, and since nobody ever triumphantly opposed any of Franklin's natural tendencies, he was soon running the section. He made partner in three and one-half years, still wearing the wing-tip shoes, the short back and sides, and the pince-nez.

He also made Marian, a joke which he did not understand when I made it. I called him Robin Hood, and he didn't get it. Marian looked like a small horse, perhaps a pony, who had read *Vogue* and believed it. She had a thin, angular frame and a terrible posture. She had more teeth, and larger ones, than Secretariat. She also had streaks of blond in her mousy hair. The idea of going to bed with her was unimaginable to any male but Franklin. Apparently he managed it, because they had three children. All of whom, to their great misfortune, favored both of their parents. To see them together was to be reminded of the Ledyard Dressage Competition at the Myopia Hunt Club, and they whinnied like horses, too. Franklin played tennis and once, when I was visiting them, dragged me to a polo match at Myopia.

I did not visit Franklin to watch polo. I visited Franklin to watch baseball. Corporate financial legal partners have certain obligations. Among them is the mandate to entertain corporate officers. A large number of corporate officers enjoy baseball. Those visiting Boston, to confer with Franklin and his spear carriers, expected to see the Red Sox. Franklin's firm has a skyview box at Fenway Park.

Ever since Bob Short cleaned Washington's clock, hauling his Washington Senators down to Arlington, Texas, and renaming them the Rangers—on the last night in town, the bosses distributed, free of charge, Manager Ted Williams' book on hitting, which the infuriated patrons ripped to shreds and discarded onto the playing field—I have been at least tolerant of Franklin and seldom missed an opportunity to see him.

In Boston. In the summer. When the Red Sox were playing at home. Otherwise, I avoided him. Franklin was useless in the winter.

It was because of that avoidance that I learned of Franklin's split from Marian about a year after it happened. The beginnings of a most remarkable change were noticeable on Franklin's face when he told me about it. As he quoted Marian, they had "outgrown" each other.

Marian had found someone closer to her own age—the service manager of the local Volvo dealership. Franklin described him to me as "nothing better'n a goddamned bookie." Franklin, also, had found new companionship: a rather fetching paralegal named Wendy, about twenty-three, who had proved most helpful to him on a complicated international finance matter he had handled in New York.

"Marian," Franklin said, with more resentment that I would have thought him able to muster, "called Wendy a cheap little tart."

Franklin told me that he did not see why Marian had to talk like that. I noticed that the pince-nez had been replaced by blue-tinted aviator glasses. I noticed that the short graying hair was no longer short. It had been blown dry. There seemed to be quite a lot more of it, and not only because it was longer either. I observed that Franklin was wearing a gold ID bracelet on his right wrist. And that his father's heirloom Hamilton watch had been replaced by a Seiko digital calculator. "I never said anything like that to Marian about that little gangster she took up with," Franklin said. "I let her have her fling. I didn't embarrass her. Nothing but a greasy little dago."

I did not meet Gene, the service manager, on that Boston visit. This deprivation I accepted with the best grace possible. But I did meet Wendy, who chewed gum. She talked of ficus trees recently purchased for their new condominium on the waterfront. From what she said, the accommodations were quite comfortable, but I begged off when she invited me to see them. From what she said, I was able to conclude with utter confidence that I could not stand her. I went downtown to the Parker House in a cab I shared with them, getting off there, instead of at the Ritz, where I was staying, because I had claimed to be meeting a friend there. All I wanted was a drink. By chance, I met Edgar in the bar.

"I was going to say I had a headache," I said. "Jesus, am I glad to see you. Tiant's finger still isn't right, I think, and Lynn was waving at sliders like they were long-lost relatives. And while all of this was going on, Wendy was massaging Franklin's bicep and talking about rock music. I had the worst hot dog I ever had in my life, and more beer'n I should've. This is the first time that I ever went to a baseball game and had a lousy time."

"You should go to court more often," Edgar said. "That'd get you used to misery."

"Look, Edgar," I said, "I told you there're no guarantees. There's a certain amount of trouble in this world, and there isn't anything that I, or any other lawyer, can do about it."

"Yeah," he said. "This I knew."

Edgar has had his ups and downs and is capable of some rancor toward whoever may be handy when he has had a drink or two. I thought a new subject might be more comfortable.

"I saw Jim Curry a week or two ago," I said. Edgar and Jim had been as close as Edgar and I, at Fordham, but I was never very close to Jim myself. For a kid out of Canton, Massachusetts, scraping through college on scholarship and financial-aid jobs, Jim had a very aristocratic demeanor, and it annoyed me. On about the fourth night of sharing his company, I asked him if he wore those chino pants, white wool socks, and run-over loafers when he was playing polo Sundays, and there resulted a distinct chilliness between us that never totally dissipated.

"That guy," Edgar said, "that fucking guy."

"He seemed to be doing quite well," I said.

"Oh, he is, he is," Edgar said. "Now. Now, he is doing all right. But back about fifteen years or so ago, he wasn't doing all right. When I dug my old friend out of the gutter; when he was just back from Vietnam and wandering around the world looking foolish, dead broke, and looking for a job that'd give him something to do, so he wouldn't have to end up spending the rest of his life in cheap saloons, telling people stories that weren't entirely true about his valorous deeds in Vietnam; back then he was not doing all right. Back then being a friend of Jim Curry's was like having a fatal weakness for stray dogs—you maybe felt kind all the time, but you always had a lot of dogshit on your floors, too, and you heard quite a lot of barking in the night."

"He seems to have quite a reputation now," I said. "Everybody I know seems to think he's one of the most talented journalists in Washington."

"Uh-huh," Edgar said, "that's exactly what I mean. He *is* talented, but he doesn't *use* it anymore. Now he's got a *reputation,* and it's a reputation as a journalist, not a reporter, and he don't need no talent anymore. Now he can coast, and loaf, and go to fancy dinner parties up in the high numbers on Wisconsin, and over on Dent Place, and way, way up on Foxhall, and he don't frequent no bars no more, because he's always having cocktails at the embassy. Some embassy. Tonight they're dining at the Watergate in some heavy hitter's condominium, and everybody there discusses what went on at Pisces, last night, where the swells meet privately to boogie, I believe the word is. And somebody says two syllables about foreign trade. Two days later, James F. Curry's got a thousand words about the balance of payments going out to influence governments everywhere, and it's all bullshit, every word of it."

"That's where I saw him," I said. "At a dinner party out in the Cathedral section."

"Naturally," Edgar said. "Bet it was black tie, too."

"Well," I said, "it was a buffet after Sills sang at the Ken

Cen, so just about everybody there was in black tie, yeah."

"Sure," Edgar said. "Sure, sure, sure. Jim Curry showers in black tie. He's got the only rubber tux in Washington. When he approaches the former Marietta Hope Dingbat, or whatever her name was before he married her, with lascivious thoughts in mind, and she's of a bollicking mood, he takes off his fucking cumberbund, and she takes off her tiara. And they go at it otherwise fully clothed, because there isn't that much time before the next gathering. He's a rotten son of a bitch, is all. Everybody told me that, and I should've known it, but I thought of him as an old friend of mine, and I didn't believe them." Edgar sighed. "They were right, and I was wrong."

"Gee," I said, "he was asking for you."

"With his mouth full of caviar, I bet," Edgar said. I did not say anything. As a matter of accuracy, I could have told him it was seafood Newburg, but the difference did not seem sufficiently important to mention. "What was he asking?"

"Well," I said, "it was mostly small talk. I don't see Curry that often, and neither one of us has much information about what the other one is doing. He just wanted to know if I had seen you, and how you were doing, and how your life was. That sort of thing."

"All of which he knows very well," Edgar said. "That bastard. You know what did it to him? It was Marietta that did it to him. She was the one with all the moves.

"You know Annie Curry?" Edgar said. "Jim's first wife?" I said that I did not. "I did," Edgar said. "*Good* lady. Dumb as rocks about some things, but she really loved him. Cared about him. She loved him so much, she knew he was screwing everything that jumped, and she just let him do it."

"That does sound dumb," I said.

"There's dumb," he said, "and then there's stupid. Annie was dumb. She kept her mouth shut. You know the old rules of grammar: neither is dumb, but both are stupid. Annie was dumb. She said nothing.

"Was she right? I dunno. There's two kinds of them women. One yells, and the other doesn't. They don't have much for lives, and they have the capacity to make it worse. Not better. Annie kept her mouth shut.

"Look," Edgar said, "what'd she have, huh? What do you think those women've got, staying home in the woods? Nothing, is what. They got diapers for a while. They got school lunches, and after that they don't have nothing. Except maybe the vanilla extract and the cooking sherry and the other girls that pack school lunches and play tennis and otherwise don't have anything to do all day. Hubby gets up in the morning and clothes his naked body and goes off to work. He comes home at night and listens to how the kids did in school and how Madge did in the ladies' doubles round robin. He has two drinks and watches the game of the week. Then he unclothes his naked body, and they go to bed and screw. Flowers and dinner out on the anniversary. New station wagon every three years. Thirty-dollar brooch, or maybe a nightie, on her birthday. On his birthday he gets a silk tie that doesn't go with anything he owns and cost fifteen bucks, from Sulka. Kids give him bookends they made in woodworking class. Every Saturday they go on a picnic or something, after he cuts the lawn.

"Then," Edgar said, "after everybody gets atrophy of the brain, a mail-order prefrontal lobotomy, for some damned reason or other, hubby gets a job in Washington. Now he's not gonna turn down 'Washington Correspondent' as a title, even if it is for three weeklies headquartered in Eagle Forks, Iowa, and she's not gonna stand in the way of his career. So in they come, the two of them a bit dazed, and they buy a house for more'n they can afford, and he goes up on the Hill in that Sulka tie that doesn't go with his suit.

"Three months later," Edgar said, "he knows exactly what is going on in that town. Or at least he thinks he does. But she's out in Rockville, making school lunches and looking for new Madges to play tennis with. She doesn't know what the fuck is going on. As a matter of fact, she doesn't even know that something's *going* on.

"When it dawns on her," Edgar said, "it is because he is not getting home in time for din-din, to hear how the kids did in school today. There is gin on his breath, and she thinks the truth is not in him. He says he has been hacking around in some bar, picking up information—which, after all, is how he makes their fucking living—and he is telling the truth. She thinks he has been hacking around with some blonde.

"She accuses him," Edgar said.

I could not resist it. "She says, 'Junior,' " I said, " 'you have been out getting your rocks off with Linda Morse.' "

"Ahh, shaddup," Edgar said. "Inna first place, any man can make a mistake. In the second place, the Lindas come later, in my experience. *After* you've been accused of a few Lindas.

"She accuses him, and she accuses him," Edgar said. "This is because she's scared. The guy doesn't understand this. He begins to resent it. He's been drinking free booze, sure, and nibbling a few canapés, but what he is doing is actually what he says he is doing, which is getting information. She doesn't believe him. Pretty soon, he figures: the fuck shouldn't I? And he does. Because there is a certain amount of gash around at those lash-ups, and it does seem like a shame to pass it up if you're getting blamed for taking advantage of it anyway.

"Now," Edgar said, "this is the pattern. But for some reason, Annie Curry did not follow the pattern. She got a little heavy, and she looked dumber and dumber, but she never drove him out. I think *he* resented *that*. The least she could've done was be a bitch and nag him into shacking up with some bimbo.

"So he shacked up with the bimbo anyway. Many bimbos. The lady from the *Trib*. A bit of slap and tickle with the kid from the Miami *Herald*. A little roll in the hay with the lady from Dallas, before lunch next day with the one who lobbied for the automobile industry, and cocktails that evening with the cookie from LA. Jim Curry. Jesus, did that guy move.

"He had two broads on the Hill, at least, and one down at State, and one worked in the White House, and another one for National Public Radio. And you know something, Kemo Sabe? Rat that he was, I liked him a lot better then.

"He looked like he'd been out drilling oil wells all night, and he had bags under his eyes you could have used to pack enough stuff for two weeks in another town. But he was working his ass off for me, and if he was fucking the rest of it off on some movie-star groupie that wound up on the presidential press plane, well, didn't scrape no tartar off my teeth.

"I never understood how Annie took it, but apparently she did and figured he'd come out of it. What I never understood was how his body did it; the man should've been dead three times over. Got more ass'n a toilet seat. Drank more booze'n Errol Flynn. Looked like hell all the time, which made me wonder some about all those women, but his work was dynamite, and all I got was praise from upstairs, I had the good judgment to hire him.

"Then he got tangled up with Marietta," Edgar said. "How that happened, I will never know."

"Well, whatever it was, it was good for him," I said. "He looks great."

"Oh," Edgar said, "I know that. I saw Jim Curry the end of last month. I was down in Our Nation's Capital, in the misguided expectation that I might perhaps call upon my children and determine whether they still recognized me, and I them, but of course, notwithstanding the most elaborate arrangements, old Mary Claire screwed it up again, and I didn't have a plane back until Sunday.

"You know something about these Election Years? They really hack the airlines. You can't get in, and you can't get out, all these Congressmen and staff types galloping back to their districts, to startle the hell out of the yokels. I tell you, Moses wanted to get his People out of Egypt, what he should've done was declare it an Election Year in Jerusalem, and there would've been no need to part the Red Sea—they would've swum it.

"Anyway," he said, "I got this friend of mine on the *Star* that I used to have a drink or two with, and I called him, and the bastard took me to Prayers at the Australian Embassy, where they got that beer that'll take chrome off a trailer hitch, and for some reason or other, Jim Curry was there, wearing a suit of all things. Looked like a movie star. Is there maybe something going on with the Australians I don't know about?"

"If there is," I said, "I don't know about it either."

"Well," Edgar said, "if Curry was there, there is something going on with the Australians. Anyway, it must've been a slow night for him and Marietta: he had on a regular suit. A pretty nice regular suit, of course. Could've chaired several meetings of the Interstate Commerce Committee in it. Nice red and blue striped tie, and a little piece of handkerchief peeping out of the breast pocket. But still, civvies. And I said to him, being pretty much of at a loss for some company, and way too old and tired to go down to Sarsfield's and look for it: 'Whaddaya say we have dinner down at Nick and Dottie's, or something?' And he looked at me, like he just spotted something suspicious on my cuffs.

"Now keep in mind," Edgar said, "this is my old college buddy. This is the guy that I hired when nobody else would hire him, and then I kept fighting off the publisher, had this very talented nephew that he was sure could do the same job, and I stayed at it until Jim finally gets the Pulitzer. This is the same cadaver, walking around, that I used to get expense accounts okayed for when he was fucking himself blind, all right? This is not some guy that I picked up at the gas station, like I was trying to cadge a free meal off of him. I was taking him at face value.

" 'Oh, hell,' he says, 'no, Edgar, no. We're going up to the Wilsons' for dinner.'

" 'Wilsons'?' I said stupidly.

" 'Up on Kalorama,' he says helpfully.

" 'The street I know,' I said. 'The fuck is Wilson?' He told me, and I still don't know. Or care.

" 'Oh, hell, Edgar,' he says, 'I'm sorry. Toby Wilson. New head of the National Endowment.'

" 'Who's *we?*' I said, and up glides this vision that he introduces to me as Marietta. I damned near shat myself.

"I know that broad," Edgar said. "I knew that broad from right after I knew Linda, when Marietta was working for the House Judiciary Committee, and she was still a broad. She used to hang out down at Duke Ziebert's, for Christ sake, and I may even have bought her a drink or two myself. Hell, I might even've bought *her,* but I was drinking so much then, I can't remember.

"I knew her when she was dating the well-known western Senator, all unbeknownst to the equally well-known western Senator's wife. Unless she happened to read the papers, wherein the broad was regularly quoted. And I knew her when she was making big eyes at a certain presidential assistant, and getting big eyes back. Now I know how Yastrzemski feels when some kid he saw with his son in Little League shows up to make the starting lineup in spring training.

" 'Jesus Christ, Marietta,' I said, 'it's been a long goddamned time.' Right," Edgar said. "Maybe I should've been tactful or something, and said: 'Good Lord, Marietta, you must be as old as the hills.'

"Well," Edgar said, "she got even with me. And I let her do it. I might as well've just rolled over, put all four feet in the air, and let her shoot me in the ear with a twenty-two. 'Too long, Edgar,' she said to me, 'much too long.' She said it in a voice that Formfit could make panties out of, or maybe Sulka could make those neckties that Jim used to get out of the kids' allowances for Father's Day.

"Those two," Edgar said, "those two've got more signals'n the Redskins ever heard of. They were calling audibles left and right at that embassy, and I wasn't even shifting. By the time they got through, they were both sure Sissy—whoever the hell Sissy is—wouldn't mind an extra man. In fact, she'd love it, and we were off to see the Wizard, the Wonderful Wizard of Oz.

"Now," he said, "you keep in mind what I said. First, I am upset, on account of how this woman that I married once, that I am paying the interest on the national debt to, will not let me see my kids. Which I flew down there at enormous personal expense to see. I was not in a good mood.

"Second, I have been pouring that depressant that they fly out of Australia on the diplomatic special down on my depression for about two and one-half hours, and it's hotter'n the clabbers of hell in the room that I am doing it in.

"Third, that I have had no lunch to speak of, because I hadda get some certain things done at the paper before I take off, and by the time I get them done, whatever lunch I'm gonna get I'm gonna get on the plane, and even though I always fly American, that is not no lunch that I call lunch.

"And besides, being scared shitless, I had three Bloody Marys.

"As a result of all of which, I am in no condition to play the kind of Mexican handball, or Arabian basketball, that these two old hookers that I used to know are playing with my head. What I was was hungry. So I said that I would go.

"Well," Edgar said, "they're not old hookers, for one thing; they used to be old hookers, but they're not anymore. And for another thing, they don't cuss much anymore. I remember Curry had a tongue on him that you could use to strip paint, and there was one night in a low-class dive that old Marietta got a bit peevish with a fellow—not, I might add, your obedient servant—and did a job on him that I would've thought you'd need a glass cutter to perform. But not anymore. Unh-unh. Now it's all 'Dear' this, and 'Darling' that, a peck onna cheek 'stead of a punch inna mouth, and where'd I leave my switchblade anyway?

"The first thing that they did, I had ridden to the embassy with my friend, they ordered up this silver gray Mercedes that they bought with the breakage from their combined incomes. It's only about as long as the Washington Monument would be, if you laid it on its side, and they got this fellow driving that used to be a bodyguard for Idi Amin but got fired because he was too big. And mean. And off we go to Grandmother's house.

"Whereupon I said," Edgar said, "as we swing up to Dupont and take other fashionable thoroughfares: 'Jesus Christ, James F. Curry, or do I repeat myself? You've come a considerable distance since I was handing out assignments. You know something about them Koreans you're not printing maybe?'

"Now," Edgar said, "I agree, this is not gentle discourse. But me and Jim is old friends, right? He is Butch, and I am Sundance. Maybe a little long in the tooth, but we always had a pretty good way with each other, and when one of us would come into the office wrecked in the morning, the other one would generally get all over him like a rash and laugh him out of it. I've known this guy for half my life. I'm congratulating him. He should know this.

"Does he know this? Maybe he does, and then again, maybe he does not. He never gets a chance to say. Because naughty Marietta horns in and says, quite haughtily: 'I inherited some money.'

"Now," Edgar said, "that is bullshit, and I know it. Marietta comes from some tank town in West Virginia, and until she got off the train in Union Station, she thought Mercedes was the first name of an actress named McCambridge. I mean, what is this shit? 'Oh, nuts,' I said, still thinking that we're playing by the old rules, 'don't give me that crap. I was just telling my old friend that I admired his car. And you, you've known me long enough yourself to know that's what I meant.'

"I guess," Edgar said, "that was not exactly the thing I should've picked to say. Because apparently Marietta had not fully listed to him previous liaisons of her own that began in various bars and, for all I know, ended there. There was this extended silence, which James F. Curry did nothing to repair,

Marietta Curry clearly wanted, and I was certain only of making worse did I dare to fix it. Therefore, with uncommon good sense, I kept my big mouth shut. For a change.

"We got to the party," Edgar said. "A rather spacious brick manse, with a semicircle drive, and carriage lights, and those nifty Mount Vernon col-yums situated two by each, on either side of the doorway, through which one could maneuver a Tiger tank without much difficulty, and all around about are stabled vehicles that cost a lot of money. Lemme put it this way: your basic Cadillac Seville is the dinghy for most of those land yachts, and it occurs to me that, as usual, I am in way over my head. And, further: why did I do this?

"To eat, naturally," Edgar said, "and I managed to unhorse myself of Rommel's staff car there and went inside.

"Now what we have got," Edgar said, "is this rented butler, which is clearly Arthur Treacher with a bad embalming job, or maybe Arthur Murray with a good one. And I stand there like a dummy in the foyer, all these women in long dresses swooping by me. All these men, freshly tailored, that very afternoon, washed, coiffed, and barbered, and I felt like I was watching Alfred Hitchcock's thing again, *The Birds,* except this time I was *in* it, and not doing any better'n the people that were in the last one did.

"From the foyer," Edgar said, "I pulled such as remained of my chestnuts and humped myself into what a lower-class guy like me would call the living room and there are fauna of many higher orders, some from State and some from Justice, others from such esoteric rookeries as the Washington *Post* and the Senate of the old U.S. I mean, you had a couple or three Undersecretaries in captivity in those precincts. One or more White House Assistants of various persuasions. A leading black. A couple of Iranians. A pride of real estate developers. One or two highly ranked amateur tennis players, each with a mean backhand. Some women that've been around since Christ rose from the dead. A guy who ran for President and lost, quite miserably. A top-ranked homosexual, of one sex or the other. A former spy. A current spy. A partridge in a pear tree. Which was me. And I looked like I had been in that pear tree for several days, too. During wet weather.

" 'Would you like a drink, sir?' this creature in a maid costume says to me, and I stood there on the astrakhan, or whatever that Oriental rug was, thinking: Actually what I would like is a rather stiff jolt of heroin, but I'm too ashamed to ask, and it'd probably make me sick anyway. So I took a path of least resistance and said: 'Yes. Gimme about as much bourbon as you can find, with some ice and some water, and go easy on the water.'

"And that," Edgar said, "was when the fun began. I told one of the Iranians that from Shah-an-Shah, I did not know, but I knew oppression when I saw it. I told our former Ambassador to the Court of the Shah-an-Shah that he knew it just as well as I did, and that he'd spent his whole term in Eye-ran playing dead, for various strategic reasons. I told the former presidential candidate why he lost, and that, in my well-considered opinion, it was entirely his own fault. Inasmuch as a moribund porpoise would've been able to read the mood of the voters better'n he had and make adjustments accordingly. I had several choice observations to make to the leading homosexual, most of which had to do with Anita Bryant, I think it was, and then I went in to din-din."

"Jesus," I said.

"I said nothing about Jesus," Edgar said. "Jesus hadn't come up yet. There wasn't none of that kind of White House Assistants around that night.

"A place was made for me at one of the tables," Edgar said. "The place was rather ostentatiously made for me. I took it anyway. It was clear to me, even in my weakened condition, that I was a *very* extra man and that had I vanished into thin air, it would have been perfectly all right with mine host, not to mention mine hostess. Whose name I still did not have when I sat down, and do not have to this very day. Nor do I want it.

"Plumped down next to me," Edgar said, "was this woman, grossly overweight, who declaimed to me, and world, that she was dieting. In which enterprise I wished her good fortune and added the observation that she could surely benefit from any success achieved in that line.

"This failed to elate her," Edgar said, "and she farted. I made appropriate mention of this reaction, which she, and a majority of our tablemates, found inappropriate.

"The subject was changed," Edgar said, "and rather abruptly, I might add. It was changed to matters of interest to the professional homosexual, who had also been seated with our little group. If there had been a professional leper in attendance, he would've been there, too. From the corner of my eye, I could see the Curry couple looking on, from the corners of their eyes, and from a much better table, too. I could also see that they were taking most inordinate satisfaction from my antics. It then occurred to me—to be sure, a little late— that they had set me up.

"You have got," Edgar said, "no idea how mean I am."

"Oh yes, I have," I said.

"From that point on," Edgar said, "I was the soul of charm, the paradigm of courtesy. Indeed, the prince of peace. I listened with attentiveness to the professional fairy. When it came the turn of the Congressman discredited by his adventures with the trollop, I maintained the peace. I drank nothing stronger than the wine, and very damned little of that. I told no bawdy stories, and I did not slurp my soup. When the quails were served, I made no comment as Madama Butterfly, to my immediate right, ate hair, hide, bones, and all. Nor any when she dumped the Beaujolais down her cleavage. I smiled and smiled and smiled, just like old Iago. And when there was a lull in the conversation 'mongst our little group, and I heard my old friend Curry saying quite stertorously that after all, Edgar was a dear old friend of his and they simply had to bring him, I introduced a harmless question that started the gibble-gabble going at our table once again.

"I tell you, Counselor," Edgar said, "drunk as I was, old John Paul Jones would've been right proud of me. I held my fire until I had the *Serapis* well within range on the broadside, and then I let all cannons go. I ate the crème caramel, and I swallowed coffee as though determined to turn dark brown by sunrise. I nodded and smiled. When they served the fruit and cheese and brandy, I ate the fruit and cheese and sniffed the brandy. I was the very model of a modern major general, and it was the worst time that I ever had, eating dinner, in my life. Were murder not against the law in the District of Columbia, I would have outdone Richard Speck and cleaned the whole joint out. Except I didn't have a sawed-off shotgun, which I would've needed to disable the whole group at once before they could bolt for the door. Because many of them lads, and all of the ladies, including the fat ones, 're very quick on their feet.

"And then, as I left, I thanked the hostess for having me as an unexpected guest. 'I didn't want to impose,' I said, 'but Jim would've been heartbroken. Ever since I found the shrink who cured him of his terrible mental and drinking problems and saved his job for him, he's considered me his best friend. I just can't say *no* to him.'"

"Well," I said, "that must've been the party Jim Curry talked about. It doesn't sound the same, but it must've been."

"What'd he say?" Edgar said.

"I don't know if I should do this," I said.

"I don't know if you shouldn't," Edgar said. "I took a cab home to the hotel from that party and thanked my lucky stars the Diamond cab came for once. Now you can either tell me or you can not tell me, and in the latter case, I will break the neck of this here Harp bottle and disfigure you for life. Because I know that bastard now, and I know that bitch he married, and I would rather have a nifty case of trench-mouth'n see either one of them again. Speak, O Muse."

"Curry told me that you'd gone downhill deplorably," I said. "Since last he saw you. He said you got loaded at a dinner party, scandalized everybody, slurred your words, and did everything but take your clothes off. He said you threw up in the coat closet, and made offensive remarks to his wife, and that he thought you were pretty much washed up."

Edgar sat back in the chair. He poured the rest of the Harp beer into the mug, let the head lie down, and raised the mug. I raised my glass as well.

"A toast," Edgar said. "It all comes down to this: after all, what're friends for?"

"I dunno," I said. "Like I said, I just came from the first ball game I ever had a bad time at. What do I know? The guy's a fool. He's going through the silly season or something. He's got this idiotic woman with him, and he looks like somebody you'd expect to see at a convention in Cleveland. How the hell do I know? If I said I knew, I would be lying."

"Then don't say you know," Edgar said. "But lemme leave you with this, Counselor: don't bet on anything that can talk."

"Huh?" I said.

"How's your love life?" Edgar said.

"Jeanne's fine," I said.

Edgar, for once, did not say anything. Erroneously I thought that I had topped him.

Five

In June, Edgar returned to Washington for a few days. He called my office right after Jeanne reported that she had not managed to shake the virus which had laid waste to her intestinal tract for the better part of a week. She said that she had stopped throwing up and therefore had nothing to contribute to the continuation of the runs. She said that she still felt very woozy. She said that she was sorry, but that I would have to take the boys to the ball game by myself.

I took that then in much better spirit than I would now. I took it in better spirit than I should have then. Jeanne is a fine lady, and I loved her dearly. But she was indisposed a great deal during our marriage. In fact, she was a pain in the ass. She took the long view of things. This was that in a hundred years, no one would give a shit what I did, so why should she be interested now? I should've told that woman where to get off a hell of a lot sooner than I did. If, in fact, I ever did.

Edgar said he was in Washington "to look around." The paper had sent him down.

"Actually, what the guy is doing is being nice to me and nailing the company for a free trip for me to see my kids. But I've been stale lately, and I probably would've gone to Portland, Maine, if somebody'd asked me to. Something about June that looks like April in Boston, I think. You live down here long enough, you get used to thinking that if it's April, it's getting warm. And if it's June, it must be. Don't even notice, there ain't no cherry blossoms around up in Boston. The sky's all gray, and the wind's raw. Just pull out your summer suits, like a damned fool, and spend the whole day freezing your ass off. Just because it's April. When it's still that way in June, you get pissed. Whatcha doon?"

I told Edgar that I was cleaning up some crap for a presentation on offshore drilling rights, which was true, and that I was bored silly, which was also true.

"Wanna have a drink?" Edgar said. He sounded as though he might have had one or two already.

"I'd love to," I said. "Thing of it is, I've got to get this stuff out before I leave. Then go home and get the kids, which'll stick me in traffic for forty or fifty minutes on the Whitehurst, and then it's an hour's drive up to Baltimore. At least."

"Call up the Orioles," Edgar said. "You're probably the only ones going anyway. Tell 'em you'll be a little late. They'll wait for you."

"Got an extra ticket if you'd like to come," I said. "Wife canceled."

"Who's in town?" Edgar said. "Sox're in Milwaukee tonight, which, unless they forget the agate type box score in the morning, I'll be able to find out how many runs each side got, and that'll be it. Bush town. No baseball, no interest in baseball."

"Mariners," I said, wishing I had not brought the whole thing up in the first place. The kids were trouble at the ball park, and Jeanne was no help herself. I was never quite certain how it was that I had gotten involved in the sport, but in retrospect, it seems to have been mostly Edgar's fault. His fault, and my perversity.

Edgar and I came from backgrounds similar economically—lower-middle-class—but greatly disparate geographically. Edgar came from the Savin Hill section of Dorchester, in Boston. I came from Northland, Wisconsin, where my father took more satisfaction from his title of professor at Northland College (biology) than he possibly could have obtained from his salary. I don't know what that salary was, but it was low.

When I was growing up, baseball was simply not a topic of discussion in my house. I guess the Braves moved to Milwaukee when I was a kid, and some fellow named Aaron was playing in the outfield, but quite honestly, I never paid much attention to them. Until I got to Fordham, I had never seen anything quite like Edgar. I have seen more of New England since then, and heard more of it, too. Hearing more has meant hearing the Red Sox games, no matter where you go, in New England in the summer. In the law, we call it assumption of the risk. In New England, they call it the Red Sox Baseball Network. The people up in Edgar's town are all nuts.

Confronted with this aberration, in college, I took to belaboring Edgar. Having a mean streak in me, I declared myself to be a Yankee fan.

I didn't know shit about the Yankees. All I knew was Ruth, Gehrig, DiMaggio (Joe), and Berra. I got that from reading newspapers, when I was not competing with someone, whose name I have forgotten, for the highest grades in history and government. That did not leave me much time. I didn't know much about history and government, except that high grades helped a lot in getting into law school. But it was enough for Edgar. It was enough for Edgar the way a small red cape is enough for a large brown bull.

The trouble was that what began as a diversion for me became an obsession. I am not proud of this. I agree with all the lofty types who believe that baseball is a dull game, interesting only to those with dull minds. I am afraid I have a dull mind. And affectation became affection. Not the team, but the game. I considered the lack of major-league baseball a major shortcoming, sincerely to be regretted, when the profit motive compelled me to move to Washington.

"Oh, good," Edgar said. "That sounds very exciting. You and me and thirteen hundred other pigeons, huddled together in eight rows along the first base line. I think, actually, that if I can't find something better'n that to do, I will just go up on the Hill with a small picnic basket and a bottle of Chablis, sit in the evening, and watch the muggings. Whyn'tcha give it a miss, and we can at least have dinner?"

"NCD," I said, which was college for No Can Do. "I promised the kids, and I promised the wife, and we were going to have crabs and oysters and beer, and now I've got to deliver."

"Well," Edgar said, "cross me off your dance card for tonight then. I'm not gonna spend two or three hours back and forth on the Ballwasher Expressway. . . ."

". . . Freeway," I said absently.

". . . to see Darrell Johnson, cast-off Red Sox manager, maneuver a bunch of misfits around an empty stadium in opposition to a bunch of guys I never heard of, dressed up in B. Robby and F. Robby uniforms. For all I know, somebody may even win, but I already had the vapors this spring and found them boring. Too boring to repeat on purpose."

"What was the matter with you?" I said.

"Old age?" Edgar said. "Middle age? A mild disappointment at the end of a mildly disappointing affair—it ended on a petty note, but to be honest with you, it wasn't very exhilarating when it began. I dunno. I just felt punk, dragging my ass around like I was eighty-three years old, and sick of it. We had a mother-jumper of a winter up there. Snow up the yin-yang. I got to the point where I was thinking of calling the Miami *Herald*. See if they could use an experienced copyboy. Wouldn't do any good, though; they probably converted to those damned little television sets that always make me feel as though the next sentence'll appear on Barbara Walters' face, and they don't need copy runners anymore anyway. I needed a change. I just didn't like the one I got."

"Anybody I know?" I said.

"Nah," Edgar said. "This J-School grad student at BU I met at a seminar. Nice enough kid, but that was what she was. Had no idea who Alger Hiss was. Is. I never really expected much from the exercise, and that was about what I got—the exercise. I didn't really, I can't really, complain, although I guess that's probably what I'm doing, come to think of it. Hey, look, I'm sorry. You gotta go. How about lunch or something?"

We agreed on the next day, but something came up, and I left word for him at the Madison Hotel that I would check back in later in the afternoon. He called me shortly after five. There was a good deal of commotion in the background.

"Nice going, Counselor," Edgar said. "Any particular reason you decided to leave me standing at the altar, waiting at the gate? Get me into Lion d'Or with all them guys from Texas, so I can watch the rich get fat and tender while I shift from foot to foot and wonder if there's enough slack left in the Mastercharge for me to order up a small basket of rolls and a short beer?"

"I called the Madison," I said lamely.

"Well, my friend," Edgar said with relish, "I am a working newsman. 'Working press,' we call it, in that crusty tradition that we have. I did pretty good to fly the Madison past the very nose of the Bob Cratchit we have got in Accounting in the first place. He would've had me in some fleabag in the Northeast section, two bucks a night, a fresh light bulb of your very own which you must turn in at the desk when you check out. Unless you really check out, but without physically leaving the room, as many of the inmates regrettably do, on overdose of one kind or another. In which case the attendants from the meat wagon unscrew the bulb and hand it in at the desk while they're handing you out on the gurney with a sheet over your face. Clean linen every month, bathroom's two blocks down and one block over, the Gulf Station. Ask attendant on duty for key.

"The only way I can get myself *into* the Madison, Counselor, is by making damned sure I get myself *out* of the Madison at a less-than-civilized hour each and every morning that I wake up billeted there. In order to consume many pieces of toast, and wedges of cantaloupe, and cups of scandalously weak coffee. In further order that I may obtain sufficient raw materials for the convincing pretext of writing columns and columns of inside stuff, filched from the very brains of the mighty by your artful correspondent. The mighty, of course, ingesting toast, melons, and coffee furiously, in order to stall while they desperately try to think of something which is both plausible and sufficiently sensational to get them prominent mention in an election year, but not so magnificent as to get people to start thinking about calling in the grand jury.

"Them melons and bread're probably nourishing, Counselor, but they ain't tasty, they don't come accompanied by no martini, and I will give it to you with the hair and horns still on: they don't make up for lunch."

"Did you get anything?" I said.

"If you mean *lunch,* Counselor," Edgar said, "as a matter of fact, I did. I had the asparagus with hollandaise sauce, a small salad for my large bowel, and crab en chemise, which was superb. While dancing attendance upon learned counsel, who never showed up, I had two silver bullets, and with my luncheon, I consumed a full bottle of Korbel Natural champagne. Then I signed the charge slip with a flourish, turned it over, and wrote your name down as my guest. So, you bastard, you'd damned right well better remember what a fine lunch we had, because I can foresee trouble with that little item when it hits Cratchit's desk—I would anticipate trouble with that one if Amelia Earhart's name was on the back and I could prove I actually talked to her."

"Well, at least you didn't go hungry then," I said.

"You have got to pay attention, Counselor," Edgar said. "Otherwise, you will never make a career for yourself in the law and will be forced to spend the rest of your life dabbling in shit and chemicals mixed by the makers of shitcans for ships in Syracuse.

"A newspaperman never goes hungry. We are just like the Army and travel on our stomachs. We travel, as a matter of fact, *for* our stomachs. Where're you taking me for dinner?

"And don't tell me *home*. I love Jeanne. I think the whole bloody damned world of Jeanne. She's kept her figure, so far, and she's kept her husband, so far, and you got two fine-looking boys, an immaculate home in one of the better sections, and even the dog is well behaved. I would imagine that Jeanne is pretty good in the rack as well, and as a matter of fact, I have imagined that in considerable detail, which I will discuss if you wish, although I prefer to keep our liaison secret, even from her.

"Anyway, Jeanne is a remarkable and accomplished woman. But, Counselor, Counselor, she can't cook worth a lick, and she knows it. I can stew up the Spaghetti-Os at home, my Morton's Hungry Man frozen turkey dinner, or almost anything that looks like food but is really something else that some mad Polack invented out in Skokie, Illinois. And frequently, I have. But when I am on the road, as Bing and Bob used to be, I eat well for a change, just to let the liver and the lights know that I am looking out for their best interests. I have a question pending, Counselor."

"I thought you came down here to see your kids," I said.

"I did," Edgar said, "and I'm gonna. But that's Saturday, and this isn't, and besides, I got to get my strength up before I go and confront that sawmill that I used to be married to and am now preserving at an annual expense only a little bit greater than that for maintaining the Lincoln Memorial. And she's not as good-looking either, although the last time I saw her she was almost as big.

"Tell me something, Counselor: why'd we marry late? And

why, if it was so we could hell around awhile first and develop our judgment, which you evidently did, and I most assuredly did not, did I pick the Vampire Lady of Teaneck, New Jersey, while you selected Jeanne, formerly of the Angelic Choir? Everybody else I know, that's at my age and in this fix, got the kid thing over with a long time ago and makes only seldom reference to his former spouses. Mostly first snapping their fingers a couple times and settling for 'What's'ername, there, my first wife.' Can you tell me that? Will you tell me that?

"Will you buy me dinner, *please?* You owe it to me. I carried you all through first-year theology and second-year philosophy, and I didn't do you no harm, neither, when the *Summa Theologica* proved a little intricate for your taste. Where would you be without me? Passing papers in Mamaroneck, most likely, instead of rubbing shoulders with the powerful. You oughta buy me dinner every night of my life, and brunch, as well, on Sundays."

"I'll call Jeanne," I said.

"Do," Edgar said, "and give her my warmest personal regards. Tell her she may join us if she wishes. But on to more important matters: to what opulent establishment are you taking me tonight, and what time should I meet you?"

"I don't know," I said. "Tell me where you are, and I'll meet you there for a drink, and then we can go to dinner."

"The Class Reunion," Edgar said. "Saloon, down on. . . ."

"Know the place," I said. "See you in forty minutes."

Now I was in trouble. Jeanne had disliked Edgar since the day I introduced them. She thought him vulgar (I said: "coarse"), rude ("outspoken"), cynical ("skeptical—he has to be, in his work"), too fond of the booze (no reply), unfaithful to his wife, whom Jeanne also disliked (again, silence), and generally no good.

Jeanne is a graduate of Marymount College, in Tarrytown, New York. She is accustomed to an orderly life, something of which Edgar, for all the remarks that have been made about him, has never been accused of committing. Jeanne would choose dinner with a viper over cocktails with Edgar. But then again, she had been ill, and while we had nothing planned for the evening, I did feel some obligation to go home. I called her up.

"Still kind of weak," she said. "Actually, the only thing I've been able to keep on my stomach is tea and toast. I'm lying down."

"Edgar's in town," I said.

"Aha," she said, "so that's it. Now I know what made me sick."

"Jeanne," I said, "he's an old friend and a good guy."

"Oh, come on, Peter," she said, "he's a ruffian. He's one of your old drinking buddies from college who thinks he's still about twenty, and it's ludicrous. He's feeding off you, and for more than food, too. Free legal advice. Free sympathy. Free this and free that. Come to your senses, honey; the guy's a loser and a leech, and you're wasting your time with him. Come home and give me tender, loving care. Tell the freeloading bum your wife's sick, and you can't go out and get drunk with him tonight."

"Jeanne," I said, "I stood him up for lunch."

"So what?" she said. "You've stood me up plenty of times. I don't recall many dinners out, in amends."

"I called his hotel," I said, "and when they told me he was out, I asked if they could tell me where he was. And he'd left word that if anyone called, he was having breakfast with the Chairman of the House Subcommittee on the Offshore Drilling Lease Law Amendment, and then he'd be at the hearings."

"Oh," she said.

"Now," I said, "twice a week, that ruffian takes that goddamned column of his and tells about four hundred and fifty thousand people in New England, which is the area I'm working on, what they ought to think about any issue that comes into his head."

"Uh-huh," she said.

"I never would've dreamed that question would interest him," I said, "but apparently it does. And the reason that I missed lunch with him today was because two papers in Maine, one in New Hampshire, and three in Massachusetts took up the cudgels against my clients today, and they were almost frantic."

"Have a nice dinner, dear," Jeanne said. "Don't come home half-drunk, if you can help it."

I located Edgar at the second table from the rear, on the right-hand side of the Class Reunion. This was not an easy task. The Class Reunion is decorated in black, mostly, and it's none too brightly lighted. This facilitates the planting of stories by White House staffers with chosen reporters. It also conduces to the safe conduct of refreshments before and after the commission of infidelities, because a customer standing at the bar would find it very difficult to identify any two people seated more than fifteen feet away.

When Edgar worked in Washington, the Class Reunion was the place where he held court each evening, from shortly after five until at least eleven. "Unless," as he put it, "something more promising turns up."

Something often did. The ratio of unattached males to unattached females in Washington greatly favors the males, and there are a good many ladies in the city who have become in consequence quite bold, as my mother used to say. Edgar arranged at least two liaisons of fair duration at the Class Reunion and, from what he said, at least, a considerable number of one-night stands. Like a great many divorced men whom I know, Edgar anticipated the official collapse of his marriage with intermittent attacks of wanderlust; he celebrated the divorce with an outbreak of satyriasis so extreme as to be almost frightening. Seldom was he seen without a woman companion, and for quite a while, it was almost never the same woman two nights in a row. At the party held at the CR, as he calls it, to observe the occasion of his return to Boston, I saw at least ten women with whom he had had casual affairs. I assume each was aware of his adventures with the others, but everyone seemed pretty cordial toward one another, loudly demanding that a plaque be purchased and installed over his usual table.

When I found Edgar that night last June, he had what he called "the usual committee" around him. There was the fellow from the *Post* who drinks grapefruit juice and vodka. There were two free-lance writers from the Coast, one drinking Wild Turkey with chasers of Heineken, the other with three on-the-rocks glasses in front of him, each filled to the brim with bourbon. There was a woman from the *Star* who was having a Bloody Maria and an argument with a neurasthenic young man who looked like somebody I had seen at Treasury. Beside him was a woman from *New York* magazine who had just done a bitchy piece about piety in the White House. Two tables away, Linda Morse sat holding hands with a young fellow from the National Labor Relations Board, who had just left his wife. She was oblivious to Edgar, and Edgar was ostentatiously ignoring Linda. Linda looked considerably older than she should have.

"And now, Ladies and Gentlemen, and Children of All Ages," Edgar said, "guard well your tongues. For here approaches a card-carrying minion of the Prince of Fucking Darkness, and he will have your ass in a sling in a moment should you affront him. I give you that rara avis, that plague of locusts upon this fair seat of government, a lawyer."

Edgar's claque applauded, some booing and others hissing.

Edgar stood up. He walked around the table, put his arm around me, and said: "C'mon, Counselor, leave this trashy assemblage, and let us proceed to table. The fuck're we going?"

"Edgar," I said, "confidentially, you look pretty drunk to me."

"Confidentially, Peter, old thing, I *am* pretty, drunk. I am also pretty, sober. But right now I am only about, oh, one-third drunk, whatever my pulchritude, and I want my goddamned dinner."

I took Edgar down the street and around the corner to

the Sans Souci, where I had made a reservation. I wanted a place close enough to reach on foot and close enough for Edgar to leave on foot for the hotel. Thirty years ago, I observed in him a startling phenomenon of Second Wind: when he is off on a toot, and he clearly was that week in Washington in June, he can drink his lunch, work all afternoon, commence with the cocktail hour at five, drink until eight or nine, eat a large dinner, and continue drinking without the slightest change in his already-boisterous behavior until around two or three in the morning.

Then he goes to bed, sleeps five hours, and appears for work at the regular time. I can't do that, and I had to be up in the morning. It was imperative that I avoid driving Edgar somewhere in my car, because it is virtually impossible to get him home, once he has gotten you out.

"Sans Souci," Edgar said, nodding, "that will be satisfactory, Counselor. Motion allowed."

We had drinks, of course, while looking at the menu, I because I needed one by then, Edgar because he demanded them.

"Much better," he said, of the martini. "Then again, of course, there is no such thing as a bad martini."

"Long day?" I said.

"If I ever had a short one," Edgar said, "it slipped my mind."

"Much footwork," I said, "with few results? Kind of day I've had, come to think of it."

"Peter," he said, "it's not that. I don't mind the tearing around, trying to trap some Congressman before he can think up a good runaround to give me. You get the 'Yes, he'll see you in a hour,' so you go do something else and then come back. That's when you get 'I'm awfully sorry, but he had to go back to the House to make roll call.' Which, of course, he had every intention of skipping, in order to grant me several sage remarks about one of his pet proposals which I could put in the newspaper. But either his Administrative Assistant or his Legislative Assistant started thinking about what was probably on my mind, and decided that it was gonna do the candidate for reelection more harm than it was going to do him good, and the Congressman slipped out the side door, while I was coming through the front.

"I don't mind that at all. I've been at this racket now since Nineteen-fifty-two, and people've been giving me the runaround, or trying to, at least since Nineteen-fifty-four. They were doing it before that probably; I just wasn't cute enough to outcute them and went around believing all their excuses, their evasions and half-truths, and probably ten or a dozen outright goddamned lies. No, in twenty-six years, I have to admit I kind of like this game.

"I dunno, always, which one of us's playing cat and who's got the role of mouse, but I don't even mind it very much when I get the rodent's role. Because they let me use that newspaper up there, from time to time, to express my considered views of threats to this Republic, and when I find some claw marks on my soft, gray, fuzzy coat, I have this thing to do: I get even. There are some folks who have left a few bruises on my otherwise-impeccable professional credentials, but there is not one of them, so far as I know, who has tried to do it for a second time. And if there is somebody that I never caught when he blew smoke up my ass, once or more than that, well, that fellow is smarter'n I am, and he deserves his success.

"No, Peter," Edgar said, "it's not the heavy physical work I mind, not even the heavy mental stuff. It's the cheap stuff, the nasty little tricks that people try to pull on you, and they're so clumsy at it that you don't really even get mad at them. All you feel is contempt.

"Catch this, willya, my friend?" Edgar said. "Must've been, let's see, 'Seventy, 'Seventy-one, and I was all tangled up in a lot of newspaper administrative hackwork which carried a title that Pharaoh would've envied but did not involve any of the kind of work I really like to do. I can handle administration. I can do it. I can also shave my face with a blade which a lady has employed to depiliate her legs, but that would leave my flesh streaming with blood, and it would hurt like hell when the Skin-Bracer hit it. So, if the lady is civil enough to tell me that she has used my razor, I put a new blade in it. And if she isn't civil enough, and I filet my face like a god-damned haddock with the first stroke, I mention the omission to her. In dulcet tones, of course.

"I may make a stupid choice now and then, which I seem to recall doing once to a catastrophic degree in a matrimonial matter, but at least give me the opportunity to make the stupid choice—don't try to hornswoggle me.

"Anyway," Edgar said, "I was vaulting around the paper. . . ."

"This was down here?" I said.

"Yeah," he said, "down here, and I got more titles'n the head of the KKK, and more dumb memos to read, about things I don't care a damn thing about, and one of those stacks was résumés from aspiring young journalists. The ones that called themselves *journalists* I put into a pile to read last, if ever. The ones that said *reporter* I read with as much interest as possible in a joint where you had four hundred résumés on hand, some from people actually quite fit for their work, and only about five or six openings at any one time with which to do a reverse Loaves and Fishes bit. And then there were the ones I read immediately, because by some clever intuition, such as a green memo slip reading *Friend of Publisher Family,* usually abbreviated *FPF,* I could sense that this applicant was unusually well qualified and should be, if at all possible, added to the payroll yesterday at a salary twice my own. If some suitable work, such as fetching coffee or covering the White House, could be found.

"Generally," Edgar said, "I was able to get Publisher off hook with Family Friend. Which, it finally dawned on me, was what Publisher wanted me to do instead of overrunning the paper with buffoons at great expense to Publisher's treasure.

So I would scrawl some noncommittal note to the effect that the lad or the lass showed promise but needed additional seasoning in the field. Like being buried in it for eternity nine miles southeast of Topeka. Which I did not add. Or that while the applicant was unusually well versed in her specialty, problems of space did not permit us to publish a daily column on crewel, and had she considered the Singer Sewing Center Newsletter?

"Then one fine fucking day," Edgar said, "when more than the usual number of things had gone wrong, putting the total up well into the hundreds, an FPF résumé came down that absolutely iced the cake. This kid, unless he was the most consummate liar since Dick Nixon, looked absolutely perfect on paper. He was Temple, in English, which at least raised the possibility that he could write a declarative sentence without falling down in a swoon of hypoglycemia as a result of the exertion. He had edited the student newspaper and interned at real live newspapers every summer starting in his sixteenth year.

"I was aware that he had probably obtained those slots as results of other FPF applications," Edgar said, "and that he could probably muster glowing letters of recommendation from his superiors, by dint of the same sort of polite request. Still, he had attached clips, and unless his FPF connections all across the globe had obtained for him in each city his own personal rewriteman, the kid was pretty good. Not flashy, not uppity, nothing smart-ass. Just good, steady reporting.

"Hard news, too. Not a damned thing about the immorality of the War in Vietnam, under the by-line of some whelp summering at Tanglewood and pretending to be a reporter. For the previous year, he had been doing a very creditable piece of work as a general assignment reporter in Harrisburg, and I figured that it would be nice if possibly I might, for once, demonstrate to Publisher that FPF was not invariably the kiss of death.

"So I wrote to this perfect kid, name of Spinelli—how the

Spinellis got to know all those Publishers, I can't imagine; probably all descended from bootleggers without regard to race, creed, or country of national origin—and invited him to come in for an interview next time he was going to be in Washington. This, freely translated, means: this is a buyer's market, kid, and we don't spend one dime more than necessary, so we have no intention of paying your expenses.

"He called two days later. He was very polite; he asked me for an appointment at my convenience, which he would meet precisely. So—all the eager ones do that, and some of them turn out to be pretty good reporters, because hungry is a good thing for a new reporter to be—I said that would be fine, and marked it down, and waited with mild interest to see if this kid was, in actual fact, perfect.

"He was," Edgar said. "His background was perfect, his clips were perfect, and damned if he was not, in person, himself, perfect. He was neat; he was clean; he had his hair skillfully barbered to the respectable length. He was polite, but there was that little edge to it that said he was an aggressive lad, if need be, and would very courteously chop your balls off if you tried to lie to him. He was Four-F, on account of some ailment that was minor for civilians but major for the military, apparently, or else his draft board had an FPF code, too. I dunno. Either way, I was not gonna have to look forward to getting this showdog all trained and then watch helplessly as they snapped him up and paid for his ticket to Southeast Asia.

" 'Son of a bitch,' I said to myself, 'here I have got one Michael Spinelli, which I can hire without flinching as I do it and get myself a brownie point or two with Publisher in one fell swoop.

"So," Edgar said, "Michael came to the big city. He was put on general assignment, and he did quite well at it. Not so well that older and less-talented hands were miffed, but well enough so that older and less-talented hands could be discreetly shifted around until they fetched up doing the Garden Page. He was, like Charlotte said to Wilbur, the Pig, *perfect.*

"For about four months," Edgar said. "For about four months he was perfect. And then I noticed that he didn't seem to have a lot of friends around the joint. Pals. Chums. Drinking buddies. People seemed to avoid him. Well, not exactly. They were just rather busy when he happened to be around.

"I thought it might be jealousy of an FPF. That'll happen. I didn't spend all my waking hours agonizing over the problem, I mean, but still, it was sort of like one of those little pimples that used to spring up behind the right ear, when you and I were young, Maggie, which you could fondle and torment while you tried very hard to look like you were thinking, while trying even harder actually to think. It sort of puzzled me, and since I am a perceptive soul, I do not like things to puzzle me.

"So, on days when I had a brief interval available for prayerful meditation, I begin to watch him. Quite covertly, of course. Now, I was working my ass off then. I came in early, and I left late, and except for those rare days when I rose defiantly from my chair, which was giving me goddamned bedsores, for the luvva Mike, and proclaimed that I was taking a long lunch, and anybody who didn't like it could go ahead and shove it, I was almost always there.

"I was there when Spinelli came in in the morning. If his shift was nine o'clock, he arrived at eight-fifty-nine. If he was through at five-thirty, his desk was neat and his jacket gone from the rack at five-thirty-one. Being a considerable slob myself, constitutionally unable to get anywhere on time, I was impressed favorably by the morning punctuality and envious of the evening's. I couldn't understand how he did that or why he wanted to. I never knew a reporter in my life, good or bad, who wouldn't sit around and bullshit for hours, quitting time or not.

"I decided the kid was maybe too perfect, and I would make an effort to loosen him up a bit. Tell him some of the things he would've picked up in conversation that would have been a hell of a lot more enjoyable than mine, if he had only joined in it.

"Besides, maybe he wasn't perfect. Maybe he was possessed of that one redeeming fault, and maybe his was just shyness, the kid from the woodlands in the big city, feeling his way along.

"Anyway," Edgar said, "I walked past him as he sat down one morning precisely on the dot of nine, or whatever it was, and said to him: 'The boss likes to get a memo from me after a new man's been here six months or so, progress report kind of thing. I like to give the boss what the boss wants. Your stuff's good, I know that, but the boss also likes to know if you're happy, and what your plans are, and maybe what areas you'd like to specialize in. So I thought we could have a couple beers after work.'

"'That's very kind of you, Mister Lannin,' he said, 'but it really isn't necessary. I'm very happy here, and I like just what I'm doing.'

"'Well," I said, 'we can have the beers anyway and just shoot the shit for an hour or so.'

"Now he begins to look worried. And I begin to wonder: is this kid maybe a fairy or something? Nobody ever sees him, he hasn't got any friends that I know about—has he maybe got some friends he doesn't *want* us to know about?

"The hell, Peter, I don't care if you diddle *goats,* in the privacy of your own backyard. But if I got a reporter that's gonna get arrested up in Georgetown in a dress some night, and he's a boy, and the cop that arrested him was a Casual Clothes Squad fellow who wasn't really interested in the best blow job he ever had, but was willing to pretend he was until he made the bust, well, I think that might be my business. FPF or no FPF, you wave your whanger where whanger waving's not permitted by John Law and get captured in the effort, you could get my paper in a bunch of very awkward trouble. And every single other one of our reporters will have to waste some energy keeping their tempers down when some hostile bureaucrat sees a nifty little insult as a way of distracting their attention.

"So," Edgar said, after we had ordered wine and lemon sole, "I said to him: 'Well, c'mon, kid. Meet up at Jenkins Hill,' or wherever the hell I was hanging out then, 'and we'll gab and maybe have a sandwich, and that'll be it.'

" 'I can't,' he says, quite firmly, which is to show me that he's scared the truth'll make me mad, but much too honorable to lie to me, being perfect and all. 'I can't, Mister Lannin,' he said. 'I'm going to law school, nights, at GW, and I have a class at six, and the traffic and everything. . . .'

" 'Why, Michael,' I said. I never heard anybody call that kid Mike, you know? I also never heard nobody call me Mister Lannin, for that matter. 'Shithead' was more common. 'Michael,' I said, 'that's very commendable. First year, I suppose?' 'No,' he says, with firm bravery, 'second. I had credits that I got when I was working in Harrisburg, and I transferred them.'

"Now, Peter," Edgar said, when the Pouilly Fumé had arrived, and he had inhaled about a third of it, "as you yourself know, I have nothing against learning in the law or ambition generally. Probably because I have very little of either myself. Lots of reporters go to law school, some because they want to cover the Supreme Court, and others because they detest their spouses but also dislike the taste of alcohol and thus must find something else to do in the evening. But this kid was the first one I'd met that was, *seemed*, ashamed of it. 'Twarnt no modesty, neither, or at least I didn't think it was. I endeavored to cheer the lad. 'That's great, Michael,' I said. 'You thinking of going into private practice, job with the government, or something?'

"Peter," Edgar said, "that was when the perfect kid lied to me, and I just discovered it today, seven, eight years later, when I ran into him up on the Hill. He said to me: 'I don't think so, Mister Lannin. I'm very happy here. But the law's a good discipline, and I figure it can only help me with my job, to do it better.'

"That lump of oleo should've put me on guard," Edgar said. "But it didn't. Michael matured in the mechanics of his regular profession and continued in law school, and one Sunday the engagement pages of the Philadelphia papers reported his betrothal to one Sharon Something-or-Other, whose background at Bryn Mawr and whose work with retarded children clearly demonstrated that she was perfect, too. It was a good picture, of a very lovely young lady.

"One night, after they were married, I ran into them having a hamburger at Nathan's, dressed in classy clothes and filled with joy by some damned Serious movie they'd seen. And as any fool would have expected, Sharon assured me that Michael had told her *so* much about me, and spoke *so* highly of me, and was just *so,* well, ecstatic about his job.

"Right. If Michael was ever ecstatic, I am Martin Bormann, and Simon Wiesenthal, of Vienna, will probably be eternally grateful to you if you give him my current address at the headwaters of the Amazon.

"Time passed," Edgar said. "and so did a number of closing hours, many of which I attended. At last I winched myself up by affixing an eyebolt in the concrete of my liver and concluded that while I had a dreadful divorce, and a hatful of bills, and a job that I hated, I was still not yet dead, which was something, anyway, and that I should get myself the hell out of here while I was still in a condition to handle my own transportation. That I did."

The fish arrived, and Edgar went at it like a wolverine. With his mouth full, he continued. "Today, since the day I left, was the first time I'd seen that little son of a bitch. He came to my farewell party at the CR, to have a couple of beers, and that, of course, was exactly what he had, two beers. I neither saw him nor heard of him since. Not that I inquired.

By then I had decided that perfect people made me jealous or uneasy, neither of which conditions I enjoy as much as reasonable inebriation, and both of which I therefore avoid.

"He was coming up the northwest steps of the Longworth Building," Edgar said. "Looked like something out of *Gentleman's Quarterly,* except more tastefully dressed. The buttons on the sleeves of his glen plaid suit had real buttonholes underneath them. The attaché case cost about a million bucks, and probably had at least that much in it.

"Michael Spinelli was not alone," Edgar said. "He had with him that rancid old whore Congressman Prideaux, who had just spent the morning in my sight, and in my vision, gutting the drilling bill, which will, of course, fuck up the New England economy *and* shoreline, if it's left the way it is now, after that performance, and the two of them're chortling and giggling like a couple of salamanders.

"Joining also in that merry company," Edgar said, "were three ladies, chronological ages around twenty-two, years of worldly experience approaching forty-five. Their names were not known to me, but their genus and species were, and while I have been away from here a long time, there are several breeds that I have met before. I would venture to say that if I went out to the Zoo, I might find a different zebra than I saw the last time, but the color scheme, I bet, would be just about the same.

" '*Edgar,*' says this engine-turned Hessian, 'this is a wonderful surprise. We were just going back to the Congressman's office—you know Bob Prideaux, of course'—and I nodded, rather curtly, I suppose—'and Bob, this is Edgar Lannin, the fellow I was telling you I thought I saw at the press table when I peeked in this morning.' "

"Prideaux returned my nod, at a discount. 'The *minute,*' Michael said, 'that I thought I recognized you, I called up the Press Gallery, and they said you were in town. Oh, and this is Kathy, and Ellen, and Judy.' The ladies made sounds like an aviary.

" 'What brings you down here, Lannin?' Prideaux rumbles. 'You know what brings me down here, Bob,' I said. 'What brings you up here, Michael?'

"He's got this grin now, that you would have to put the dimmer on if you were crossing the Key Bridge with him late at night in a convertible, and he decided to turn it on. 'Business, Edgar,' Michael says. 'I'm with Capstone Consolidated, and we're very interested in this drilling bill, and as you know, Bob is, too. And I thought we might renew old acquaintances and talk about it over dinner.'

" 'And will the ladies be able to join us?" I said.

" 'Of course,' says Michael. 'As a matter of fact, Judy, here, came along especially to meet you when we said we were going to try to find you. And during dinner, we thought, maybe, at the Montpelier Room, we could explain to you a few of our thoughts on this thing, and then go to Pisces.'

" 'This,' I said, 'would all be off the record, I assume.'

"Well, he ain't perfect after all. He doesn't know when somebody's giving it to him. 'Oh, no,' Michael said, 'strictly on the record. Just not for attribution.'

" 'Thank you,' I said, 'that's what I thought. Unfortunately I have another engagement. Ladies,' I said, 'Gentlemen, I must go. Do have a lovely evening, and may I suggest, Michael, even though I am not versed in the sacred mysteries of your learning, that I would think it fairly probable that the five of you could deduct all personal expenses, under the heading of occupational seminar?' "

Edgar finished his fish, finished his salad, finished his vegetables, and finished the wine. He ordered espresso, and brandy, and pêche melba. He belched, softly. His voice was much quieter than before.

"That little shit," he said. "That little shit. Look, I'm not saying that I made him, and he owes me. The kid had talent. All I did was plug him into the paper. And I don't object to his occupation—hell, you do a lot of the same thing, and I don't object to you. I've gotten a lot of good stories from good lobbyists, large numbers of whom know a hell of a lot more about what's going on in this Congress than the idealistic little turkeys actually running it.

"But just the same," Edgar said, "I did trust that kid with responsibility when I certainly didn't have to, and it didn't hurt him any when he did what he obviously planned to do anyway, after he developed his press contacts and got his law degree while pretending that he had no such idea in mind.

"So," Edgar said to me, "why does he pay me back by trying to buy me with a dinner and a bimbo? Does he think a dinner's gonna make me print his propaganda under my by-line, which is what Not for Attribution means, and means that it's therefore Attributed to Lannin? Does he really think that he can use me for his whore, and use his whores to get me, and get me all that easy? Is that all a friend is for here?

"Jesus," Edgar said, leaning back and cradling the brandy snifter in both hands. "There are some times when I think I should've joined the convent. I'm just too goddamned naïve, I guess. You think?"

"No," I said. "If you were, somebody would've bought you and bagged you on this drilling thing by now."

Edgar did not want to go carousing for once. I walked him back to his hotel, got my car, and went home. I told Jeanne that there had been no point in outlining my clients' views on the drilling legislation that night. "Edgar," I said, "was too tired."

"Too drunk, you mean," she said, over the *Newsweek* she was reading.

"Somehow," I said, "I have to doubt that. I'd hate to think he's smarter drunk, than I am, sober."

Six

Toward the first of July Edgar stopped in Washington on his way home from a conference on the law and the media. He looked like hell. I told him so.

"Of course I look like hell," he said. "Have you ever been to a conference on the law and the media? Have you ever had a proctoscopy? Have you ever taken a chain saw, on purpose, and cut your goddamned foot off? Of course you haven't. You've got more sense'n that.

"You wanna hear some more?" Edgar said. "Hey, these're pretty nice offices you got here, Counselor. That some kind of fuckin' Klee over there onna wall?"

"Kandinsky," I said. "Print, let me add."

"Looks nice," Edgar said. "That house I used to own, out in Silver Spring, I had some spackle wallpaper I put up in the kitchen, all by myself, looked a lot like that. Paid one-eighty-nine a roll, and it was greaseproof and washable, too. And it really was: put it over the stove and never had a bit of trouble keeping it clean. Could've gotten you a good price on a sheet of it twice as big, framed it better'n that in the woodworking shop I used to have in the basement. Gave that away, too. Hope the bitch severs all the tendons in her wrist, using the bandsaw. What can I do for you?"

"You came here," I said. "This's my office, remember?"

"Oh, yeah," Edgar said. He looked at me. "You're looking *very* trim, Counselor. See you in May, you look pretty good; see you in June, you look downright dashing. Now it's July, and you look even better. You sure you're getting enough to eat? I mean, Jeanne's a great girl and all, but you don't want to lose too much weight.

"Oh, sure, Edgar," I said.

"Make the clients worry," Edgar said. "See this guy, works too hard, all tired out, thin, haggard, make them lose confidence in your ability to deal with Very Serious Matters. Gotta get enough good food and booze to eat, you know. Make sure you're getting laid, too. You know what JFK said: he didn't get laid at least once a day, it made his head ache. Bet the divvil never had a headache in his life. You gettin' laid enough, Peter?"

"Everything's fine, Edgar," I said.

"Good, good," Edgar said. "Everything's fine with me, too," He looked out the window, over the rooftops toward L Street. "Ah, yes, a fine July evening. Makes me remember the days of my youth. All nostalgic, in fact. Not that I was getting any," he said. "Free for dinner? My treat. Well, not mine exactly, but Bob Cratchit's so sick of my outrageous lies that he usually doesn't bother asking me anymore. I'm in an expansive mood. Pick a restaurant, any restaurant, and you better grab it while you can, because Halley's Comet will be back next week, and it's gonna be the end of the world."

"Can't," I said.

"Oh, nuts," Edgar said, "you can catch the new exhibit at the Hirshhorn next week, when all the proles go. You don't need to hit the deck with all the heavy hitters that know about as much about art as you do and've got pieces of Armstrong kitchen linoleum framed in their offices, too. Forget the cheap champagne in the plastic glasses. Come on and have dinner with me. Pick a joint and tell Jeanne, meet us there."

"Can't do it," I said. "Jeanne's not in town. Jeanne took the boys to Poughkeepsie to see their grandparents for two weeks."

"Lucky man," Edgar said. "Still sure about the JFK thing?"

"Look," I said, "I've got to be someplace in about an hour and a half. I can have a beer with you here and leave from here, or I can leave now and dawdle around until it's time for me to go. What'll it be?"

"Oh," Edgar said, "that's enough talk about you, Counselor. Let's talk about me. I'll have the beer. Heineken, please."

"Sorry," I said, punching the call button. "Dos Equis is what I bought this time."

"Dos Equis it is," Edgar said. "I turn into Pancho Villa halfway through the mission, it'll be your fault. The last time I was in this office, I had one bottle each of San Miguel and Kirin, and by the time I left, I didn't know whether to besmirch the memory of Ramón Magsaysay or bomb Pearl Harbor. Decisions, decisions."

The beers were fetched.

"I also like the sculpture there," he said. "Very attractive. I'm a cultivated man, so I can tell. That is either an imitation jade T'ang horse, or an abstract, or the late Marilyn Monroe's ass. You got class, Quinn, sheer, unremitting class. Does my heart good, I can tell you, see you prospering like this."

"Where the hell've you been?" I said. It was after hours, and I loosened my tie and put my feet on the desk.

"Sirrah," Edgar said, "I have been to The Greenbrier. The Greenbrier, Ladies and Gentlemen, is a resort hotel, which is located either in Warm Springs, West Virginia, or Hot Springs, Georgia, or both of the above. Maybe in Arkansas, I dunno. It is most difficult to determine which, there being almost no empirical data, virtually no one of the age of reason giving a shit. The only man in the world who knows where The Greenbrier is is Sam Snead, who used to visit it now and again when he was the resident golf pro there. Or so the oral tradition of the prophets has it.

"At any rate," Edgar said, "as one of the leading lights of contemporary columnists, I was hauled off to The Greenbrier, quite docilely, considering that a weekend in a costly resort might be a pleasant interlude for a humble scribe, particularly when all of his expenses were to be vouchsafed unto him by his employer. And, Peter, as you have excellent reason to know, I am a fucking *artist* with an expense account. I can foul those things up so it would take Houdini to catch even a glimpse of what I did with the ninety bucks I claimed to have spent upon a feast of squabs, and I don't have to worry none, because Houdini's dead. And no matter what he said, Houdini is not coming back, however much it grieves him."

"You also look good, Edgar," I said, "although you also look like hell, too." It was true. He had good color. He had lost some weight, and his eyes were clear. He did not snuffle.

"Thank you," Edgar said, "I *do* look good. I have taken serious steps to improve my goddamned appearance."

"Working out?" I said.

"In a manner of speaking," Edgar said. "I awoke one morning in my quarters, more than usually alert, and got a close look at myself, more closer than is usual. And I said to myself, I said, says I: 'Lannin, you bastard. You look like sixty-three miles of badly paved road through the mill towns of southern Connecticut. You should do something for yourself. Or to yourself, whichever may seem more emergent and likely to do good. You are a wreck of a once-fine figure of a man. Furthermore, you look like hell.'

"Just like you said, Counselor. Except the hell I look like now is temporary, curable by a good dinner and some rest, and the hell I otherwise looked like was correctable only by the application of the skills of an accomplished mortician. So that mourners would say: 'My, doesn't he look natural.' And Friends to See Mister Lannin would respond: 'No, as a matter of fact, he doesn't. If he looked natural, he would look like

101

hell. As it is, he looks much better dead than he ever did alive.' I'm bushed, and I've got big bags under my eyes, and I'm hungry and that goddamned car that Mister Avis loaned me, for an exorbitant fee, just about drove me nuts coming through the Shenandoahs, but I think I'm gonna live. I've had lots of fun at wakes, but never at one where I was dead. Where was I?"

"You were going to tell me how come, underneath your pallor and exhaustion, you look so good," I said.

"Ahh, yes," Edgar said.

"You took up exercise," I said.

"No," Edgar said, "I did not. I gave up exercise. I gave up exercising the hand I use to drink hard liquor. Then I went down there and went to hell again, but just for a short time."

"Really," I said.

"Yes," he said. "I understand, from unusually well-informed sources, that the economy of Tennessee has been seriously depressed from the past couple weeks, nobody being quite able to understand what the hell went wrong. Further, the gin industry, as a whole, has lost an average of three-point-eight on the New York Stock Exchange since I made this decision, but now, when I look tired, there is a very good reason for it—it is because I have not had enough sleep, and not because I have gashed myself, fore and aft, with the claws of a mature raccoon. If you follow me."

"I do," I said.

"Thank you," he said. "The beer industry is up, and the wine industry is holding its own, but the Visine people and the Bufferin people are rumored to have investigators out upon the streets, even as we speak, and there is trouble afoot in the land of commerce."

"You can do it to yourself on beer, too, you know," I said.

"That you can," Edgar said, "and I have personal knowledge of several who have. One generally completed his first case of Little Knicks by noon, and the other, being more advanced, had but a few cans of the twelve-ounce Buds remaining by one in the afternoon.

"But they were truly enormous gentlemen, able to contain gases adequate to support the Goodyear blimp, and men of strong stomachs, also, who could abide the noxious fumes resultant, Counselor. That was why they shared an office. No one else could. I am a gentler soul, indeed, one of those who seldom entered that office, for that very reason, and consume no more than half my weight in beer each day. Besides, apparently I have a bladder of limited capacity. Compared to theirs, that is. Did I drink as much beer as they, I would get in training for the Boston Marathon merely by rushing to the men's room to relieve my painful condition. Where was I?"

"At The Greenbrier," I said.

"Of course," Edgar said, "at The Greenbrier.

"The Greenbrier, Ladies and Gentlemen, is a resort to which may repair a forty-eight-year-old-man, on an expense account, with no female companion whatsoever, let alone, and perish forfend, a younger one, and by the very act of registration, lower the average age of the guests by three-point-six years."

"Oh, come on," I said.

"Ah," Edgar said, "the credo of the press—I know a lot of this stuff today, keep in mind, because I've been gorging it all weekend, at Tara."

"I thought you said it was The Greenbrier," I said.

"And so I did," Edgar said. "It is Tara, masquerading as The Greenbrier. Ceilings of a height, the like of which Louis Quatorze would have envied, tasteless bastard that he was. Verdant walls and stately white pillars. Staircases fit only for a Scarlett O'Hara to descend, tumbling, thus intentionally miscarrying Rhett Butler's ill-gotten get. Chandeliers and rolling acres of immaculate carpet. Conference rooms well suited to international conferences of undertakers, so sepulchral are they. All the chairs are padded white and painted gold. All the plants are forced, and all the servants need the same treatment. The bacon is greasy in the morning, and there is not much to be said for the eggs either. The toast, once you say *cold,* needs of description nothing further. The coffee is bearable, if you are a slum kid, as am I, and used to work the grease pits down at the Mobil station. Otherwise, breakfast is not so hot.

"Then comes luncheon," Edgar said. "The best thing to say about the luncheon is this: the less said, the better. Not the better luncheon. The better, less should be said about it.

"Dinner is a real treat," Edgar said. "The food is tolerable, I guess, but the hotel won't serve strong drink to you in the dining room. Wine, yes. Strong drink, no. Strong drink must be bad for senior citizens, or something, although I had a great-uncle who demonstrably did not believe that and outlived everyone else in the clan. Maybe it interferes with the cardiac monitoring devices I suspect they have installed in some hidden place in every guest bed. It's a wonder they don't serve the meat cut up for you and get their vegetables from Gerber's. 'And tonight, for dessert, we have apple cobbler or tapioca pudding.'

"In those stimulating surroundings," Edgar said, "gathered a pride of the weightiest journalists—it looked like somebody, years ago, had crossbred Arthur Sulzberger and James Reston and then cloned the offspring about two hundred times—and a veritable herd of Honorables and Learned Brothers of the law. Cowpunching this assemblage were men and women of appalling erudition, at great expense imported from the citadels of law at the University of Chicago, Stanford, Columbia, Harvard, Yale, and Boalt Hall. There was a guest star visiting from Boston College Law School, and a man from Georgetown Law, but I think they were strays.

"This august college met in plenary session for breakfast. Over acres of warm orange juice, cold, cold toast, and a tepid beverage proffered in reluctant compliance with a request for something else, such as a cup of coffee, the invited guests mostly disregarded gluey scrambled eggs and fought off the urge to go back to bed.

"This was in order to benefit from the opportunity to hear remarks of the late Honorable Bernard Cammon, former Associate Justice of the United States Supreme Court. Justice Cammon retired in Nineteen-ought-four, I think it was, and died a couple years later, but refused to do the decent thing and lie down. Since then he has been traipsing around the country, sitting in various federal courts and appeals courts as a Senior Justice, and thereby creating a great deal of havoc and commotion.

"By this transparent means," Edgar said, "Mr. Justice Cammon has attracted the attention of the press, of course, and it must be said that he appears not at all averse to it, making a damned fool of himself in precinct after precinct, and a colossal mess of every life that is brought to him in trouble. Consequently, he is known for—and in his introduction he was praised for—his intense interest in the sometimes-conflicting claims of free press and fair trial.

"Now you have got to keep something in mind," Edgar said. "This lash-up wasn't plotted by the lawyers. For one thing, there was no immediate money to be made from it, and my understanding is that lawyers only really get their hearts into scheming when there is obvious profit to be made. This exercise in cross-pollination was decreed by the lords of the free and responsible press, aforesaid, so they were the ones who did all the bucking up, for both sides. They invited Cammon because Cammon is the media's pet judge.

"Cammon doesn't look like much," Edgar said. "Either a little Irish pawnbroker or a little Jewish saloonkeeper. He doesn't sound like much either—he's got the high, scratchy voice of a superannuated fishwife. He's very clearly a pathological egomaniac, who should be put on Thorazine or some other powerful immobilizer, if necessary by use of one of those dart guns that Marlon Perkins uses to incapacitate rhinoceri on *Wild Kingdom,* lest he bite himself and reinfect himself with rabies.

"He's entertaining, I guess, if you find it amusing to watch senility under treatment by provision of a large audience and a public address system, but otherwise I would rather listen to my ex-wife at breakfast. When I was still married to her, I used to skip breakfast, and it was a better breakfast'n The Greenbrier served, too.

"Anyway," Edgar said, "Cammon proceeded in the classical fashion, first citing enough Cardozo, Frankfurter, and Warren decisions to sedate all the lawyers present, then stupefying all the newspapermen present with lavish references to Mencken, Broun, Hecht, Swope, and Pulitzer. The lawyers thought that sounded like a good name for a partnership. The newspapermen imagined themselves listed in such catalogues fifty years from now, and the television types had never heard of any of the folks mentioned so far. But Cammon is shrewd, and provided something for the illiterate broadcasters as well: he dwelt at length upon the major contributions to liberal First Amendment contributions made by Fred Friendly and Edward R. Murrow, which made the TV boys feel more secure. I forget what he said about them and whatever the hell it was he claimed to admire. I didn't know what the devil he was talking about, but that was all right because he didn't either.

"We met at eight, and he started talking at eight-forty-five. By ten-ten, as near as I could tell, he was only up to about Nineteen-fifty-six. And he still hadn't mentioned John Peter Zenger, which I understand the statutes governing such meetings require you to do. He had Tom Jefferson's line about a country without government or a country without newspapers, to get through, and the old son of a bitch was just beginning to warm to his subject.

"The guy who introduced him had apologized that time had not permitted printing of the advance text; by now many of us knew the truth, which was that the *New York Times* had respectfully declined to print that speech instead of its usual Sunday edition. People were running out of cigarettes. People were running out for cigarettes, and also to make farewell calls to kith and kin whom, they had become convinced, they would never see again. The more optimistic were canceling appointments made for three weeks hence, and one guy reached his son at kindergarten to apologize in advance for being unable to make the kid's graduation from Oberlin. Lifelong unbelievers were muttering imprecations at the Deity, and the more devout of our number were joining in prayer, no less fervent for its silence, that God would see fit to clasp the Honorable to His bosom at ten-twenty at the latest. God, having omniscience and no desire whatsoever for enduring what would follow, did He elevate Bernard to His Great Bench Up in the Sky, did no such thing and maintained the old bastard in noisy good health until slightly after eleven-thirty.

"By then there remained less than an hour before the plenary luncheon session, a fact which infuriated the golfers in our number who had anticipated a full eighteen holes between the toast with little butter and the toast with chicken à la king. The thirsty, which was most of us, thought that ample time to bag a Bloody Mary, or perhaps even two. Some with varicose veins were getting desperate, and those lacking the bladder capacity of the mastodon, which was the vast majority, were prepared to make wind sprints to the men's room."

"There weren't any women there?" I said.

"Not officially," Edgar said. "Not many, at least. The ladies of the law and the press have only recently shown up in numbers and talent sufficient for some of them to achieve, say, your eminence in the profession, and mine in mine. Probably take them awhile to come up with a gross or two of pompous old windbags. Of course, my invitation had a lot less to do with my accomplishments than it did with the fact that Billy Dacey, my editor, has been to several of those dog-and-pony shows before, and had his fill of them. I must ask Bill what it was I did to him to deserve this kind of treatment.

"On the other hand," Edgar said, "there were some ladies around, but they were 'my assistant' or 'my niece.' Something like that. They were all much younger than the gentlemen they accompanied, and I thought it was, ah, sporting of them to save the law firms and the newspapers and the networks the expense of renting separate rooms. Few of them seemed to venture forth into the sunlight. Probably getting their beauty sleep and then spending the day improving their minds by reading Proust for the third time. Generally only saw them at night in the bar."

"Oh," I said.

"The Master of Revels arose, as Cammon subsided to perfunctory applause, and thanked him profusely for his 'extended' remarks. Cammon seemed to think that was a compliment. The Master then introduced the head-table guests, reminding everyone of the auctioneer at the old Lucky Strike ads. To our immense relief, the closing speaker, a gentlemen of taste and decency from the San Francisco *Chronicle,* said that he would defer his brief remarks until another meeting in the program. People were trampled on their way from the hall. Later, when it was discovered that the bars were not open, there was a near riot, but several, including your obedient servant, had had the foresight to pack refreshments in with the fresh underwear, and most repaired to their rooms. Even though I was behaving myself, I had emergency supplies. Beer's too bulky.

"The twelve-thirty meeting," Edgar said, "was not punctually attended, and by now those who had observed the importance of the convocation by wearing ties and sport coats had, most of them, joined the rest of the ragamuffins in slacks and sport shirts. Lacoste sport shirts for the tonier, and unspeakable garments with foliage for the trendy.

"The haberdashery choices of the scribes and the pharisees, I thought, were a nifty little piece of evidence of their differences in outlook: they were indistinguishable. These are the gentry, and their opinions actually are very much the same.

"Oh, sure, they argue all the time, and sometimes they even fight a pitched battle or two, but when they quarrel, it's because each of them has a chunk of the same thing, which is wealth and power, and now and then gets greedy for a little more. This endangers the other's chunk and makes him fighting mad. Because there is only so much of that stuff. Those guys don't bother much with principle, because they've all got the same principles, and those're pretty high actually. What gets them to pulling hair and gouging eyes is which of the principled fellows is going to get the bigger slice of the pie, because the pie is pretty good, and it's not unlimited.

"Those conferences are like talks over arms limitation. They also give guys who would secretly like to be Senators the chance to pretend they're in the Senate, for a little while, without all the fuss and bother of running for office.

"Over the chicken," Edgar said, "an organizational briefing was delivered by an owlish-looking gentleman from U-Chi, who looked to be about fifty years into the mission and was well skilled at being earnest. The professor repeated every single syllable in the invitation pamphlet, for those of us newspapermen and lawyers who never learned to read. For the television types, it was probably a service, since many of them obviously cannot, and even those who can do not believe a thing is so until a talking head has told them that it is. Wine and beer were available for those with the temerity to drink outside their closets, in the small number of which I am proud to count myself.

"The purpose of the conference, we were informed, was to hash out law-press problems by the Case Method. The professor condescended to explain to the scribes that the Case Method is the way the law is taught in school. For the retarded, he said that the approach was also known as the Socratic Method. Certain facts, known as The Case, would be stated, and those facts in turn would present an insoluble dilemma involving the freedom of the press and the fairness of the trial.

"It was pretty obvious," Edgar said, "that what the organizers wanted was a fight. What we like to call a fair and frank exchange of views. Such as, for example: 'If you really think that, you're an asshole.' Honest to God, Peter, it was like the group leaders, or whatever the hell they called themselves, were bucking up to choose sides for a sandlot baseball game in a grimy neighborhood. Silliest thing I ever saw.

"What you had was the reporters—most of whom haven't covered a story in years and spend all their time sitting around long tables, flogging the actual reporters—on one side and the legals on the other. From cursory inspection, I would have to say that no more than three of the legals've seen the inside of a courtroom since Nineteen-sixty-five. Except for the judges, of course, whose views on trying cases can be pretty annoying themselves.

"We set forth in serried array to battle for the victory standard, the Constitution, and the Bill of Rights, Rampant on a Field of discarded briefs and newspapers from the day before yesterday.

"Well," Edgar said, "we dispersed after chocolate pudding, some of us contestants, some of us observers, all having agreed that the transcripts of the meetings, sure as they were to be replete with wildly provocative statements, should report what was said, but not who said it. Except for the professors, whose reputations as incisive gadflies would scarcely be enhanced were their brilliant ripostes not attributed, thus materially reducing the likelihood that they would be selected for the next commotion, probably in Hawaii. The reason given for this was to permit the judges to express themselves without fear of censure upon issues possibly lurking in cases pending before them. In other words, they were not to be caught in the act of admitting how they were gonna rule. But it also eliminated the possibility that one of the estimable journalists might be caught saying something on the record and making a fool of himself in the process. The thing that a journalist loathes and fears most in the world is being journalized.

"We began on Tuesday morning," Edgar said. "We finished on Thursday night. Three days, or a year and a half, after we had started. We did not accomplish one goddamned fucking thing except, perhaps, permanent damage to our digestive systems. Except for those who had brought their own bottles, we did not have sufficient to drink, and those, like me, who had not thought to invite nieces did not get laid. Although a couple of the more rambunctious attempted preliminaries with the nieces of other gentlemen, and some nasty scuffling broke out. When the goddamned thing was over, those who still had played no golf, and wanted to, remained overnight to get a round in today, while those of us who thought golf to be preferable only to a day in an iron lung went out of that circular drive into the twilight of the Blue Ridge Mountains at paces so rapid as to diminish in mere hundreds of yards the depth of tread on Mister Avis' tires by wear equivalent to thousands of miles of normal driving. These are estimates; your mileage may vary.

"Peter," he said, "it was awful. I was driving all night to get away from that mausoleum, and then I had to get up around eleven today to do *Panorama,* and since then I've been trying to get some work done. Now I'm hungry."

"You did *Panorama?*" I said.

"Sure," Edgar said. "I used to do *Panorama* when Maury Povich was hosting it. And the new lady I knew when she was with Channel Four in Boston. Which is why I didn't have any lunch. Briefing starts at eleven-thirty. Pat does news, noon-twelve-thirty. Show starts twelve-thirty, goes till two. You're way the hell up there on Fifty-one-fifty-one Wisconsin, you can't get back downtown in time for a decent lunch, so you go across the street to the Trattoria and pretend that what they're serving you is lunch. That's why I'm hungry."

"Why do you do it then?" I said.

"I do it because everything feeds on something else," Edgar said. "That goddamned show is amazing. You try to put on a show in Boston at that hour, and you will titillate more housewives in a week'n you could reach if you were giving away free pantyhose at the supermarket, the only condition for a year's supply being the donor takes crotch measurements. But down here, goddamned if everybody doesn't watch that thing. People with actual power. Somebody gives you a ration of shit on the Hill today, zing him a couple times tomorrow on WTTG. That'll get his attention. It'll get his attention because he won't be able to go to a dinner party tomorrow night, which he feels he has to do, without getting a whole bunch of sympathy from people that he knows don't mean it, about what a vicious attack you made on him. I am telling you, those that can't watch the show have somebody watching the show for them. Maybe in their office, maybe at home. But it's instant revenge, and for an out-of-town writer who can go home and goose the bastard in a paper where he'll never see it, it's pure gold to have a slingshot of your own, right there in the Georgetown alley where he parks his car."

"Yeah," I said, "I guess it would be."

"You get on there," Edgar said, "and you got three guys who would've been interior decorators, except they had athletic ability, so they're dancers. And they leap around like gazelles gone mad, with their genitalia showing. Then you get the guy who says every women should get a free abortion every week, whether she wants it or not. You got the widow of somebody famous, who is plugging her book, and the singer booked this week at some hotel, or the rock group from the Cellar Door.

"You got a Congressman from Utah who breeds snails for cooking, and the Senator from some place who eats nothing but broom straw and welcome mats, because fiber's what's important in your diet. You got your Serious Novelist, and your drama critic, your movie producer, and your evangelist. Life is a cabaret, old chum, come to the cabaret.

"If you do it good, and you do it often enough, you get on *Meet the Press,* and *Face the Nation,* there to do ferocious things to Cabinet secretaries and presidential hopefuls. And your boss, who does not see them programs because they don't come on late enough on Sunday—around noon—for him to've gotten out of bed, hears about how you bearded the entire Joint Chiefs of Staff and decides that you're the Prince of Players. Furthermore, all them folks that're supposed to take time out of their busy days so you can make a living have with them always the uneasy, gnawing feeling that if they refuse to see you when you want something for the papers, you may turn up as one of the interviewers when they get on one of those national shows. For which they did have time. And you will take that opportunity to de-pants them. The disposition of a scorpion's no good for you at all, unless people know you've got it, and know you have got a little grotto from which you can emerge to sting them. I nailed the Chairman of the House Committee on Banking, years ago, on *Panorama* less than two hours after he lied to me about the interest rate bill. He never lied to me again.

"That's why."

"Makes sense," I said.

"What doesn't make sense," Edgar said, "is why *my* old friend, with his wife out of town, can't join *his* old friend for dinner."

"I told you," I said. "I've got something to do."

"Does that involve, perhaps, dinner?" Edgar said. "A very good dinner, in fact?"

"Yes," I said, "as a matter of fact, it does."

"Perhaps," Edgar said, "a dinner in a private home?"

"Yes," I said.

"But you can't invite me," Edgar said.

"No," I said, "as a matter of fact, I can't."

"Hmm," Edgar said, "would that perhaps be because while the former Mrs. Vernon Capeless is a free lady, as well as a Cordon Bleu cook, and a lady of considerable public admiration in this town for the way she put up with the rotten bastard all those years before she finally threw him out, the current Mrs. Peter J. Quinn, though in Poughkeepsie far away, might prove less tolerant of a public, shall we say, linking of Mr. Quinn with Mrs. Capeless than she has of Mr. Quinn's habitual late evenings twice a week, on Tuesday and on Thursday?"

"Jesus," I said.

"Because if that is the reason," Edgar said, "hear this: I

am hungry. I do not wish to eat alone. I knew Maggie Capeless years ago, when she started that show for WTOP that everybody said was gonna fall flat on its ass, and I come back here years later, and it's still doing fine. Further, Maggie knows that I like Maggie. I hate Vernon, which I think I told him to his face one night, but I thought she was wonderful, and I am prepared to believe that she still is.

"I also like you, Peter. And I have no real wish to complicate your life, nor any intention of doing so. I won't hang around very late, and I won't make any snide little comments if I see some of your shaving lotion on the counter in the bathroom, as I expect I will. I will depart, in my Avis car, as soon as the brandy is finished, and the two of you teenagers can go at it like a couple of hot warthogs, without me mentioning Word One. To anybody.

"Not, Peter," Edgar said, reproachfully, "that I'd have a hell of a lot to add to what's public information as it is. You don't know anything about fooling around, do you, old pal?"

"Well . . ." I said.

"Not a blessed thing," Edgar said. "Now listen to me for a minute, all right? I'm not trying to talk you out of this, understand? I don't disapprove of my old pal Peter fooling around with my old pal Maggie. Hell, I'm jealous, more'n anything. If I could get into Maggie's pants I would do it at once. Matter of fact, if you want the truth, I tried it once, when Vernon was still living with her and dickin' that woman who sells real estate and looks like a Mississippi state cop, and she would have none of it. 'No,' she said, to my astonishment, 'if I'm gonna live with that rat, then that is what I am gonna do, and I'm gonna do all of it. You're kind of cute, Edgar, but I'm kind of married. There're days when I wish to high heaven I weren't, but I am.

" 'Now,' Maggie said, 'don't stand there like a little boy, rubbing your feet together and biting your lip and trying to think up some tactful way to spring the big news on me, so I'll get mad enough at Vernon to go to bed with you. To spite him. I don't spite people. I either get complete revenge, or I let it slide. I know what Vernon's doing, and I know the woman he's doing it with. And I must say, I'm insulted. It was one thing when Vernon was seeing that youngster who works in the children's department at Woodie's. At least she was cute. Stupid, but cute. And I certainly couldn't complain that he was giving her anything that belonged to me, because I didn't want any more of what he wanted to give me. Will you tell me something, Edgar? Why does a man want to fuck a woman in the ass?'

" 'I don't know,' I said to her. 'Never held much interest for me.'

" 'Well,' she said, 'I don't know either. Vernon and I got married when we were both juniors at the University of Virginia. We didn't know anything, really, but we were smart and ready to learn. Vernon didn't want to do any of that stuff then. He was perfectly content with the missionary position, and so was I. Vernon and I were married for almost twenty-one years, and we had a pretty good marriage for about fifteen of them. But then he got a little weird, wanting to tie me up, and then the other thing.

" 'I went along with it for a little while,' Maggie said. 'Up till then Vernon'd been a good husband. He worked hard, and he made a big success for himself. And that's not easy to do in this town, running a liquor store on the prices they set on the Hill, so they can buy booze on the cheap. He took good care of me, never pestered me about not wanting to have children, gave me presents, took me places, and listened to what I had to say.

" 'Then all of a sudden,' she said, 'he changed. He went in for all that kinky stuff, and I really didn't enjoy it. He *hurt* me, and I finally came right out and said it. If you want to do that stuff, go find somebody else to do it with. I won't do it, not any longer, but if it's that important to you, and you can find another partner, go ahead and do it.

" 'I don't really know what I expected him to do,' she said.

115

'I guess I hoped it'd snap him out of it. Maybe I hoped he'd walk out. I don't know what I thought. But I had to do something. I have to go to work every day to produce that show, and I have to be able to sit down when I get there and talk to people without squirming around all the time because my ass is sore and raw.

" 'Well,' she said, 'I find out how important it was to him. Now what I have to decide is how important he is to me. That's a big decision, Edgar,' she said. 'I can't handle more than one big decision at a time, and your proposition comes under that heading. Forgive me?'

"At the time," Edgar said, "I did. What I don't forgive her for is making the decision about Vernon while I was out of town, and then making the decision about you before I had the opportunity to renew my inquiries. Ah, well, when you work in Boston, you miss your chances in Washington, and when you work down here, there's probably something promising slipping right by you up there.

"Anyway," Edgar said, "what I was thinking was this. . . ."

"How the hell did you find out?" I said. I did not tell him that I had not known before why Maggie divorced Vernon.

"Remember Hooper?" Edgar said.

"Sure," I said, "Hooper S. Hooper and his wife wife, Teddi Teddi. What's Hooper doing?"

"Hooper Hooper's making good use of his legislative experience on the Hill. He's teaching political science at Goucher College, and he called me up to pick my brains about Boston politics for a book he's writing. Exchanged me a little gossip. Hooper's mummy lives in Executive Towers. Hooper is a devoted son. He visits his mummy one night a week, and he happened to pick one of your two. What is it, Peter? Is it Tuesdays and Thursdays?"

"It varies," I said.

"Well, anyway," Edgar said. "Hooper called me, and he asked me if you were seeing Mrs. Capeless. See, Hooper gets all of his fine vintages from Vernon, and he buys quite a lot of them. Has for years. So Vernon and Maggie had Hooper and Teddi over to the house one night, and then another and another, and Hooper got so he could recognize Maggie. He saw you arrive with her one night, and then again the next week. So he asked me if you had a little something going with Maggie."

"What'd you tell him?" I said.

"Peter," Edgar said, "my problem is that I always think the worst of people. 'Of course not, Hooper,' I said indignantly. 'Peter's a happily married man with a family. Community leader. Lovely wife and however many lovely children. Peter's way too straight to be sneaking around with Maggie Capeless.'

" 'Jeez,' Hoop said—this was in February, I think it was, end of February—'Jeez, she lives in the same building with my mother, and if he's not always there the night I visit her, his car is. He got a blue BMW coupe?'

" 'Dunno what he's driving,' I said. 'Haven't seen him in a while. Peter likes a good meal, though, and I don't think his lovely wife's too capable in that line. Peter and Maggie're probably just friends.'

" 'Probably,' Hooper said. But I kept my nose in the air, and within a week I had the facts. I do admire your taste, Peter, and I absolutely demand my dinner."

"This is blackmail, you know," I said, reaching for the phone.

"Counselor, Counselor," Edgar said, "many things are. Some are sinful, some are criminal, and some are downright reprehensible. But this is done in the Lord's name. I am fucking hungry, and I wanna eat with my old friends."

"Maggie," I said, when she answered, "lay on another plate. Edgar Lannin's coming."

"What'd she say?" he said, after I hung up.

"What did she say?" I said. "She said: 'Son of a bitch, I haven't seen old Edgar since VJ-Day. Bring him over.' "

117

Seven

Two weeks later Edgar got to see his kids. He was back in Washington, griping about the weather again. This time he was complaining that circumstances had forced him to leave Boston, where it had become very pleasant, and dragged him back to Washington, where it had become too hot for his taste. "And wait till August,' he said, in the Admiral's Club at Washington National Airport, his tie pulled down from his collar and his shirt bedraggled. "Now it's just hot. In August you'll be able to lose ten pounds, waiting on the corner for a cab.

"You know something, Peter?" Edgar was wearing one of those disreputable Haspel cord suits which looks fine in the morning when you put it on, and wretched an hour later if you have ventured outdoors while wearing it. "The way this town runs the cab business stinks."

"This is Alexandria," I said. Edgar gets on my nerves occasionally.

"Sure," Edgar said, "and it's government property as well, so if you lose your property here, and think it might've been stolen from you, don't do no good to call the cops in Virginia. Cops in Virginia tell you: 'Call the FBI.' FBI tells you: 'Go downstairs, give some money to the flower girls and Jews for Jesus, which wouldn't be parading around the goddamned place anyway, it wasn't a government reservation.' "

"You wouldn't be parading around in the papers either," I said. "They get to parade around because of the First Amendment, which hasn't given you a bad life, I can see."

"Paper flowers and Gospel pamphlets," Edgar said. "You know I almost missed my plane the last time because of all those idiots accosting me on the way to security? Why is the Boston plane always at Gate Twelve? Do they do that just to annoy me? Next time that I come down here, I don't think I'm gonna bring my rock collection. I keep this up, I'm gonna hurt my back. I got a couple friends with bad backs, and I've listened to them, and it doesn't sound like something I would like to have."

"What brings you down here?" I said.

Edgar ignored me. He was drinking a Bloody Mary, which was odd for him, at three in the afternoon. "Time I get to Gate Twelve," Edgar said, "I might as well forget about the plane and walk the rest of the way to Boston. Wouldn't take much longer."

"What brings you down here?" I said. "This is Monday, and you're going back. War break out over the weekend?"

"Probably," Edgar said. "I had a small one myself. I finally got to see the kids. Jesus Christ, I can't believe it. One full weekend per month: that's all I asked. Pick 'em up Friday, take 'em back Monday. March: nope, something came up. April: half, Little League game for the youngest on Saturday, church trip, the two oldest Saturday night, Sunday morning. Sounds like a movie title, doesn't it? Gonna take a goddamned school bus out to some river somewhere in Virginia, pitch all those tents and cook some stew, and sing around the campfire, rah-dee-doo-dah. Screw Daddy."

"Hey, Edgar," I said.

"Oh, lemme up," Edgar said, waving his hand. "I don't object to them having their friends. I don't object to them playing baseball, roasting snakes, singing hymns, or groping choir members of the opposite sex silly in their sleeping bags before the fire, rah-dee-doo-dah. If I were in their shoes, I'd much rather do those things 'n spend the whole goddamned weekend in a Shakey's, woofing down the pizza while Dad drinks the beer, before we hit our third dull movie in two days. How many pinball machines've they got in Maryland anyway? You wanna take my count? I think we've seen most of them. You know your Baltimore Orioles that I refused to go and watch the last time I was down? I went and watched the Baltimore Orioles this time down, and it was just like I told you it would be the last time: me and the kids and thirteen hundred other pigeons watching the Chicago White Sox pretend Minnie Minoso's still playing. Up the Ballwasher, down the Ballwasher, and back to the motel. Where, on my limited budget, I have to stack the little bastards like cordwood.

"Lemme tell you something more, Counselor," Edgar said, "that ain't no fun. It costs like the devil, and a cold-water enema with a forty-pound pressure head compares favorably in pleasurability. By the time you get up in the morning that room smells like a locker room and looks a lot like a herd of wild boars got in there during the night and went rooting through the dirty underwear without finding what they wanted. You know what the airfare runs me for one of these paternal visits? Well, it beats the everlasting shit out of a hundred bucks, is what it does, and by the time I figure the parking and the tolls and the rental car and the ball game tickets, and all those other confounded things that drive me into bankruptcy faster'n I can haul myself out, if I start out with three hundred bucks on Friday afternoon at Logan, I'm lucky I got cabfare by the time I get back to Boston. Three hundred bucks I haven't got, for approximately twenty-one hours of excruciating agony with three kids who've presumably been looking forward to seeing the old man since February, which was the

120

last month she didn't manage to screw up, and didn't really get one goddamned chance whatsoever to talk to me at all. You ever try to tell your old man something personal in the goddamned breakfast nook at the Holiday Inn, with all the other kids looking on? Damned right, you didn't."

I tried to cheer him up. "Edgar, as a matter of fact," I said, "I never tried to tell my old man anything personal anywhere. I was chiefly afraid that he would find out something personal. I got my education in the gutter, where the best lessons're given, and I excluded him from everything I possibly could, unless I was discovered. Then I pretended I'd just been too scared to talk to him about it."

Edgar was not about to be consoled. "Nuts," he said. "That was your choice. My kids haven't got any choice. You gonna ask me, confidentially, it's okay to pull your joint, when you're standing next to me, the salad bar at the Sir Walter Raleigh Steak House? You are not. Maybe, we were all by ourselves, watching the fire in the timbered living room of a New Hampshire farmhouse, with fuckin' *wolves* howling outside in the snowy evening, you would not ask me then either. But at least you would have the choice.

"Well," Edgar said, "what I'm doing with them, when I'm allowed the chance to do it, which is about one out of three, and that one discounted by two-thirds, comes under just about the same damned sort of category, which is pony-loping. It looks like fun, and it's supposed to be fun, but it's not much fun at all. Doing it alone, anything, is not much fun.

"Peter," Edgar said, "I have, at my advanced age, at last discovered why it is that folks build houses. It is so they will have some place to live and will not be forced to consort unwittingly with strangers when they are with their families. There is something intimidating, and vastly destructive of candid conversation, to taking one's familial meals at a table jostled every so often by some jerk in a double-knit maroon jacket from Toledo, going up for his fifth helping of dessert, after his nineteenth pitcher of beer, and people calling out order

121

numbers of various pizzas and sub sandwiches over loudspeakers mounted just above your ear. While some snotty-nosed teenager racks up the volume on the newest Fleetwood Mac record on the jukebox, next to your table. What the papers say is that the father gets to see the kid, and the kid gets to see the father, and that is *all* they bloody mean, too. You *see* each other. What I got involves no talk. No continuity. No reliance. No reciprocal satisfaction. For nobody. I got visitation rights, and by God, when I get them, that is what I got: I am a visitor. It sucks."

"I know," I said.

"You *don't* know," Edgar said. "Have you ever been alone in Washington on a Saturday night when you didn't expect to be? If you expected to be, you wouldn't have been, but you didn't, so you are. Have you ever done that?"

"No," I said.

"No," Edgar said. "Well, let me give you a brief summary. If you are forty-eight, which you damned right well are, you are too old to hit the hot spots, as we oldsters quaintly call them, because there is something inherently ridiculous in a forty-eight-year-old man hitting the hot spots. Unless he is hitting them with a woman. And unless she is between forty-five and fifty, there will still be something inherently ridiculous in it. So, if you have any sense of dignity at all—and I don't have much, but I've got enough for knowledge that I should not go out on purpose and make a damned fool of myself, doing it often enough, as it is, without meaning to—you will not do it.

"The guys're not around, not even the guys that're always around. The ones that're married, still, go home on Saturday night, or else they don't leave the house all day, making up for the sins of the workaday week. The ones that aren't married anymore have got plans with their kids or are enjoying a little candlelight and wine, either with a lady or some friends. No matter what you do, you are gonna be Ishmael, and that is all there is to it. Ain't many whalers setting out from the pier down off Maine Avenue, particularly on Saturday night, and if there were, it wouldn't matter much to me, because I've got to get back to Boston anyway. There're folks up there under the impression I do work for them, and they get restless when they don't see my charming face around the premises. In addition to which, I probably wouldn't be any good at whaling either. Shit."

"Well," I said, trying to calm him down a little, "these things will happen, you know. Mary Claire probably didn't know about the church thing when you set up the weekend. Something's always getting scrambled, no matter how hard you try."

"Oh, *more* shit," Edgar said. "Of course, she didn't know when we set it up. But she fuckin' goddamned right well knew it before I took off on Friday. Life's a busted straight, but goddammit all, when you draw the second ten, instead of the jack you expected, the least you can do is tell me before I blow the egg money on a useless trip. I asked Teddy when this trip of theirs came up, and he told me he thought it was about two weeks ago, and Mary Claire said the same thing. Which, of course, explains that unexplained clothing expense of eighty bucks she suddenly needed an advance on the support for this month. Oh, she knew about it all right. She helped to plan it, likely. She was just blocking my hat for me."

"Maybe she didn't want to disappoint you for the third month in a row," I said.

"Try the fifteenth *year* in a row," Edgar said. "And when you do, I'll tell you what a jerk you are. If disappointing me was a course of graduate study, that woman'd be a tenured professor at Harvard, occupying the Mary Claire Murray Lannin Chair in the Department of Disappointing Edgar. Hell, she'd get the Nobel, easy. What an everlasting bitch. What little money that I've got that she can't get her hands on, she tricks me into wasting. If it was not against the law, I would kill her cheerfully, and not with any gun either. I would use my bare hands, so as not to miss any of the pleasure of it. She is a rotten human being, and I hate her guts. Except for that, she's pretty much all right."

"You know, old pal, old buddy," I said, "you were no paradigm of virtue before you moved out on her."

"I haven't been since then either," Edgar said, "but then, I'm not asking her to support my bad habits, and she does expect me to support hers. Which, now that I think of it, you know something about."

"There was nothing I could do about that that I didn't do," I said, "and you know it. I told you about that old moss-backed son of a bitch, that one reduced alimony before he thought of what he was saying, and then he had to check into GU Hospital for two weeks on the dialysis machine. Hell, one of my partners. . . ."

"Which one?" Edgar asked. "Bradley, Bellow, or Knight?"

"Nobody on the firm name," I said. "Recent partner. Only been practicing law about sixteen years. Needs a little more experience in his field, which is domestic law, before we charter members think about adding his name after *Quinn*. If he lives that long. In his area, I'd be worried."

"How come you're tail-end Charlie on that thing, Quinn?" Edgar said. "Short straw?"

"Ed Bradley," I said, "was Undersecretary of State. Ben Bellow was Director of the Internal Revenue Service. Joe Knight was a U.S. Senator for fourteen years and Chairman of the Democratic Party. I was Special Counsel to a President now dead, but they thought I showed promise. Why didn't Covington defer to Burling, if alphabetical order is the way things ought to be?"

"I dunno," Edgar said.

"I dunno either," I said. "And nobody else does either. Or whether any of it makes any difference. Anyway, one of my partners once asked that judge to give our—male—client custody of the children, and the judge went up in a sheet of blue flame. I told you what was going to happen when we went in there, and you told me to go in there anyway. Hey, I'm not your keeper—I'm your lawyer. I tell you what I think you ought to do, and I assume you think about what I've told you, and then you tell me what you want done. And if it's not illegal or fattening or liable to get me disbarred, I obey your instructions. Most of the time. Unless doing so would make me, in addition to the above, look like a goddamned fool, in which event I tell you to go plague another lawyer."

"Yeah," Edgar said, "well, I admire your balanced view of law and precedent, Counselor, but it's still my goddamned money that she's dining out on with her boyfriend."

"Boyfriend?" I said. "My, my. Clairesie's got a boyfriend?"

"Certainly has," Edgar said. "Saw him with my own baby blues. Big as life, breathing in and out, got a lavender pink T-Bird that's so big he must have to tack it around the corners, yes, indeed. Jesus, Peter, remember how great those little two-seater Birds were, the first ones? This thing looks like a Continental that suddenly lost its nerve and decided to become a Mercury. Looked like a boyfriend to me. Either that or he's her main man and she's working Fourteenth Street in white vinyl boots at night. One or the other."

"Son of a gun," I said. "She serious about him?"

"I think so," Edgar said. "No, I don't think so. I suspect she may be. She's losing weight.

"That usually means something," I said.

"Did with every guy I ever knew," Edgar said. "Every guy I ever knew, the first thing he did, when he got a little honey on the side, was go out and get a new wardrobe, usually including shirts with big collars and flowers on them, that he wore without an undershirt and left unbuttoned all the way down his big, fat, hairy belly to his belt buckle. Lot of cheap jewelry, too. Then, and only then, did he begin to take some pains about sprucing up the redecorated premises of his belly, and of course, when he did, he ingrew the new wardrobe and hadda go out and start over again. Of course, by then he generally didn't have the new honey, just hopes of getting a newer honey, so he had a little bit more sense and dressed like something besides a fourth-rate fence.

"So I figure," Edgar said, "it applies to the guys, it probably applies also to the girls. And I would have to say old Mary Claire is probably down now to about, oh, one-fifty, one-fifty-five."

"She was never that heavy," I said.

"I know that," Edgar said. "She had a pretty good haunch on her, though. For a slim little heifer in that wedding dress, she fattened up real good, you got to admit. Got so when you saw her in those white slacks, all you could think of was weisswurst, and that thought didn't make you hungry neither."

"I wouldn't know," I said.

"Course you wouldn't," Edgar said. "Jeanne was as slender as a snake when you two got married, and the last time I saw her, she still was. She evidently gives enough of a shit about you to keep herself in shape, instead of going all to seed like an abandoned farm, and I am telling you, my friend, that that can make a difference. She catch on to you yet? Don't answer that.

"Who the hell wants to climb into bed," Edgar said, "on a summer's night, when there's a bit of a brownout and the air conditioners aren't quite keeping up with the humidity, just letting it get a little bit of a lead on them, when you know there's a big fat walrus already in there, roaring away like an engine running out of oil? Not me, Jack."

It occurred to me, soon enough, I am glad to say, that I ought not to utter what I thought, which was that Mary Claire probably would have answered his question the same way he did, back when they split up. I work out three mornings a week at the Y. I'm no kid, but my weight's all right, and I have reasonably good muscle tone. Edgar, who ran rings around me in college intramural basketball—he was a very capable backcourt man—had let himself go terribly. His face looked puffy and red, and his middle expanded every year.

126

He was becoming round-shouldered, and his eyes were full of blood. But Edgar had come back nicely in Boston. Now only his clothes looked shabby.

I had a pretty good idea of the principal reason for this decline. If he had not been in the mood that he was in, I would've have mentioned it to him, and in no uncertain terms either. Edgar will take a certain amount of guff from me, as I will from him. As a matter of fact, Edgar is probably the only man on earth from whom I will take guff, unless the man happens to hold high office, or I need him. Edgar would probably say that I am the only human being from whom he willingly accepts criticism, though he seems to get a hell of lot from other sources whether he likes it or not. Anyway, if Edgar had been mellow, I would have said something to him, but he was in a very quarrelsome mood, and I thought that criticism might do more harm than good.

"There's usually a reason for that, if you look hard enough," I said. "Women getting fat like that."

"I did," Edgar said, "and there was. There were several, in fact. The first one was that she was safely married, and we was them, what is it there, them Roman Catholic type fellas, so that was one thing out of the way. Sort of like getting a job with the post office as a sorter right after you finish your hitch with the Army. Show up for work, keep doing it until you're sixty-five, and the government'll take care of you for life. Fuck the mail—who gives a shit about that? The paycheck, then the pension. That's what counts.

"Them broads of that persuasion of our vintage," Edgar said, "the Catholic ones, I mean, that was exactly the attitude they took. You can't blame them individually. It was the attitude their families took. They had it bred into them, like little tits, or big feet, or something. It wasn't conscious—it was genetic. Once you stumbled to the altar, so horny you could barely walk, and scribbled something on the dotted line, they had you.

"Oh," he said, "I don't mean that they thought they could

127

commit armed robbery and get away with it. They took to braining you with a bleach bottle while you slept, probably you would leave them. But short of the bleach bottle, you couldn't and even the bleach bottle would not be enough to get you to divorce them. Because, after all, you were Catholics, and Catholics didn't do that. Only Protestants."

"Well," I said.

"It's true," Edgar said. "To them the marriage contract was as guaranteed as the one you get when they let you into the United Mine Workers. Nothing short of one or the other of you falling down dead was gonna break it. Literally.

"Now you take these young ballplayers," Edgar said.

"Look," I said, "this is all very interesting, but aren't you waiting here to catch a plane? It's almost quarter of four."

"I am," Edgar said. "I took a chance and came out here to catch a plane without a reservation and I lost, and the first one I could get was five-twenty-five. When that steward comes along, flag him down.

"You look at those young ballplayers that have one helluva rookie year and get themselves long-term contracts for umpteen million dollars a year for the rest of their lives and think about how come so many of them're downright lackadaisical. Don't run too fast—might sprain an ankle. Don't crash into the fence—might hurt your shoulder. Don't slide too much—might tear a muscle. Is it a little cold today, Poopsie? Better not pitch—arm might tighten up. Be careful crossing streets, woo, woo; don't eat sweets, woo, woo; cook your meat, woo, woo; you'll get a pain in your tum-tummy.

"In other words, don't hustle. Dog it just an imperceptible little bit, so you'll live a long time and generally feel pretty relaxed, and you can plan to live forever, and quite well also. Because, after all, who knows what wickedness the club will think up to perform upon you if you extend yourself too far and get hurt? And besides, why should you? You've got nothing to strive for. You get paid just as much for loafing as you do for working."

"Hey," I said, "wait a minute. Running a household, raising children: that's not loafing. That's damned hard work, and it's boring as hell, too. I'll tell you something—I wouldn't do it. I'd rather bust my ass on the Hill all day, and maybe get nowhere, than spend a whole damned day doing the same damned things I did yesterday, so I can be ready to do the same damned things tomorrow. I wouldn't touch it. Not for twice the money I get now."

"No," Edgar said, "you wouldn't, and that's why you never demanded it. Because you didn't want it. But the ladies, Counselor, the ladies did. That was what they thought they wanted, and that was what they demanded. Get married, keep house, raise kids, about nineteen years after the last kid was born when they become full-time mothers and retired from being wives.

"Play golf, tennis, canasta every afternoon. Do a little swimming. Get plenty of rest. Drink too much. Get involved in a few charities. Do a lot of shopping, and generally be about as useful as a dead skunk in the middle of the road. No wonder they get dull as hell, hog-idle and stupid, too.

"It's a better deal'n the post office, come to think of it. If hubby lives, and doesn't bolt, you got the joint checking account and generous nagging rights. If he dies, you got the insurance. And if he lives, but he bolts, you got the alimony.

"And why the hell can't you go out and work, you lazy bitch? Because you haven't gone to work in nineteen years, at least fifteen or sixteen of which you spent alone in the house munching chocolates all day, and nipping at the cooking sherry, while the kids were in school. In other words, you can't work because you've been hog-idle too long. If you wore tie shoes, you'd have to have somebody else around to make the knot for you. Jesus."

"Well," I said, "there's one thing. . . ."

"You know what they tell you to do, you run over somebody in Arabia," Edgar said. "They tell you to jam the damned shift in reverse and run over the bastard again. Because it's cheaper to compensate the family for the corpse than it is to support the poor maimed bastard for life. That's what we should do with ex-wives in the United States. First the divorce, and then you run over them twice with a Buick station wagon, unless they agree to go to work."

"If I can finish," I said.

The steward came back, and Edgar ordered "a double beaker of Wild Turkey and a Heineken." I ordered a Coke.

"Finish," Edgar said.

"If she's got a boyfriend," I said, "that could put a considerably different perspective on your situation."

"Ahh," Edgar said, "they'll never get married. She's too cute for that. She's bouncing around like Catherine Daneuve. A bit porky for the role, perhaps, but all decked out, a simpering, whimpering fool again. But she's not gonna get married. What's she gonna get married for? She's got the paycheck, mine. She's got the boyfriend. She's got the kids, and she's got the house.

"You know something? I hate to sound like a materialistic old son of a bitch, which I most certainly am, but while I love my kids, I cannot really complain about the job she does with them. Except the job she does *with* them on me. Otherwise, she is fine. They are good kids, and I ain't been around much, enough, to take the credit for it. True, not even Solomon in all his glory was arrayed as are the lilies of the field, but most of the nasty kids I've seen, which is a fair and substantial number, bear interesting resemblances to their upbringers in their most disgusting respects. And mine don't. So, while I miss them, I can't say she's done a lousy job with them, because she hasn't. I doubt I could've done as good. But then, of course, I've had to work.

"What I had to work to do," Edgar said, as the drinks arrived and he paid for them, "was to provide the environment and the three squares apiece a day, and the glorious raiments with which they are bedecked, and that goddamned house I gave away like a chump because I hired a lawyer that was cheap and got the services of a damned cheap lawyer. Which ended up costing me a great deal more than if I'd hired somebody decent in the first place, because there was a certain amount of equity in that vine-covered cottage, and there is gonna be a lot more, and I ain't gonna get none of it. That is one thing that pisses me off.

"The other thing that pisses me off," Edger said, "say, can you have me committed, if I say something to you that's really crazy?"

"Nope," I said, "attorney-client privilege. Course if you say it too loud, and one of these other folks hears it, doesn't come under the privilege anymore, and they might do it on their own."

Edgar looked around at the blue chairs, men and women dressed in suits sitting in the chairs and self-consciously making telephone calls on credit cards, the aircraft beyond the windows. A seedy-looking fellow in a brown seersucker suit was gazing vacantly at us from one of the tables while he held a phone to his ear. "I'll take my chances," he said. "These folks're all too busy showing off.

"What really pisses me off," he said, lowering his voice slightly, "is the goddamned fucking shrubbery. The rosebushes. The forsythia. The fucking goddamned hollyhocks, for Christ sake."

"What's the matter with it?" I said.

"*Nothing's* the matter with it," Edgar said. "*That's* what pisses me off. That little brick ranch was as bare as a baby's bottom when I bought it in my domestic period. I was out there every weekend, potting and pruning and seeding, and I made it look damned nice. *Damned* nice. The dogwoods bloom, and the rhododendrons blossom, and the bees flock to that house like there wouldn't be no honey in the supermarket next year if they didn't visit the Lannin homestead. No, it's beautiful. It's beautiful because there's an item in that goddamned budget of hers to pay for the kid that does the gardening that I put in, that increases the value of the house that I bought, that she got. That, Peter, pisses me off."

I waited for an instant or two to see if he had subsided. "Edgar," I said, "could I possibly talk now?"

"You can talk," he said, "but you won't make any sense. You've got a happy marriage. Apparently. Two of them. Jeanne and Maggie. You won that in the lottery. Nothing you know's gonna make one atom of sense to somebody who knows what I know."

"I wasn't going to talk about marriage," I said. "What about the boyfriend?"

"Well," Edgar said, with noticeable effort, "I don't know. I've met him. His name's Roger Shanahan. I know he's a nice guy. He's about thirty-five, and he's never been married. His family lives out in the horsey part of Virginia, where they got big white barns and miles of white rail fences. And horsies, horsies, horsies. He's teaching the kids to ride horsies, and they love him, and when they talk about him, they also make him out to be a very nice guy. He's out at my house most of the time apparently, although the kids're very discreet about arrangements made for sleeping and most other activities often occurring after sundown, and I like him. He's all right."

"What does she think of him?" I said.

"Mary Claire?" he said. "She's convinced he's the bear's nuts. I think I'm supposed to get jealous, but except for certain odd moments, I really do not hate the broad, and I'm glad to see her happy. I just wish she'd stop taking all my money, of which there was not a whole lot to start with. I'd like my electric garage door opener back again, for one thing. I never used to get wet. I opened the door with the clicker in the morning and backed the car out, and I put it in the garage at the office. At night when I got home, I hit the clicker, and the door opened, and I drove the car in, and I hit the button again, and once again, I didn't get wet. She has got that, too. My door opener. Son of a bitch, I'll bet old Roger's got the other one, so he can come in at night and leave in the morning, and none of the neighbors the wiser. That crafty bastard."

"All right," I said. "Is it remotely possible that they *are* in love, and that if, as you say, she's as happy as you seem to think, they *might* get married and at least let you up from all that alimony?"

"Peter," he said, "what're you doing here?"

"Meeting one of the partners from our corresponding firm in Nashville," I said. "We're going on to New York tonight, for a meeting about regulations in the market in petrodollars."

"Good," Edgar said. "Nothing to do with real life, then, I take it."

"I suppose you could say that," I said.

"Would the Nashville lawyer be a lady, by any chance?" Edgar said.

"If so," I said, "he'll be very surprised to hear it. His name is Wendell Sparrow. He's about fifty, and he's not my type at all."

"Good," Edgar said. "Now, back to the real world. I *know* Roger Shanahan, and I have for some time. I know him because I used to see him every Sunday when I was still going through those paces. Roger is the assistant pastor of St. Theresa's Church. He was the guy running the camping trip."

"Oh," I said.

"You can get divorced, Counselor," Edgar said, "but you can never get unmarried."

Eight

Edgar, by the end of July, had begun to adopt a rather superior attitude. "It's hotter'n hell down here," he said, wearing that same disreputable Haspel suit.

"Have you had that thing cleaned?" I said.

"What thing?" he said. "Why're your offices so goddamned *hot* anyway? You suckin' up to *El Presidente,* same as everybody else? You wanna be Secretary of Energy, like that tightwad old Jim Schlesinger that got resurrected?"

"They lock the goddamned thermostats," I said. "First time they did it, one of the more intransigent associates stuck a screwdriver in his pocket on the way out of his apartment that morning, jimmied the lock, and racked the wheel down to a civilized level. They put on a new lock and cranked her back up to eighty. He brought in a tire iron and busted the lock again. Now they've got something on it made by Mosler Safe, I think it is, and Willie Sutton couldn't get into it. We're thinking of retaining Dirty Harry and his Forty-four to blow the thing off, but until we have a partners' meeting and decide to do it, we swelter."

"They give you something off the exorbitant rent for this sacrifice, I assume," Edgar said.

"They *add* something to the rent, for the extra cost of giving us less power that costs more to leave us sweating," I said.

"The hell you do?" Edgar said. "You rent this goddamned suite from a bunch of lawyers?"

"No," I said, "from a bunch of landlords. Worse. Lawyers fuck you, but kiss you first, and they tell you that they love you afterwards. Landlords don't respect you in the morning. Don't change the subject. *I* had a question pending. You had that thing, that suit, cleaned since I saw you last?"

"When was that?" he said.

"Two weeks ago," I said. "Looked like you'd been basted in it then, and it looks like you've been basted in it now."

"Two weeks ago," he said. "Lemme think. I had it rendered once and retrieved enough oil to run my lamps for the summer months. Yes, I had it cleaned, too. Not since then, though. As soon as the tailor gets finished with the new stuff, I'm gonna throw this thing away. But I had it cleaned. Also pressed. Cleaned *and* pressed. Did that on the expense account. Paper sent me out to Memphis, see if Elvis was still dead. Well, if they were actually gonna bury him again in that crypt. Got the suit cleaned at the hotel. Made the valet do it. Stuck it on the bill. I was gonna have a bit of dental work done, too. Maybe have the fangs capped. But I hadda go home before I could get an appointment. But, yes, I had it cleaned. Why? Look a bit scruffy?"

"*Scruffy,*" I said, "is one word that comes to mind. Not to mine, of course, but, very likely, to the minds of many others. You look like you slept at the Seamen's Mission."

"In days gone by," Edgar said, "I would have had to admit that I very well might've. But now I have reformed, and I know very well that I did not. I have been behaving myself. I hate it, but I have been doing it. And I am getting new clothes."

"For same reason?" I said. "The reform, I mean."

135

"You mean fear of death?" Edgar said. "Like we had in college when we got drunk?"

"Yeah," I said.

"Partly," Edgar said. "Partly, it is fear of death. Partly, it is love of life. Would that make a title for a soap?"

"Sure," I said. "Very good one in fact."

"I thought so," Edgar said, nodding. "How old Maggie?"

"Old Maggie fine," I said.

"Where old Maggie?" Edgar said.

"She's in Vineyard Haven, in the house she took off old Vernon, and it ain't bad neither. Nice view of the Sound, nice set of weathered stairs leading down to nice private beach, nice French doors leading into master bedroom off sundeck, through which summer wind blows in the morning, off the sea, when the sun comes up."

"Ahh," Edgar said. "Bet a man could have a small grill down on that beach at sunset, throw on a steak or two, crack perhaps one or more bottles of wine, and sing George M. Cohan favorites until even his Irish sweater was not quite enough to ward off the evening chill. And then to bed."

"Very possible," I said. "Tell me, did they bury Elvis?"

"Far as I know," Edgar said. "What I did was watch it on television. Couldn't get near the goddamned mansion. Last year. Too many screaming teenagers, age around thirty-five, leaping about like . . . there's this guy I know that freaked out of the newspaper business, couple years ago, and decided to become Thoreau, up in Maine. Log cabin, everything. Grows his own goddamned food, including chickens. Every week, goes down to the general store, puts in a dime, calls me collect. At the paper, of course. I accept the charges. On behalf of the paper, of course. I ain't no goddamned *fool*. And every time, it's when'm I coming up for Natural Dinner?

"I finally got sick of it," Edgar said. "I drove all the way up to this town in Maine that you could hawk a lunger across on a windless day, and I inquired of the natives, all of whom were noncommittal, but finally I found a dirt road, and I went up it, feeling like Erskine Caldwell, and I came to this place, which would fall down if it had the energy, and there is my old friend. Looking like L'il Abner, but with a terminal case of whiskers and a serious case of seriousness. Guy's been eating oats or something.

"I got out of the car," Edgar said, "I've got on this sport jacket and this pilled shirt and a pair of pants that, quite honestly, could stand a bit of attention, and he stands there looking like something Grant Wood painted with a pitchfork, and I thought: Why the fuck did I do this? And he says to me, he says, says he: 'Edgar. At long last.' And breaks into this grin that shows more teeth'n Jimmy Carter.

"All of a sudden, I knew something. I knew quite a few things, in fact. I knew why he kept calling me, and I was wrong, and I knew what he was doing, digging around in the dirt. I knew why he was living in a fucking tepee, and doing it with a woman who looked like she could nest birds in her hair and not even notice. She wasn't even half his age, but she was as serene as the Archangel Gabriel, and *she* was glad to see me, too. Challis tie and all. There's dogs all over the place, and cats to the number of eighty-five, and when it comes to Jeeps being pulverized for parts, Guam never saw anything like it. The corn was as high as an elephant's eye, and so was the mary-ju-onna.

"Peter," Edgar said, "I am close to fifty years old, and I'm damned glad of it, all things considered. One of which is that if I weren't, I would be dead, and my enemies would derive considerable satisfaction from that development. I'm sot in my ways, and I'm a pain in the arse in the morning, but there is no one on this earth who can truthfully say that I dumped a friend or ducked an obligation. I maybe didn't carry through, but I tried like a fucking bastard, and that is about all that I can manage.

"I went inside," Edgar said. "It was a converted barn, and there are still, in the air, the lingering aroma of cowflaps. I didn't give a shit. So to speak. They poured some wine, which

137

I drank, and they served some cheese, which they said they made, and we crouched on our haunches and made fun of the fatheads, which is easy to do, and not that much different from the dinner parties down here, except that the fatheads we were mocking are the people who go to the dinner parties down here. Adrian and I took turns telling war stories to Lisa, about the dumb things people'd made us do when we were working down here four, five years ago, and then she told us some of the dumb things the people at her paper made her do when she was working up here—and she's from Louisiana—right after I left. Which was how they ran into each other, covering some half-assed press conference at State. And they had a few drinks, and they rolled around together some, and pretty soon it started getting serious between them.

" 'It's funny the way things happen,' Adrian said. 'I swore I'd never get married again. I hadn't been married for years, and I missed it not one bit. I thought. No kids, no alimony, my folks're in Chicago, both in good health, prosperous and active, and when my sister got married, she moved to Seattle, and we finally gave up all pretense of being interested in each other. My sister bored the ass off me. I don't see how two parents who could produce a fascinating fellow like me contrived to whelp a bovine creature like that.

" 'I had my house in Georgetown—it wasn't very big, to be sure, but it was mostly mine, and it was decorated the way I wanted it, and it had a great kitchen and a wine cellar that was the envy of many a richer man. On Saturday mornings, I read the papers in the Café de la Paix and drank filtre coffee with my croissants. I drove out to Middleburg on Sundays in my British racing green Healey, for brunch at the old tavern. I had friends with condos in San Juan, for when the winter got dreary, and friends with tennis courts in their yards in the Northwest, for when the summer evenings were pleasant. I had a cottage for a month on Cape Cod, and while I am not by any means afflicted with satyriasis, I am nevertheless a man, and I was a single man in Washington, and that is something like being the only woman at Dienbienphu. I never had much interest in clothes, so I didn't have a lot of them, but the ones I had were damned good. Before I met Lisa, I had everything I ever wanted, and I wasn't even forty years old.'

" 'It was really funny,' she said, 'I wasn't in anywhere near the same position, but when you thought about it, I was. I didn't have any education beyond high school. All I had was no doubt whatsoever in mind that I was going to get my ass out of the Louisiana boonies, no matter what it took. Unless it was putting out, and if I was not out by the time I was thirty, I was going to give *that* some further thought, too. But I could make a typewriter sound like a machine gun, which was a good beginning. And I could take dictation and give back something that looked like English, and do it before the week was out, and I knew how to work. So pretty soon I wasn't taking dictation from the boss anymore—I was taking it from the reporters, and some of them couldn't write English with a quill pen, let alone dictate it, and it was a small paper, so what I did showed.

" 'There was a guy on that paper,' she said, 'a great big man named Wilfrid. He was about fifty years old, and he looked like a sumo wrestler. Gigantic man. They called him the publisher and the city editor and the national editor, and every other title they had available, because Wilfrid made it that way.

" 'There was only one thing in the world that Wilfrid wanted,' she said, 'and that was for every soul under his command to do the best work possible, and the most of it. When Wilfrid saw that I could do rewrite, he took me off dictation and put me on rewrite. When I told him that I wanted to do features, he paid me thirty-five bucks for every feature that I did, and told me it was chickenshit money for that kind of work but all he could afford to pay. When I wanted to go on special assignment, he took me off rewrite, and advanced me my expenses, and sent me up to Baton Rouge and told

139

me to keep my eyes open, my mouth shut, and my pants on.

" 'I was at that little paper for less than eighteen months,' she said. 'When I went in there, I had a letter that certified that I could type ninety words a minute. And that was all. When I went out, I had a Newspaper Guild card and a job with the *Times-Picayune,* and I was twenty years old. I also had, as I did not know, a telephone call from my Wilfrid to the *Picayune's* Wilfrid, and when I was twenty-two, I was on my way to Washington.' "

"She must be good in the sack," I said.

"No," Edgar said. "I don't think so. Well, she probably is good in the sack, but I don't think that's how she got to Washington. I dunno much about the way you fellows run your trade, but I know enough to make me think that you don't run yours the same as we run ours.

"See," he said, "there's lots of you. And until Woodstein pulled down a President, there were nowhere near as many of us. In addition to which, we got a lot of plain riffraff in our shops."

"So've we," I said.

"Per capita," he said. "You like that, Counselor? Little Latin there, just to work the kinks out? Per capita, you probably got more riffraff. But you're more heartless than we and do not put the hopeless ones to work on the obits and the religion wrap-ups. No, you triage them, because you've got to make a living in this world, and if a lawyer is so bad he cannot make a living, pretty soon he goes and does something else. Or else he starves to death. Either way, it's the same result for the legal profession. Whereas we scribblers go back for the wounded and often support them well into their tenth and final bout with alcoholism, while wincing at the stuff they produce for publication in the paper.

"Anyway," Edgar said, "you show us somebody who has really got it to burn, and most of us commence to use our teeth and elbows in the corners to push the kid along, because we need all the help we can get. It ain't our money that the kid is getting, and we don't own the goddamned paper, but it is our goddamned paper nonetheless, and anything that makes it look good makes us look good. There're a lot of ladies who will fuck, if approached with sufficient tact: 'You wanna fuck?' 'Sure.' There are very few ladies, and very few gentlemen, who have got enough snap on the fastball to make it from the bayou to the Hill in less'n four years, and those who did it in that time did it on quality and damned hard work.

"Which was what she said," Edgar said. " 'I busted my ass,' she said. 'I mean, I *really* busted my ass. I thought I was busting my ass before, but it was nothing, compared to the work I was doing in Washington. I wasn't up as early in the morning, and I was asleep each night by one, but I wasn't ever off-duty. I was working from the minute I got up until the minute that I went home, and there were one or two guys who would've liked it if I had held office hours in the bedroom as well. More'n one or two. Everything I did was work. If I went out for a beer, it was work, or might be, because I might hear about something and have to go back to the office and check it out. If I went to dinner, I was working, and if I went to a show at the National Theater, I always had it in the back of my mind that the desk might be interested in how the leading lady from LSU was reacting to the Big Time.

" 'I never really thought about it," she said. 'I was just like Adrian. I was making more money than I ever dreamed of, almost twenty-three thousand dollars a year. I had a little red Lancia that I couldn't afford, even though it was used, and I got all my clothes at Loehmann's, where they sell the same stuff I couldn't afford when it was at Saks, but they were still Labels, and I looked damned good. I never screwed a Congressman, but I still had no trouble running into one whose wife was back in Duluth and who needed a companion for a White House reception. I loved it, but I didn't think about it.

" 'Then,' she said, 'I fell in love with a guy. I didn't move in with him, and he didn't move in with me, but we were an Item, I guess, and he had just the same kind of life I did. Which made it seem like it was nice. We went to dinners, me in my Calvin Kleins, him in his John Weitzes, and if we didn't use my Lancia, we used his Porsche. The network was paying him about three hundred million bucks a year to look handsome while standing on the White House lawn with a mike clipped to his tie, and even though it was the very devil to get him to part with a penny of it, unless it was for himself, he was still getting it. Now and then, when he was absolutely bushed, I could talk him into a weekend on the West Coast, and once, when he was about to have a breakdown, I got him to Nassau. But he had the breakdown anyway. I think the price of the room was what made him snap.

" 'Still,' she said, 'it looked ideal. There was no conflict of interest, like when you're sleeping with the head of the Senate committee you're covering, so you have to go to the boss and tell him that your boyfriend just gave you a box of candy and you'd better be reassigned to the National Institute of Health. The reason that it wasn't ideal was the same reason: there was no conflict of interest because there was no interest.

" 'I finally broke up with him,' she said. 'I didn't have any special reason for breaking up with him. But hell, I didn't have any special reason for starting up with him, any more'n I did for buying the Lancia. I thought he was something that I wanted. The reason I gave him was that he was so goddamned *cheap* I thought I would scream every time he added up a dinner check. But the real reason probably was that there wasn't any reason; hanging around with him was like hanging around with myself, except I was never embarrassed, leaving a table alone, by the size of the tip I'd decided on, and I was when I left after he decided.

" 'I went into some sort of funk for a while,' she said. 'It wasn't anything serious. It was just like I was resting or something. Saving up my strength. Regrouping my forces. I was really doing that. Getting in shape for the next fight. Working out, getting plenty of rest, lots of fruit juices and good fresh air. Not having to worry about packing a change of clothes in my overnight bag, in case Charles invited me to stay, so that people in the office wouldn't leer at me the next day, when I came in in the same outfit. It was easier, but it was also temporary, and I knew it. That was when I met Adrian, right when I was just about finished being on the mend.'

" 'And we started up in exactly the same way,' Adrian said. 'I acted the same way with her that I acted with the other ladies I knew, and she acted the same way with me that she did with him. We ran each other ragged, and we allowed the town to run us both ragged, and that was just the way that things were supposed to be.'

" 'We were turning,' she said, 'into Beautiful fucking People, and it sucked.'

" 'Yeah,' he said, 'and we didn't even have the brains to know it. And then, one day, I had the most astonishing thought, which was that I was happier when I was with Lisa than I was when I was not with Lisa. Much happier, in fact. Happier'n I'd ever been in my life.

" 'So I sat back on my little stool in the Senate Press Gallery, while William Proxmire discoursed to a chamber populated only by the President pro tem, several bored pages, some clerks, and John Tower chatting quietly with Alan Cranston off in the corner near the door to the cloakroom, and it crossed my mind that perhaps I should devote a bit more attention to what was happening to me. Not to prevent it, not by any means. Appreciate it, maybe. Savor it. Not miss any of it. Because apparently I was engaged in doing something that I had not done before. And it was rather pleasant, too, unlike most of the experiences that I had dwelt upon in the past.'

" 'What I started doing,' Lisa said, 'well, the first thing was that I went into an absolute fit of panic. I was really scared. When I was a kid, I had this dog. He was a nice little dog, brown and white. Nothing you'd walk on a good leash in the malls rented out to the smarter shops, but still, a nice little brown and white dog. He only had two problems: he chased cars, and when he had to go to the vet, he turned into a Bengal tiger.

" 'Well,' she said, 'it was the first one that finally got him, one sunny day when he attacked a Pontiac GTO with a nasty kid behind the wheel, but there was nothing we could've done about that, and therefore, it was bound to happen sooner or later: somebody would swerve a car into him faster'n he could swerve his body out of the way. So that was all right. But for the longest time, all his life actually, we battled that little dog to get him to go to the vet for his shots without having to knock him unconscious first, and that was a losing proposition.

" 'I must've been in Washington before it dawned on me that that dog had two personalities, one of which was when he was being Lisa's little brown and white dog, and the other when he was getting ready to take your leg off at the knee if you even showed him a hypodermic needle. When he saw a vet, he went into the second personality.

" 'If we'd never shown him a vet, just let him take his chances with ringworm and heartworm and distemper and rabies and all those other things that the rest of his buddies in the neighborhood faced without the benefits of medical science, we never would've seen the ugly side of him, and as far as we were concerned, it would not've existed. Which would've made it a lot easier for us to look at him with complete affection, because we wouldn't've known about that streak of ferociousness he had in reserve.

" 'Now,' she said, 'I was always pretty happy with myself. Nice, uncomplicated life. Hard work, maybe, but I never minded that. And not insulated. I had my share of chuckles. I wasn't going to wind up in a rest home in my nineties, fantasizing about all the men who wanted to get into my pants. Because there were, there had been, quite a few men who wanted to get into my pants, and when I had had similar feelings about one of them, the two of us generally ended up with no pants on. I could always spot a turkey from the time that I grew tits, and I guess I must've never appealed to the weirdos, because nobody ever tried to beat me up. Which was fine by me. There was one lady who got herself drunk one night in The Dubliner, after a long day on the Hill, and invited me to try something a little different, but I had a pretty good buzz on myself and didn't figure out what she'd actually had in mind until the next morning, by which time I had long since staggered home alone and unsullied.

" 'If one of my manageable beaux was out of town, at least two of my regular beaux were in town, and I was as free calling them as they were calling me. At least until I started hanging around with the cathode-tube Adonis. And even he didn't put many scratches on my paint when I was involved with him.

" 'I was,' she said, 'like one of those Congressmen from the Middle South, anointed by the fellow vacating the seat to run successfully for the Senate, and unopposed for each of his subsequent ten terms. While there might've been a lot of things I couldn't get away with doing, there wasn't anything that I wanted to do that I couldn't get away with. I don't know if my wants were simple, or just so vulgar that a majority approved of them, but either way, they were satisfied. I maybe wasn't happy, but I was content, and that gave me about a two hundred percent lead on just about everybody else I knew.

" 'I was out to dinner once, with one of those safe-seat birds,' she said. 'He was good company, and there was about as much sexual stuff between us as there is between a polecat and a big green alligator. This made everything very relaxed. We were at some place, I forget where it was, but it was nice, and the waiter came around to see if we wanted dessert. Well, sometimes I did, and sometimes I didn't, and sometimes I just wasn't sure. 'Go ahead,' says my escort. 'Whatcha got?'

said I, and the waiter started talking about this brandied pear done up in some kind of mocha custard that was frozen, I forget what they call it. Cost about four hundred bucks, and the chef apparently was just about beside himself, he'd thought of it.' "

"Pavé glacé Montmorency," I said to Edgar.

"She didn't say what they called it," Edgar said.

"That's what it is," I said.

"Whatever it is," Edgar said. " 'I don't like pears much,' she said, 'in any condition. I don't mind frozen custard, or even R.C. Cola, but I wouldn't eat a pear in any situation. I don't like the texture of pears, no matter what you've done to them. Pears're grainy and slippery at the same time. I don't like the way they make my mouth feel. Like when you pull the cotton out of the aspirin bottle, the way your fingers feel.'

" 'Baby fingers,' Adrian says. 'Nerves too close to the skin.'

" 'Shut up,' she said. 'The Congressman apparently didn't share my prejudices. He's one of those guys who came out of a small city in a rural state, with the average amount of straw sticking to his clothes, the usual amount of cowshit dried on his shoes, and the customary bagginess in the pants of his cheap suits. But with the understanding, which is not usual, that there may possibly be a somewhat better way of doing things.

" 'He got himself off the farm, selling insurance, and he got himself out of the insurance business when he learned banking. He got himself out of banking when he learned commodities markets. And he got himself out of commodities markets when he studied politics.

" 'By then he had a lot of goddamned money, all earned while gainfully employed at honest labor, as he liked to call it, and he was beginning to read Tolstoy and think about what Thackeray really had in mind. When that guy quoted something from the Hudson Institute, it was not because some staff speechwriter was an intern from the Fletcher School of

Law and Diplomacy—it was because that guy'd read what Kahn's people had to say.

" 'People were always underestimating him, so he'd end up on the Armed Services Committee, because somebody thought he was unsophisticated and would make no trouble. And he would commence his European seminars in personal improvement at the expense of the taxpayers. Then he made trouble. He became a terrible hawk. He kept his rump-sprung wife, and he kept his rump-sprung suits, and whenever he went back to the cornfields, he took both and nothing else. And that was about the only place that he got into either one. That man knew his limits.

" 'So,' she said, 'when the waiter finished slobbering about the pear, my friend licked his chops and shook his head. "No, thanks," he said. "I've already got more bad habits than I can afford, and I'm not going to get another one. It doesn't do to be greedy." '

" 'That was what I thought about,' she said, 'when I started noticing a few palpitations about Adrian. If I wouldn't try cocaine when I was in New York, no matter what anybody said about the rush that it would give me, and if I turned down two tickets to see Mick Jagger and the Rolling Stones in person, even though I really wanted to go, because they were being scalped at me for seventy-five apiece, what the hell was I doing messing around with some goddamned emotional thing that could leave me a hell of a lot worse bankrupt, a hell of a lot faster?

" 'There's a lot of pears in this life, and you can either have a reasonable assortment of the ones you kind of like or go bearshit over the one version that absolutely knocks you for a loop and leaves you fit for nothing else. My mummy taught me to be cautious: "Never mind the handsomest boy who's the dreamiest dancer," Mummy said. "Dance with the boy who's a little clumsy, because you can smooth him out some, and he will ask you out again. But the other boy will have too many choices, and he won't choose you." My mummy's a smart lady. For two days, I didn't return Adrian's calls.'

" 'Drove me nuts,' Adrian said.

" 'What'd you do?' I said," Edgar said. "I've known Adrian a long time, and I don't care if he is younger'n I am, I still like him, in spite of that.

" 'I did the Br'er Fox Number,' he said. 'I laid low. I chewed my nails down to the quick, and I fretted quite a lot for a few days, and I didn't hear anything, and then I woke up one morning and the air was clear and the sun was out. I was alone, but I didn't have to go to work, and actually, while I didn't feel as good as I'd somewhat become accustomed to feeling, I didn't really feel bad either. "Once . . . I was . . . alone. Just . . . dreaming . . . of Para-dise . . ." you know the rest. Well, if it once nearly was mine, this is closer'n most come, and I was still pretty well off. Doesn't do to bitch. Tempts the goddamned Fates, which're always out looking to do somebody dirt, anyway, purely on a volunteer basis.

" 'Screw it,' " I said to myself, toweling briskly after a long shower. "Probably a mirage anyway. Wouldn't've worked out in a million years. Woman probably never existed. Something like the Ghost of Christmas Past, I think it was, the product of an undigested bit of mutton. Nice, dry day. Sensible thing for a man in my position to do is play a few hard sets of tennis, see if the Healey'll fire up again, and take nourishment in the company of good friends." So I did. Called up a long-suffering friend from the bureau and obtained the loan of his wife, who absolutely runs my ass ragged on the court, and from her wangled an invitation to dinner. When this woman says: "Potluck," get the rights to lick the pot and offer to bring the wine. They live halfway to East Jesus, out in Virginia, but the gleanings're good no matter how far from the Chain Bridge cutoff you may find yourself.

" 'The trouble is,' he said, 'that her tennis and her cooking're no better'n his fresh vegetables and vodka martinis and only slightly better'n the red wine I had had the foresight to stick into the trunk along with my tennis gear. The exercise, and the superior fare, left me quite exhausted by the time the eleven o'clock news came on. . . .'

" 'Drunk,' Lisa said.

" 'Drunk,' he said, 'as well. So I gratefully accepted their anxious invitation to say the night and hack my way through quarts of Bloody Marys and mountains of sausages and eggs in the morning. Instead of heading home and probably obliging the Virginia or District police to hack *their* way through the twisted wreckage of my Healey with the Jaws of Life, in order to extricate my battered body from the car's clutches. By the time I got home it was midafternoon on the Sabbath, and I was feeling quite cheerful indeed as I picked up a beer and the magazine section of the *Times.* The telephone was next, and my opening line was sparkling. "Hello," I said. "Hello," she snarled.

" 'Well,' Adrian said, 'this did not seem to be a particularly promising beginning, so I tried to take it from the top. "Hello?" I said. "We've been through that already," she said.

" 'Now,' he said, 'I was well rested, well exercised, and consequently pretty well disposed toward most things. But I have my limits, too.' "Not lately," I said, "and not for lack of trying on my part either."

" 'Where've you been?' " she said. Not seeing how it was really any of her business but being more forbearing than usual, I said: "Bowling, of course. Saturday's my bowling night. You know that. I was in the semifinals. We won those, and lost in the finals by eleven pins, and I just came up from rinsing out my purple sateen shirt. It was all sweat stains under the arms." "I've been trying to reach you for two days now," she said. "Frustrating, isn't it?" I said. "I know the feeling. I tried to reach you for two days as well. Gets tiresome. I gave up on it." "Well," she said, "are you dead or not?" "Yes," I said, "I am either dead, or I am not. Whaddaya want?" '

" 'And that,' Lisa said to me," Edgar said, " 'that was the

question. So I said: "I don't know. But it's apparently not simply what I've got, and I thought it was, and that scares me." And he asked me if I wanted to talk, and have some coffee, and I said I guessed I did, and I ended up moving in with him.'

" 'Not,' Adrian said, 'without further commotions, which gradually became fewer and farther between and more and more trivial as we gradually came around to deciding what was worth fighting about, what was not worth fighting about, and what was just plain silly to fight about. Finally, we got to the point where most of the fighting chances were clearly silly, and we stopped fighting altogether.'

" 'Ain't love grand?' I said," Edgar said. " 'Now you're in fucking Maine, tilling the goddamned soil and living off of turnips and berries and shit like that. You doing any work? Or is that a silly thing, too?'

" 'Sure, we're working," Lisa said. 'Tilling the goddamned soil. The soil does not bring forth turnips in abundance, unless it first be tilled. Not that our soil brings forth any turnips, because the day I catch it doing that, we will have some fresh soil underfoot and give it one damned good talking to before we do any tilling of it.'

" 'That's not what I meant,' I said. 'I meant: you're a couple of talented people. At least one of you is that I know about personally because Adrian whipped my ass on a story that happened right before our very eyes too many times for me to think he's not, and I will take it on faith that you must be, too, or else you wouldn't be here with him. So, are you rusticating to write books exposing the whole mad enterprise, or are you just rusticating? What the fuck *are* you doing any-way?'

" 'An interesting question,' Adrian said.

" 'What happened was this," she said. 'What we *think* hap-pened was this: my family wasn't poor. We weren't rich, but we sure weren't poor, not by the standards of Jefferson Parish, at least. My father worked, and he worked steady, and since his work happened to be in the Sheriff's Department, it left him a fair amount of time to himself.

" 'He liked to build,' she said. 'When I got to be around ten, eleven, he built on a bedroom for me, really a bedroom suite, with a little sitting room. He expanded the garage for his tools, and he finished the cellar. He put the siding on the house and the paper on the roof. He hung new doors and planed the old ones so they swung freely. He ripped out all the cabinets in the kitchen and put in new ones. He put in a dishwasher, and a stove top, and a double oven. He air-conditioned everything he couldn't insulate, and when he was through with that, he tore out the bathroom and put in double vanities and sinks with gold-plated fixtures. My daddy liked to work with his hands.

" 'One day, when I was home sick,' she said, 'Daddy came home early, looking for something to do. The people that owned the house before us had put the original indoor plumbing in, but left the outhouse standing. It wasn't standing very well by the time that Daddy got home that day. As a matter of fact, it was leaning pretty good. And Daddy got out of that prowl car and stood with his hands on his hips, looking at it, and then he went in and drank three beers, and put on his old pants, and no shirt, and went out in the yard with a big old crowbar and a shovel.

" 'He got that there crowbar underneath the northeast corner of that outhouse, and he heaved her up, and over she went, on about the seventh try. He just broke her off her foundation and tumbled her all down in a heap. Then he took that crowbar like you would take a baseball bat, and he stood there in the sun, the sweat streaming down his chest and belly, and he started to whaling the shit out of that outhouse, until there wasn't nothing left but a big stack of rotten old kindling.

" 'And he put that crowbar down. He picked up the shovel, and he shoveled all that kindling into the hole, and it didn't come near to filling it. Then he went back to the garage, and he got the barrow, and he wheeled the barrow out, and he flung the shovel into it, and he went down by the trees in the back and started digging. He'd fill that barrow and bring it up and dump it in the hole, and then he'd go back again, and every time he emptied that barrow into the hole, after about the fifth time, he would jump on the dirt several times.

" 'At first you could hear the wood breaking under him and the dirt, and then after a while you couldn't, but he kept filling the barrow and emptying the barrow, and the sun went down, and he was out there in the twilight, emptying the barrow and jumping on the dirt.

" 'He came in about eight, eight-thirty,' she said. 'He was filthy, and he was all sweaty, but the land was nice and level, and if you didn't know that outhouse was there in the morning, you would not've know that it had ever been there that night. Just fresh earth, like somebody'd turned her over and got sick of it and would start again tomorrow, making a garden.

" 'So I said to him: "Daddy, you gonna plant something there?" And he said: "Nope. There's human shit down there, and lots of lime. It's old, but it's there, and if the one of them things don't poison you, 'tother one will. Best a man can do is make it look better. Think it looks better?" "Surely does," I said, and it did, too.

" 'Well,' she said," Edgar said, " 'I think that was what happened to us. At least, to me. Once I got the crowbar under the corner of my life, I just tipped the whole thing over and threw it down on the ground. But it didn't make any sense to just leave it there, all broken, useless, and unsightly. If . . . if I was going to turn around and look at myself in the mirror and admit it, say: "Well, Lisa, now you built that whole thing up, the life on the job, and the life with Charles, 'NBC News, Washington,' and now you're tangled up with this guy and he's getting a little daffy, the thing is, what do you do now?"

" ' And that was when I decided that I never really thought anything out, through and through. I had one thing that I did at a time. I got out of that little town. I got out of that little paper. I got out of that little romance with Charles. I got into this wonderful thing with Adrian. But every time I got something I wanted—and I wanted all of the things I got—I didn't know what to do next.

" 'See,' she said," Edgar said, " 'I know, for somebody that was supposed to be able to put words together, I know I am not doing what you would call a hell of a damned good job explaining this. But anyway, once I got Adrian in my life— and I don't mean this the way it sounds—what was in my life before was all out of proportion to him. Smaller scale. It was like the old outhouse. It was there, but nobody used it anymore, and it was just sort of falling apart, because what was indoors was so much better. And I was getting funny looks and some complaints about the way I was doing my job. People started asking me if I was too good to hang around with them all night at some dumb cocktail party, when I'd been home with Adrian, having dinner, reading a book that didn't have anything to do with my work. Or maybe just making it with Adrian all night.

" 'At first I lied, and I said I had something else to do. Or I didn't feel good. And that made me feel like a hypocrite, so I turned around one day, when somebody asked me something like that, and I told them the reason they didn't see me at some damned function or other was that I didn't want to go. I wanted to go home. And that was the night I told Adrian I was thinking about demolishing the life I had, that I worked so hard to get, and what did he think about that? Burying it. And he said that was all right with him.'

" 'I was the same way,' Adrian said. 'All of a sudden I was consumed by this thing we had. I did the same things as before, and they bored the hell out of me. I was *aware* that they bored the hell out of me. I did something, and I thought to myself: "This is not important to me. Lisa is important to me, and the rest of the stuff I do is not important to me anymore." '

" 'So,' she said, 'one night, spontaneously, I started talking

153

about it, and he said he'd been thinking exactly the same thing, and we both said: "Well, why're we doing these things, then, if this's the way we feel?" And we couldn't think of a reason, so we decided to stop. And we came up here.'

" 'The Healey alone,' Adrian said, 'brought almost forty-five hundred. I had the land, and the house didn't cost much, the house here. The furniture's simple, and I paid for the stuff and the roof that's over it with what I got for the stuff in my house in Georgetown alone. I don't have the clothing bills; she doesn't have the parking tickets that the Lancia got out on the street. We got the Jeep for practically zilch, and we've still got almost ninety thousand dollars that I got for the house.

" 'It costs us,' he said, 'we figure, somewhere in the neighborhood of thirty-eight hundred bucks a year to live. We get upwards of sixty-three hundred in interest on the ninety, and we don't spend it. We grow most of what we eat. What we used to spend on tennis, for exercise, we get free now, walking in the woods and looking at the animals. We chop our own wood and make our own hard stuff from the apples that we grow ourselves. We do buy wine, but it's jug wine, and we don't drink much coffee anymore. When we want a trip, we sell a piece on Natural Living, one place or the other, and then we go to New York. We maybe look a little country, but we'll live forever, and when we die, we'll die happy.'

"For dinner," Edgar said, "we had fresh roast chickens. And I mean fresh. Adrian went out to the chicken yard behind the house and grabbed a hen that hadn't been producing up to snuff. Took a piece of cord out of his pocket, hogtied her feet, and hung her from the clothesline upside down. Grabbed another hen—and they all had names; first one was Agatha, I think, and the second was Louise—tied her feet, got her by the drumsticks, whomped her head down on the handy stump nearby, pulled the hatchet out from the side of the stump, and chopped her head off. Blood was flying all over the place, Louise's next of kin looking on stupidly while Louise

154

flopped around headless in the dusk, and Agatha watched from the clothesline upside down. Adrian took Agatha down, laid her across the stump, and guillotined Agatha as well, with about the same results. 'How about the rest of them?' I said. 'Your feathered boarders. They know this's gonna happen to them someday, they end up in the pot?'

" 'Chickens're not very bright,' Adrian said. 'I doubt it. Wilbur over there, the pig, he may have some idea, but the hens don't seem to reason well. Course, if they do, it works to our advantage. I'm not gonna eat a bird that's belting out the eggs.'

"I will tell you something, Peter," Edgar said, "I am no great fan of chicken. I can get it down, but I am not a fan of it. Ordinarily. That night I damned near gagged. I knew a broad named Agatha once, same name as the first chicken, and she could've used having her head cut off. Would've improved her appearance considerable. And for all I know, there was somebody who ate her. But it wasn't me with her, and I wished that it had not been me with the fucking chickens. I would've taken turnip cheerfully, and I *hate* turnip."

"So I take it," I said, "that you came to tell me that you're convinced of the good sense of their position and intend to complete your present tour of duty, retire to the woods, and meditate, and commit felonious assaults upon chickens."

"No," Edgar said, "I don't. Oh, I had a good time with them. Agatha and Louise cooked up pretty well, and the wild rice was as good as any that I've had, which is to say terrible, because I hate rice. The beefsteak tomatoes were great, and the lettuce was crisp. They had had the white wine jug hung on the rope down in the well, so that while you had to be damned careful of the rock walls when you hauled it up, it was damned good and cold and quite tasty indeed. Even out of jelly glasses. The coffee had chicory in it, which I dislike, but it was strong, and the raspberries were perfect ambrosia. I praised the fresh cream they poured on the berries, because I have known Adrian for quite a while, and while I am impressed at his newfound abilities in the execution of chickens, I do not think him up to butchering a milch cow and consequently sought to plant the seed of dissuasion in his mind.

"After chow, we smoked a home-grown joint and listened to eight-track tapes of Fleetwood Mac, and neither of those things, nor the hard cider, did a damned thing for my serenity. But that was already considerable. I slept that night on a bedroll, in my underwear, before a low fire, which was needed even in the summer. And the black flies and mosquitoes and other flying varmints did enter through the window and make revenge in behalf of the rest of the kingdom of the fauna for the indignities visited upon Louise and Agatha. But it was pleasant. And I am not gonna do no such thing."

"What are you going to do?" I said.

"With what remains of this evening," he said, "I am going back to the Madison, wash the accumulated grime from my body and otherwise get cleaned up. Then I may have a drink or two and perhaps dinner consisting of the flesh of an animal to which I have not been previously introduced. Together with wine chilled in a bucket filled with ice, of manufacture by artificial means."

"Because," I said, "before you ask, I can't. This is Getaway Day for me. The wagon's loaded, and the bicycles're lashed down on the roof, and we set forth like pioneers for summer quarters in Dennisport as soon as the rush hour's over."

"How long for?" Edgar said.

"Five blissful weeks," I said. "Five blissful weeks for them, at least. I fly back from Hyannis Monday morning. And back to Hyannis Friday night. And back from Hyannis Monday morning. And so on. Until the last two weeks in August. I only get *two* blissful weeks, it being necessary in every such strategic operation to leave one operative behind in muggy Washington to earn the tariffs for the rest."

"A dedicated family man," Edgar said. "God love ya, Peter, and the wonderful work that you're doing."

"It's nothing," I said.

"It ain't a helluva lot of fuckin' much," Edgar said.

"It's better'n eating Agatha and Louise," I said.

"I would prefer it," Edgar said. "I would not like it, but I would prefer it. The trouble is, Adrian and Lisa have gone a little too far. Well, a lot too far."

"What do you mean?" I said. "They sound like they're both absolutely nuts, to me."

"That's what I mean," Edgar said. "Of course they are. They're holy fools. They got a handle on a little bit of the truth. That much, I envy them. They got some priorities straight. They decided what was important to them. And they put that first. It's obvious. They're crazy about each other. Wonderful. I wish I could be that way about somebody. I envy them.

"The trouble is," Edgar said, "they then decided that what was most important to them was *all* that was important to them, so they spend the whole fucking day digging in the dirt and tormenting the beasts of the field and completely denying all of the other things that they were good at, because they discovered what was really important to them."

"Still," I said, "you sound like you had a good time with them."

"I did," Edgar said. "I had a good time, and I learned something. I don't think they've got a handle on the whole world, but they had a grip on it that I lacked. Both of them went after something that they wanted, and they got it. Then they began weeding out the stuff they didn't want. Except for the fact that they got a little carried away and threw out just about everything else, they had basically the right idea.

"Now," Edgar said, "my motto, as you know, is moderation in all things, particularly moderation. There are a few things lacking in my life that I would kind of like to have in there, so I propose to make careful plans over my dinner and then carry them out. I figure by the time I have a large steak and a large drink or two, I will have a workable battle plan on how to get what I want.

157

"Now," Edgar said, "when you get what you want, according to them gurus of mine, up there killing chickens in the woods, it tends to crowd your time. Because after a certain age you also have a fair number of things that you perhaps do not want, but cannot be rid of. And then there are some things that you have, and don't want, that you can pitch with impunity.

"That inventory is my personal task for tomorrow," Edgar said. "I will go up on the Hill and beard several staffers resentful of the fact that their bosses're getting nice tans on their vacations, while the lackeys labor in the tombs of government. Then, early tomorrow afternoon, while you are still making the day hideous with the snoring of your weariness from the trip to Dennisport, I will board an air-conditioned airplane and return to Boston in comfort. There to prepare a good week and a half of contributions based on malevolent gossip— all true—about people who will not enjoy their vacations quite so much when they read it. By the time we land at Logan, I will have my whole life sorted out. I will know exactly what I am going to do."

"What are you going to do?" I said.

"Ah, Peter," Edgar said, getting up, "I haven't had my dinner yet. I haven't thought it all out yet. Don't be so impatient. In time, all things will be revealed to you."

"Edgar," I said, "I'm an old friend. Doesn't that matter?"

Edgar looked at me. "No," he said, after a pause, "it doesn't."

I will say this for Edgar: he may be a son of a bitch, but he's never lied to me.

Nine

Edgar returned to Washington in the middle of August, and I was damned glad of it. Until early afternoon I had spent a quiet, productive, and profitable day in my office, canceling a luncheon engagement at Jean Pierre, settling happily for a tuna on toast and a carton of milk at my desk. With only two days remaining before I joined Jeanne and the boys on the Cape for two weeks in the sun, I had come in to find that efforts of three months had suddenly coalesced, enabling me at one fell swoop to scuttle three proposed regulations of the Environmental Protection Agency.

Those regulations would have played the very devil with the marine equipment manufacturers that I represent as Washington counsel. Primarily as a result of efforts by Sumner Beale, a good friend of mine at Sharpe, Beale & McClintock, the agency had undertaken a review of existing regulations regarding coastal discharge of untreated products of marine heads and, on the basis of that review, had asked for comment on new rules relaxing the standards.

As the regulations stood, my clients had the market virtually to themselves, having developed rather complicated, fairly expensive systems which incinerated solid wastes and treated liquid wastes in such a fashion as to reduce the coliform bacteria count of the discharge to negligible levels. Sumner's clients were manufacturers of traditional marine waste disposal systems which put the wastes into the water, and out of the boat, in pretty much the same state as they were when eliminated from the human body.

Reduced to essentials, my people—Joe Brann—make and sell sophisticated, costly, effective, on-board treatment systems, the sole advantage of which is that they do not permit marine waste to pollute the waters. Our systems are subject to breakdown. They are heavy. They drain power supplies. Their market history is recent, so skilled repairmen are not always available in every port.

Sumner's people, on the other hand, make reliable, comparatively cheap, easily repaired lightweight devices, the sole disadvantage of which is a rather more than esthetic displeasure occurring from observation of what they put into the water. While they can be fitted with holding tanks, collecting the waste on board until a pump-out facility can be reached, those tanks tend to complicate the simple system and to stink up the boat as well.

Sumner saw the issue in terms of principle: "The little guy should be able to afford to take a shit on his little boat, just as much as the rich guy should be able to on his."

I also saw it in terms of principle: "There is nothing, Sumner, which is quite as objectionable as having a large brown turd wash up against your shoulder while you are teaching your kid to swim in shallow water."

The zeal with which we advocated our contradictory principles, of course, was attributable to the fact that nobody would buy my machine if they could get away with using the devices that Sumner had to sell, while nobody would buy Sumner's gadgets if they couldn't use them or had to cart their crap around with them for days until they got to open water or a pump-out station. There was no way to compromise on a division of the market and thus to propose a different amendment giving each of our interests a reasonable share (not that either of us would have been able to persuade our respective clients to choke down anything less than total victory, if it had been possible) of the booty. Either my people kept the regulation mandating the use of their equipment, thus giving them a practical monopoly of the trade, or else Sumner's people got the new regulations, transferring the monopoly.

We lobbied that issue all summer. Beale, a very good man who knows his business thoroughly, extricated a wrathfully populist statement in support of his position from a wrathfully populist Senator who spends most of his time railing against meddlesome bureaucrats. This had a good deal to say about the limitless oceans and clearly implied that people who do not enjoy swimming in shit ought to go home to their private swimming pools.

Quinn, countering smartly, provoked a wrathfully populist statement from a prominent consumer advocate, declaring that all yachts are the playthings of the rich, who should at least be required to clean up their own messes since they appear to be unwilling to support tax reform to assist the downtrodden who can only swim in the shit.

Beale's people produced studies by independent university scientists—the universities remained independent, but the scientists got paid for their work from Day One by Beale's clients, en route to their conclusions favorable to Beale's clients— showing that human waste was not only harmless to the little creatures of the sea but positively nourishing to them, particularly the scallops. I admit I was surprised when Beale made that statement: I had three New England seafood distributors ranting to the press by noon that they did not sell shit-eating scallops. The battle continued all summer. Beale and I holding friendly discussions with each other, late on warm afternoons, over gin and tonics at the Federal City Club, eating peanuts under the umbrellas on the terrace and congratulating each other on a particularly neat riposte. The agency—while the small sailboat owners backed Beale with identically worded letters complaining that their craft did not have power reserves adequate for my fancy equipment, and the large motorboat people, in letters which strongly resembled each other in wording, objected to regulatory changes on the ground that increasingly crowded anchorages and harbors would soon become pestholes—dithered.

On that muggy August morning I had arrived at the office in good spirits, probably because I had had no company for several weeks outside the office—Jeanne being on the Cape, Maggie on the island—and looked forward to human society. I had no sooner poured a cup of coffee than I received a call from one of my clients who spends his vacation in a Bertram cabin cruiser of obscene length, leaving six-foot rollers in every harbor between Camden, Maine, and Port Jeff, Long Island.

Donald loves his marine telephone. He has three of them. Donald once had a marine operator page me at lunch at Le Périgord East, in New York, to jeer at me for working while he was bounding along at fifteen knots, twenty miles off Kittery, Maine. I took it very well, I thought, and billed Donald's trade association four hundred bucks for "telephone conference with association liaison."

Donald told me, this August morning, in very guarded tones, that he wished to read aloud from a local newspaper, published in the town where he was docked. For once, when he finished, I was filled more with excitement than cupidity.

The gist of the article was that the county health people had conclusively identified as diphtheria the disease afflicting a member of the local board of selectmen and his wife; a family of three, summering from sweltering New York; a yachtsman from Boston, prominent in the electronics industry; a secretary from Boston, who was employed by the electronics company; all four musicians and three managerial types of the Classical Gash Rock Band, from Bedford, Illinois; and the pastor of the local Congregational Church. Each of them, it developed, was felled after dining at the Spindrift Restaurant, a thriving business seating an average of 263 people every night, located out on the end of the town wharf.

"I don't get it," I said. "If they're serving that many people every night, and that's the place the fifteen victims got it, how'd the other two hundred and forty-eight escape?"

"Shut up and listen. Over," Donald said.

"I'll listen," I said. "Over."

By calculating the incubation period of the disease, from the dates when the patients contracted it, and by interviewing members of their families and friends, the board of health had determined that each of the victims was among the last of the restaurant's patrons on the night when he was infected. "We had abnormally high, and abnormally low, tides that week," Donald said. "Moon tides. Apparently what the restaurant does is, they're plugged into town sewage for the rest rooms, and they've got town water. But they drain their sinks into the harbor, which seems harmless enough, and probably is, until you get a tide that drops just low enough to give you a backflow up into the sinks and probably into the whole water system and brings a little untreated marine waste up with it. Whaddaya thinka *that?* Over."

"Very interesting," I said. "Over."

"There's more," Donald said. And he went on to read the quotes which the newspaper had dug out of its files from the previous year, when the harbormaster, challenged for his failure to enforce the ban on solid waste discharge in the harbor, had declared the regulations to be unenforceable, silly, and a waste of time.

An hour later the courier in the chartered plane had twenty copies of that edition en route to my office in Washington. In the meantime, I worked from verbatim notes transcribed by my secretary. By midmorning, local television crews were filming reports by correspondents standing in the sunlight in front of the restaurant, each of them astonishingly well versed

163

in the ramifications of the proposed regulatory changes. The owner of the restaurant behaved pretty well until one of the Boston stations arrived by helicopter, and the donkey who was to do the standup asked for permission to stand by the pestilential sinks, divulging that NBC was planning to take the feed for the Evening News. Then the proprietor, out on the wharf, seized a cup of beer from one of the townspeople and threw it on the commentator, and that was what John Chancellor showed to the nation that night. Having advance knowledge, I was able to insure that the agency people would not miss it. Their unanimous reaction was: "Oh, Jesus."

With that out of the way by one-thirty—my call to Sumner, inquiring whether the bereaved wished flowers to be omitted and memorial donations made to a favorite charity, did not elicit his usual wit—I was settling back happily to mop up routine correspondence when Zena Martinez called from the Hill.

I have to begin by saying that I like Zena. Half high Hidalgo, half rat-poor Mexican-American, she went through what was then CCNY on full scholarship and extra nerve, respectfully declining the advice of her father, a cabbie, to acquire a background in hairdressing. She worked for RFK in '68, for as long as Sirhan Sirhan saw fit to permit, and then she picked herself up, dragged it down to Washington and hit the chief of the Northeast Congressional Caucus—which is a large name for a small office that tries to prevent Senators and Congressmen from New England, New York, New Jersey, and Pennsylvania from voting to cross-purposes on bills affecting all of their constituencies, and occasionally succeeds—for a job. She got it chiefly because she was willing to do menial tasks for little money and work like the devil. Very shortly, her energy and brains were remarked, and she took over office management for a Congressman from the Middle South, lasting a year in that job before joining Senator Fawcett's staff as majordomo of the office, though she was carried on the payroll of the Subcommittee on Nuclear Energy.

When Dan Fawcett passed away this year, it was none too soon. His friends were still able to speak of his statesmanship, and his selflessness, and his devotion to his family. His appearance had deteriorated somewhat, but not enough for the casual television viewer to notice, during the increasingly infrequent, increasingly brief such displays his staff permitted him to make of himself. But the plain fact of the matter was that his narrow loss of the 1972 Democratic presidential primary in Illinois, accounted in the national press and in his own mind as the death knell of his ambitions, somehow activated a side of Fawcett's nature theretofore successfully suppressed: while he had earned the mantle of the elder statesman and Senate sage, he began, incongruously at fifty-eight, to strive for the reputation of the Senate's playboy. Each of those distinctions requires quite a bit of work and can be won only by years of diligent practice of its tasks. Fawcett, having earned the first, disdained it and went after the second, against strong competition, twenty years his junior.

His health could not stand it. Previously a man who had considered Campari and soda to be hard liquor, Fawcett took to using Old Overholt as a morning mouthwash. For years considered monumentally dull in matters extracurricular, he made a plain fool of himself with women barely old enough to vote. The Senate huddled protectively around him, hoping against hope that one of his popsies would not take it into her head to write a book, or leap from the top of the Washington Monument after first preparing a touching note, and deferred to him even more than they had previously (and then it had been so pronounced that one President had called it "kowtowing"), wistful in their desire that he would snap out of it or die, whichever might be accomplished more swiftly.

Zena called me because I owed Fawcett, dying as he was, for old favors. I therefore owed her. I left the White House when the Republicans came in, and there was blessed little that the former President could do for me. But Senator Fawcett, then eagerly grooming himself for that chair, was sufficiently interested both in forming his own shadow government and in rewarding what he told me was my skill that he more or less adopted me as his protégé. I was introduced to people as a former Special Counsel, but I was retained by people who had somehow learned that a very powerful Senator, perhaps destined to be President of the United States, had great respect for my abilities.

Therefore, when Zena on the long death watch called for reinforcements, I had to respond. The switchboard operator would tell me that Zena was on the line, and groaning, I would push the button, say: "Hello," and in response get: "Mayday." I usually said: "Jesus," and she usually said: "He wants to see you." Then I would cancel everything, take a cab up to the Hill, scutter through the New Senate Office Building to his hideaway office, take off my coat, loosen my tie, and listen once more to what he had told Harry Truman about nationalizing, MacArthur, and sending nasty notes on White House stationery to critics who disliked Margaret's music. Generally, by five, he had had six whiskeys to my two and would pull himself erect to go and meet his bimbo of the evening, graciously declining to comment to reporters wandering in the corridor on the state of various pieces of legislation, speaking clearly and distinctly, betraying no sign whatsoever, except the breath of an alligator, that he had been drinking. And I would struggle back to the office, there to find pink message slips from twenty people who were mad at me for not being in when they called.

I say "struggle," because while Senator Fawcett had his limo waiting to take him to his assignation, I had no such conveniences and in those days had to depend upon cabs or the largess of friends happening by. I have the BMW, of course, but it's impossible to park on the Hill after 6:45 A.M. The friends were surprisingly plentiful, given the exodus from government buildings which could get a man trampled just after five, but they were not reliable. And the cabs were scarce.

On that mid-August day, when the Senator called me out of my tolerably conditioned office into the mugginess, the haze, and the heat, I was grouchy but resigned. After all, I had had a good morning, and the reason that I had good mornings was partly due to the Senator's strenuous promotion of me. But in the early evening of that muggy, sodden day, as I stood helplessly watching the rain sheet down on Constitution Avenue without seeing one cab, I did not feel anywhere near as charitable toward the old son of a bitch. I had to get back to the office, if for no other reason than to retrieve my car in order to go home. But the thunderstorm that had come up—while Fawcett discoursed on the Kellogg-Briand Treaty or some goddamned thing—had washed away even the hardiest of cabdrivers. Around me, people bought copies of the Washington *Star* and used them for hats and capes; I like the *Star* pretty well, but it makes a lousy raincoat, and I have cats in my family tree somewhere—I hate getting wet.

That was when Edgar tapped me on the shoulder. "Hey, buddy," he said, "you gotta dime for a cuppa coffee?"

"Son of a bitch," I said. "What're you doing here? You look great."

It was true, and not only because of the rain outside. Edgar wore a lightweight blazer, gray slacks, a neat button-down blue shirt, and blue knit tie. His shoes were polished, and his hair had been attended to by someone who knew what he was doing. His face had lost its puffiness, and the bags had vanished from his eyes. He had a deep suntan. "I certainly do," he said. "I feel like hell, but I look just great, if I do say so."

"What's the matter?" I said, thinking, if the truth be known, of Fawcett.

"Peter," Edgar said, "if the stringent demands of private practice do not preclude a drink with an old friend, I will tell you. In the comparative privacy of the Monocle."

"I've got to get back to the office," I said.

"Well, Noah," Edgar said, nodding toward the rain outside, "you're gonna get powerful wet before you get back to that office."

"I was waiting for a cab," I said.

"I'm waiting for the Parousia myself," Edgar said. "Or else it's Godot. I forget which. But then, of course, I have something which you lack." He held up a Totes umbrella.

"Yeah," I said. "I do. But then, I don't know how much good it'd do me anyway, considering how long a walk it is back to M Street."

"Plus another thing which you lack," Edgar said. He held up a plastic key fob, with four keys on it. "A nifty little Dodge Aspen, thoughtfully loaned to me by Mister Avis and parked, actually quite legally, down across from the Monocle. And there are only two things that you have to do in order to find yourself seated comfortably within that soothingly air-conditioned little buggy: you have to share my umbrella on the slow walk down the street, and you have to have a minimum of two drinks with me at the Monocle. Neither of those activities will get you very wet on the outside, at least, and the way you drink, probably the second won't even get you very wet on the inside."

"Deal," I said, erring, in my eagerness for transportation, by failing to inquire closely about what Edgar meant when he spoke about a slow walk.

"Edgar," I said, "have you got a load in your pants or something? You're waddling along here like a ruptured duck, and while far be it from me to utter a word of disapproval of your wonderful umbrella, it's not the biggest one I've ever seen. Can we maybe move it along just a little?"

"No as to both, as you lawyers say," Edgar said. "No, I have not got a load in my pants, and No, we can't move along any faster. I am running at top speed this very instant and suffering greatly for it, too, I might add."

"You hurt yourself or something?" I said, becoming alarmed. People our age have a tendency to come down with mysterious ailments, and to do it suddenly. After a couple reports of Hodgkin's disease, Huntington's chorea, Paget's syndrome, premature cardiac arrest, petit mal, Lou Gehrig's disease, and lung cancer; after a few years of reading obituaries of those roughly the same age as you, give or take ten years, who had had the decency to drop out of view for long months of illness during which they lingered, invisibly, in excruciating pain; after forming the habit of reading the death notices with the sort of morbid fascination which attends the picking of a scab not quite ripe for the plucking: after that, you come to dread the perception of infirmity in someone close to you and to prefer news of almost any injury—a sprain, a strain, a nifty set of ligaments torn in a no-holds-barred game of handball—to the gloomy reply that "I've been having some tests. Doctors say they aren't really sure yet what it is. Probably just one of those half-assed prostate things." I like a doctor who is sure. When the doctor is not sure, I am, and I do not for one instant like what I am sure about either.

"Depends on how you look at it," Edgar said. "I didn't hurt myself, but I, of my own free will, went and allowed a confounded butcher, disguised as a doctor, to hurt me, and he made the best of his opportunities, too, I can tell you."

"What the hell was it?" I said, figuring the news would be that of a small lump on the left testicle, and that for best chances of permanent recovery, it would be preferable to chop the whole scrotum off. I had a thin tingle of apprehension across the surface of my brain, similar in feeling to what I imagine a dog feels in his ear when one of those ultra-high-frequency whistles is blown.

"Oh, nothing serious," Edgar said, pitching along from side to side. They always say that. Eleven months later you are making a modest contribution to the American Cancer Society in lieu of flowers. I had completely lost my concern about getting my trousers wet. "What it was was my new girlfriend."

"Jesus Christ," I said, "what the hell'd she give you? A fistula? Tell her to keep her hands in her pockets when you're grinding away. She'll feel just as good, and you'll be able to walk afterwards."

"That's pretty good," Edgar said, laughing. "The last time somebody made an assumption on that point, he wanted to know if there was some kind of VD that they cured by progressive amputation, like docking a Doberman's ears and tail. Nah, she didn't give me anything, except maybe an ultimatum."

By then, in the rain, we had reached the corner before the old Carroll Arms Hotel, now converted to office space leased by the government, the memories of decades of seedy assignations in those cramped rooms obliterated by weeks of tedious wrangling over unimportant issues, conducted on chairs of green vinyl that stuck to your pants when you got up to leave.

"What it was," Edgar said, "she didn't want me to give *her* anything, such as a baby. So, after kicking and screaming for a few stormy nights, I gave in and had a vasectomy. Sounded a lot more harmless'n it turned out to be. It's not harmless. It hurts."

"Good Lord," I said, as the light changed and we advanced slowly across the street and down the hill. "I don't know. Letting somebody near my balls with a knife? That's contradictory of the basic principles I've lived by."

"Yeah, Peter," Edgar said, negotiating the curb with difficulty, "but there's a certain luxury to the indulgence of your principles. See, you're still married to the same woman. Rules were set a long time ago, 'fore the ladies got liberated, and you're still playing by them. But once you get waived out of that league, like I did, you find yourself in a new one, with different rules entirely. Option years, no-trade clauses, right-to-approve trade clauses, collective bargaining: all them complicated things. You're still playing against Ty Cobb; I got Reggie Jackson's free-agent status to contend with.

"See, Peter," he said, wincing each time he took a step, "there used to be three choices. You had children was the first one. That choice you still got, except I am way too old to choose that now, and I imagine my lady would probably hit me with a blunt instrument if I seriously proposed it.

"The second one was that she either did something, so you didn't have children, or else she didn't, in which case you either had children or neither one of you did anything, for days at a time, and hoped to the dear sweet Jesus that the Pope's physicians had the temperature charts and the numbers right when they said it was finally all right again for you to do something without taking any precautions."

"What about the Pill?" I said.

"There's very few ladies've got a great deal of enthusiasm for the Pill," Edgar said. "These days, at least. It sold better'n Hadacol there, for several years, but then the ladies started coming up with all these clots and things, and that sort of reduced the appetites of the other ladies for the little candies. Same thing with those IUD things, with which, apparently they enjoy about as much as you or I would with a red-hot arrow up your ass.

"This leaves," Edgar said, "the third thing, the Right Honorable Rubber. For Prevention of Disease Only, of course."

"I always hated those things," I said. "I only tried them once or twice, but I hated them." We were passing Annie's trailer, morning papers, soda pop, junk food, and dirty magazines wrapped in cellophane, where the early-afternoon editions are scooped up every morning by Senate press assistants. Who repair to the Monocle at eleven-fifteen to start in on the serious business of the day, which is lunch and gossip.

"You hated rubbers," Edgar said, "because they prevented two diseases in addition to the clap and syph: they prevented pregnancy, which is why most people use them, but they also prevented pleasure, at least for the boys. Pleasure being a disease, too, I guess. But the boys used them anyway. Besides, it was status symbol, have a rubber rolled up in your wallet. Ready for anything. Like Custer was at Little Bighorn.

"Now," Edgar said, "I used condoms a few times when I was a kid. Damned near ruined the back-seat upholstery of a borrowed Chevrolet convertible one summer on the Cape, when we were in college and I used a rubber for the first time.

"I got it on all right, while she discreetly looked the other way, resolutely looked the other way, in fact. People've worked themselves unassisted into straitjackets with less trouble'n I had with that thing. By the time I got it on, it was more a tourniquet'n a birth control device. Then I shot my load in it, presumably while I was installed in her, though damned if I could tell, and she made it clear that I should withdraw that wader from her private parts. I did so.

"Lacking the brains to get it on without giving myself an embolism," he said, "I naturally lacked the brains to get it off without spilling the beans, as it were, all over the basket-weave upholstery. What followed was much scrubbing and rubbing on my part and much scorn on the part of the lady. After that fiasco, it's no wonder I didn't make out—it was too goddamned much trouble." Edgar gimped along past the parking lot, reserved for cars with government stickers only, and totally vacant in the rain, after five in the afternoon.

"So," Edgar said, "at my advanced age, I find myself once again attacking a woman in much the same clumsy fashion as I did thirty years ago and more, but this time with considerably greater chances of success. The both of us having been married before, and fooled around some since, if the truth be known, we are about as starry-eyed as a couple of loan sharks, when it comes down to discussing the basics. While it is true that Charlie Chaplin, siring offspring in his fucking eighties, the old goat, was probably something of a geek. . . ."

"What's a geek?" I said.

"A geek is what the carnies called the Alligator Boy who bites the heads of chickens off and the Three-Headed Lady and the Wondrous Walter Wimple, Half Man, Half Fish. Which is a woman with severe skeletal deformities of the shoulders, a young man with a severe case of psoriasis, and an old man with a less severe case of psoriasis. Freaks," Edgar

172

said, ". . . still the chances are that I remain a mathematically potential stud. You wouldn't breed your favorite mare to me if you really wanted to be sure of foaling her in time for the Nineteen-eighty-one Preakness, but like they say in the National Football League, when Tampa Bay plays the Dallas Cowboys and Cosell has to think of something: 'On any given night. . . .' I think it's pretty unlikely that I could impregnate many maidens in my weakened condition, but that's probably what Charlie Chaplin thought when he did it, and he had a helluva lot more money'n I do, to hire nannies and stuff to soften the blow.

"Now," Edgar said, "having an enlightened and reasonable discussion with the lady, who had as yet experienced no hot flashes whatsoever and has every reason to believe that she's still fertile, I found myself beset from every side by the logic of her arguments. She took the position that she was not taking any more positions with me, whether diagrammed in the *Kama Sutra* or just passed on by word of mouth, as it were, until adequate and reliable measures should be taken to restrain the frisky little devils that I would otherwise contribute to her pelvic area, as soon as I got half a chance and word that even sounded like encouragement. Or else no further contributions of my bodily fluids were going to be accepted.

"I brought up," Edgar said, "well-known twentieth-century advancements in contraceptive research, mentioning Doctor John Rock, and Enovid, and Mini-Pills, and Copper Sevens. And she made harsh observations about strokes, perforated uteri, and hemorrhaging, and pregnancies that occurred despite the presence of base metals in the neighborhood familiarly known as the cunt. I got the strong notion that I was not making a great deal of progress. Which was when I made my big mistake, the one that made Napoleon's decision to visit Russia in the fall look comparatively minor. I suggested that she have her tubes tied."

"She didn't like that," I said.

"Put it this way," Edgar said, making slow progress to the

bottom of the hill, "she said No with that quiet firmness faintly reminiscent of the late J. Edgar Hoover's manner with an obstreperous young agent. This, Peter, is a very tough lady. She is the kind of lady that it is fortunate for the nightingales that she likes them and does not like cats, because if it was the other way around, she would teach birdcalls to her cats. If she had cats, which, I am glad to say, she does not."

"I would get a new lady," I said.

"Peter," Edgar said, "I grow old. I have gotten a great many new ladies. Not exactly a great *many* new ladies, but most of the ladies I have gotten, however pitiably few in number, have been extremely new. Competent in the sack, perhaps, but lacking severely in stimulative abilities at table and in other refined situations. I am not desperate, but I am weary, and I am willing to haggle. I am sick of being told that I am *interesting*. I want to be told that I am one goddamned stallion, far superior to those callow studs who simply paw and grope, and being extremely demanding, I want it said with sincerity. That this lady does. I am prepared to be reasonable. By reasonable, I mean this: tell me what you want, and if it does not endanger my life and limb, I will do it. I know what I want."

"A knife at the balls," I said.

"It was a bit of a grimace that followed the suggestion," Edgar said. "Her suggestion, I mean. My grimace. Of course, I was in an awkward situation, having suggested minor surgery to her, as I had. If I was that hot for minor surgery, how come her, and not me? Therefore, I did not expostulate, but allowed as how that might be one possibility. Because I really did enjoy getting into her pants. 'Damned right it's a possibility,' she said, and before I knew it, I was making an appointment with the guy that filets you."

"Is that operation entirely safe?" I said. We turned right at the corner and headed up the street toward the Monocle.

"Peter," Edgar said, "crossing streets, the way we have been doing, is not entirely safe. There may be a semitrailer coming, with a full head of speed, and the next thing you know, Saint Peter will be calling up the clearance of your Mastercharge to see if you can afford to pay for your room in American dollars. Or Peter's Pence, as the case may be. No, it's not entirely safe. For one thing, all it does is block the lines. The calls still come in, but the phone don't ring. Those balls of mine will continue to produce the frisky little devils, but the frisky little devils will swim upstream in the vas deferens, or whatever the hell it is they call that plumbing, and will promptly find themselves hoist on my own petard. They can't get out.

"Now," Edgar said, "the interesting thing is where they go, after they get frustrated, finding that they can't get out and go happily in search of my lady's egg, there to dance the hootchy-kootchy and cause everybody one big mess of trouble. They don't go out for a couple of beers. They don't have tickets to the ball game. Where the hell do they go? Those old spermatozoa."

"Where do they go?" I said.

"The doctor tells me," Edgar said, "they go and get themselves *ree*-sorbed. I meant to tell you, the guy in the smock with the knife is a boogie. I let a boogie with an evil grin and a knife in his hand grab my *nuts* and start cutting. Have I lost my mind or something? Probably. But I did it, nevertheless. Wearing rubbers is like eating frozen food while it's still frozen—I guess it would probably do you about as much good as it does after you thaw it out and cook it, but it's not something that appeals to me somehow.

"Nope," Edgar said, "it was either they could fit me with an on-off switch, single-pole, single-throw, or they could disconnect the power. Well, they haven't developed the switches yet, it turns out, so I had the Disconnect."

"Must hurt," I said, somehow managing to squeeze my legs together while continuing to walk.

"What hurts most," Edgar said, "is the idea. Before they do it. When they do it, the only thing they add to the idea is the jab they give you, the novocaine. Then they just hustle right in there, and snip, snip, and a few weeks you'll be Safe to Be Near. There may be some soreness for a few days. What I hope they were not leaving out is that the soreness only lasts a few days because, after the few days, your cock falls off."

"What happened?" I said. "It turn green or something?"

"You know, Peter," Edgar said, lumbering along, "I'm not entirely sure I'm glad I confided in you. You mask it pretty well, but there's a decided undercurrent of amusement in your voice at the projected departure of my manhood, and I'm not sure I like it. No, my equipment turned black, and since I've grown rather attached to it, I have to confess I'm worried. As well as sore. I would like for the soreness and the worry to go away and for the other stuff to remain. Ain't gonna be much fun back in the saddle again if I'm riding sidesaddle." Edgar belched loudly.

"Does it give you gas, too?" I said.

"No," he said, "Chinese food gives you gas. Preparing for this sortie down here today, I was by airline schedules prevented last night from seeing my lady, since the plane takes off from Boston, and she does not, and I had to be here at an unseasonable hour this morning. So I got home to my humble pad, in wretched pain, and I was lonesome. So I called up these friends of ours and said to them: 'Whatcha doin', guys?' 'Goin' out for Chinese food,' they said. 'Wanna come?' 'I hate Chinese food,' says I, 'and you know it. Why can't we all go out for a nice little pizza with a lot of mushrooms on it and maybe a pitcher of beer or so?' 'Nope,' they say, 'it's Chinese food, or you can just sit around by yourself and watch *Laverne and Shirley.*'

"Well, that didn't make Chinese food sound bad, when I thought it over, so I went and met them, and we went to this restaurant that has a Chinese name, but does not serve Chinese food. It serves this great soup, which is supposed to have a tree in it or something, and it serves ribs, and it serves some kind of beef they got a special name for, and some shrimp they also got a special name for, and these peppers and these green things that I don't know what they are, but you put this napalm on them before you eat them. And then, while you are still gasping, they come lunging out at you with this huge platter that's got duck all over it, and bread that looks like what they serve in the Greek restaurants, and of course, the minute I tasted the soup, I was starving. So I ate it all. While I was eating it all—there were three of us and I would say we got enough food to make a reasonable meal for eight people—while I was eating it, I drank quite a lot of beer. Naturally."

"Edgar," I said, "I'm shocked."

"And," Edgar said, "as a result of those two activities, I got drunk, which I have been known to do before, and I also glutted myself, which I have never done before. Therefore, I woke up this morning feeling awful, with this big, overstuffed belly, but not big enough to conceal the problem below it from me, since the landlord thoughtfully installed a mirror on the wall right over the hopper, and I had to look at it in its deplorable condition while I peed and broke wind and wondered if the headache and the belching would ever go away. I've been thinking about it since about seven this morning, and I've decided that they're probably not. And just before I walked out this morning, the lady called me to chew me out because she called me around midnight last night and I wasn't there, so who was I out fucking?

"That, my friend," Edgar said, "is the wreck of a man that you see before you this evening. Hung-over, still bloated, about to complete the process of being gelded, unable to walk, and no longer that much interested in trying. You got any idea where I could go to get somebody to drive a stake through my heart and get my mind off my troubles?"

"Maybe you should think about getting embalmed," I said.

"I'll consider it," Edgar said, "if the idea's carefully presented and I get some reason to believe it would improve my disposition."

"Otherwise?" I said. We were at the ramp leading us up to the door of the Monocle.

"Otherwise," Edgar said, "I may settle for embalming myself from the inside out. The only thing that holds me back is that the treatment makes me pee, and that means I have to look at the poor shriveled object again. I dunno. I'm depressed. I need a drink. A little liquid depressant, get my mind off the other kind."

We struggled inside, paused at the steps to the right, selected the turn to the left, and took a table for four next to the cloakroom. Edgar sat, gratefully. He said: "Ahhh."

"Edgar," I said, "as one old friend to the other, could I ask you what makes you inflict travel on yourself when you're disabled like this?"

"Certainly," he said. "Two things: greed and obedience to the stricture that one avoid the occasions of sin.

"Greed, because if I don't do what the editor wants, he will shortly have me cashiered of my column, stripped of my rank, and demoted to General Assignment, where there lurk horrors the like of which make Nessie, the Loch Ness Monster, resemble a big friendly dog. Among these is lower pay. If my pay gets lower, I better begin finding a way to cadge more quarters'n the next guy at the Park Street Station, because I will be going under.

"Occasions of sin, because when I am around the lady, I want to sin, and I ain't capable of no sinning right now, which is frustrating."

"You look pretty prosperous," I said.

"Aw, shucks," Edgar said, "it's nothing. Just a few odds and ends I picked up, down the Army-Navy Store. Tailor didn't do a bad job, did he? Actually, Peter, I am *not* prosperous. Not by your exalted standards, at least. But for the first

178

time in about a hundred years, I have got a couple coins in my pocket, which don't go bad neither."

"Hit the number?" I said.

"Regrettably, no," Edgar said. "This could be because I do not play the number, having had an adequate supply of losing propositions in my life without adding another one, at any price. No, what I did was agree to write a book."

"Impressive," I said.

"Absurdly easy," Edgar said. "I wished I thought of it before. 'I would like to write a book, Mister So-and-So.' 'Good for you, Mister Lannin. What sort of book would you like to write?' 'I dunno. Something that would make me, say, well-to-do? Not rich, now, you understand. I ain't proud. I don't know a hell of a lot about all the President's men, and the ones I do know about are not terribly interesting.' 'Well, Mister Lannin, what do you know about?' 'As a matter of fact,' I said, 'I know quite a bit about saloons. I know a lot about saloons, as a matter of fact.' 'Saloons, eh?' 'I know, I know: if *McSorley's* didn't make that much of a hit, what chance've I got?' 'Don't be too hasty, Mister Lannin. What else do you know?' 'I know a lot of stories that I heard in saloons,' I said, 'and most of them're true.' 'Never sell,' they said. 'What about politics and that kind of horsing around?' I said, which is really the same thing they said would not sell, but I'm not gonna enlighten them. 'I know quite a bit about that, too,' I said. Which happens to be true. And could I give them a couple sample chapters and an outline, and I said: 'Sure.' And I did, and they gave me five thousand dollars, which my agent let me keep forty-five hundred of, and I got some new clothes and had my balls cut off, so when I die, I will be all pink and firm, like any other castratus, but nevertheless well dressed for the first time in my life, as well as for the first time in my death. Peter," he said, "I want to tell you: I have got a blue pinstripe suit, seventeen pieces, that will be just great when I am laid out in it, and in the meantime, I have a very flattering offer from the Vienna Boys' Choir. In case I don't get the book done."

"Edgar," I said, meaning it, "this is great news. I never knew you were thinking about writing a book."

"Peter," he said, "I wasn't. I told you she is a tough lady. It was her idea. That lady has good ideas. I hope to God I retain enough circulation of the blood, when I have recovered from my current disability, to deal with the more carnal of them."

Edgar got me back to my office after two drinks, the rain having stopped and the streets of Washington wet and glistening in the sunlight, almost deserted. In the car I said to him: "She sounds like a hell of a woman, Edgar. I'm glad for you. What does she do in Boston?"

He stared at me again. "Nothing much," he said. "Not a hell of a lot, as a matter of fact. But what little she does, she likes."

"Anybody I know?" I said.

Edgar stared straight down the road now, and a horrible suspicion began to metastasize in my brain. The question was forming in my larynx, but my brain shut it off. I dreaded the vacation with Jeanne and the kids, and then I had to get through it. I could not take two weeks of that, with some additional distracting doom to worry about.

Ten

At the shag end of the evening of the Thursday before Labor Day, I sat in Baxter's Landing in Hyannis with my family and saw Edgar in a blue nylon windbreaker get out of a blue Nova sedan, pull a seabag from the back seat, and, after thanking the driver—whom I could not identify—walk down the road toward the Hi-Line dock, where the last boat to Martha's Vineyard lay easily upon her lines. He was too far away for me to hail him, and I was in no mood to do it anyway. We sat there, Jeanne and the boys and I, in our Irish sweaters, for which we were by then grateful, having lugged them all over Nantucket in the heat of the day, and I watched Edgar disappear into the vessel. After a while, in the twilight, the lines were dropped, and the boat backed around and headed out through the narrow channel, leaving a broad wake in the calm water, attended by a few strident gulls. Jeanne sipped absently on a daiquiri, while the boys filled their mouths with fried clams, onion rings, and french fries, quarreling as they chewed. We were all exhausted, and it was probably just as well.

Having planned originally to fly up to the Cape when I finished work the Friday after I saw Edgar on the Hill, I had been abruptly forced to change my plans. One of Ed Bradley's major clients, a midwestern industrialist about fifty years old who might have been expected to know better, came to Washington that Thursday, ostensibly for a conference with other businessmen equally concerned about certain proposals then pending before the Interstate Commerce Commission. The trouble was that this pillar of society in a middle-sized Illinois city somehow wandered out of the Sheraton Carlton after the dinner meeting and, obviously in a confused state, probably the result of a minor stroke, went up to Fourteenth Street, where the skin flicks, dives, and hookers are, instead of retiring to his rented quarters at the Georgetown Inn.

Ed was out of town, vacationing at his summer place in Nova Scotia. Ben Bellow was in Atlanta, and Joe Knight was in the air, returning from a business trip to Manila. The industrialist had for several years seen to it that our firm had received somewhere in the neighborhood of $135,000 from his company, which circumstance decreed that if the industrialist could not gain access to the senior partner regularly handling his inquiries, he got one of the others.

Ordinarily that would not have occasioned much inconvenience. While we do not routinely master one another's files, we all do pretty much the same kind of work, and an hour with the folders is usually enough to afford the Designated Hitter sufficient acquaintance with the matter to substitute effectively for the absent lawyer. The trouble, in this instance, was that the industrialist did not require immediate, emergency attention to an ICC ruling that no one had any reason to expect; his problem was with the Casual Clothes Squad of the District police.

Hearing cries of outrage issuing from a window open on the fifth floor of an extremely seedy hotel in a very dilapidated area, the attention of the cops had been attracted to a young lady. She was black, naked to the waist, and leaning out the

182

window with her ample breasts flapping in the warm nighttime breeze. She said that someone in the room with her was trying to kill her.

In the best *Starsky and Hutch* fashion, the cops conducted further investigations, breaking down the door of the room in question, to the genuine relief of the young lady and the outrage of the naked white man who was standing behind her, flogging her back and buttocks with the buckle end of his imported belt of Spanish leather.

Officer Munoz, reporting for the Friday shift two hours early, a courtesy which I appreciated, rubbed the sleep from his eyes, put his booted feet on the desk, slurped bad coffee from a leaking paper cup, and told me there was quite a lot of gore.

"When we kicked the door open," he said, "your friend was as naked as a snake, the lady's back and ass were all gushing blood, and he was swinging that fuckin' belt like Frank Howard used to do with a thirty-eight-ounce bat. And he didn't even notice us. Must've been *drunk out of his mind.* There he is, bollicky bare ass, beating the shit out of this poor, honest, hardworking whore, two cops jumping him, and all he can do is scream, 'Mummy, Mummy, Mummy, you never liked me, Mummy.' While whipping the hide off of her.

"Counselor," Officer Munoz said, "you got one hell of a goddamned client there. We get 'em in here, somebody rolled them, lifted their eighteen-karat ID bracelets, tied their silk pants in a knot and swiped their Gucci wallets, always containing sixteen hundred American, give or take a half a buck. We get 'em in here, they were innocently watching two broads eat each other out onna bandstand, and somebody took the wallet while their attention was occupied elsewhere. We get 'em that ask cops to blow them, and we get 'em that ask to blow cops. We get hookers that their main men whacked with hammers, and we get main men that their hookers whacked with hammers. But we don't often get a nice fat honky here that beats up black hookers while crying for his mummy and

183

takes three cops trained in subduing riots to bring him in. You know something, Counselor? I dunno what else your client is, but I can tell you one thing: for a fat shit, he is *strong*. I wouldn't wanna tangle assholes with that fucker on an everyday basis."

"Look," I said, "I don't know what got into him. As a matter of fact, I don't know much about him at all. I was introduced to him once, I think, but I can't be sure. Something must've snapped."

"This," Officer Munoz said, "this we knew."

"Where is he?" I said.

"Where is he?" Munoz said. "He's inna fuckin' cage, is where he is."

"Is he all right?" I said.

"He don't have many marks on him, if that's what you mean," Munoz said. "No more'n were absolutely necessary to get him quieted down. He got slapped around some, but then, when somebody gets you across the face with a belt buckle, you're liable to react hastily and without thinking. Even if you are a cop. That fuckin' *hurts*."

"Oh," I said.

"Gun butt," Munoz said. "Look, all right? Francesco's been a cop for nine years now, and he's pretty well housebroken. But he's been a guinea all his life, and you know how them Latins are. You roundhouse an Italian across the face with your belt, he's liable to get mad. Your guy's lucky Frangie didn't waste him."

"Yeah," I said. "Sounds nifty. Look, what about the girl?"

"Right now," Munoz said, "she is lying on her stomach in the hospital, and she ain't used to the position or the accommodations. She's also not making any money from either one of them, and her pimp's worried about where his next Caddy's gonna come from, she doesn't get back pretty soon into more familiar surroundings and positions. So, for the anger of it and probably for the sheer novelty of it, she is bringing charges.

She signed the goddamned complaint before we even read it to her."

"What it is?" I said.

"Little assault," Munoz said. "Little battery. Little dangerous weapon. Little attempted murder. Oh, yeah, and some minor stuff. The usual: drunk, disorderly, disturbing the peace, resisting arrest, A and B on a police officer, three times, on account of how there was the three of us there, and he didn't play no favorites. We didn't charge him with profaning Mother's Day, although we probably could've."

"What's the bail?" I said.

"Ain't no bail set yet," Munoz said. "Reason is, defendant ain't fit to be arraigned yet. Dressed in a blanket like he is."

"For Christ sake, Officer," I said, "you mean you didn't let him get dressed?"

"Counselor," Munoz said with fatigue, "of course, we let him get dressed. He ain't no fuckin' Adonis, you know, you get that spiffy suit off him. We couldn't take him out onto Fourteenth Street, bare ass, and we wouldn't do it. People would've thrown up in the gutter. No, we let him get dressed. The trouble is, once he got in the pen, he got himself undressed. Again."

"Oh," I said.

"Now," Munoz said, "we got more'n one tenant in the bullpen this morning. Them as weren't sleeping should've been, and they were disturbed by your client."

"More?" I said.

"This," Officer Munoz said, "is what led to the additional charges that will be filed today, mostly having to do with destruction of government property."

"What?" I said.

"Oh," Munoz said, "the blanky. The mattress. The pillow. You ever smell cheap feathers burn in a room where the usual smell's one-third urine, one-third body odor, one-third shit, and just a hint of disinfectant, to make it interesting? He took off all of his clothes, apparently found some matches in one of the pockets, and set the whole shebang on fire. The guards told him to put it out, and he did. He pissed on it. We didn't charge him with no offense for burning his own clothes. I don't think he can wear them, though."

"I see," I said.

"Well," Munoz said, "he can wear them if he wants to, but the pants're pretty well burned out in the ass, and the coat and vest're singed in places, and the shirt and tie don't look so good, neither, on account of what ain't scorched is stained. With piss."

"How about the shoes and socks?" I said.

"Shoes and socks're all right," Munoz said. "He had them on, for the second game of this here doubleheader. Garters, too. There he was, standing there, all these fuckin' off-the-wall drunks yammering about snakes and lizards and goddamned dinosaurs, peeing on his clothes and bedding, raisin' one hell of a fearful stink, wearing black wing-tip shoes, black socks, and goddamned garters. I'll tell you something, Counselor: it was a sight to see."

"I can imagine," I said.

"So that's the situation you're in," Munoz said. "I leave it up to you, Counselor, and you can make your own decision. You want me to call up the clerk and have him sked a bail hearing in twenty minutes? I can do it. Your client's got a right to it. He can waltz his bouncy white ass right into the court, with his shoes and socks and garter belt and the new blanky that we issued to him, and if it suits him, he can expose his genitalia to the judge, and the two of you can see where that gets you. Up to you."

"Somehow," I said, "I don't think that's exactly what we had in mind."

"Somehow," Munoz said, "I didn't expect it was."

Knowing precious little about the criminal law, I was not about to escort the client into the criminal court. But, knowing precious little about the criminal law, I knew damned few criminal lawyers, let alone competent criminal lawyers. By six-fifty-five in the evening, I had arranged for the client's luggage to be picked up at the hotel and brought to the lockup. Reasonably certain that he was getting dressed again, I turned to the matter of getting counsel for him. That took me until after seven-fifteen, the criminal lawyers in the District having habits similar to those of the civil lawyers on August Fridays and tending not to return after lunch.

My reservation on Delta Airlines, for Hyannis, had been for four-twenty-five. I think I shocked my secretary when she reported that the best she could do was a standby on the last Eastern flight to Boston. "Fuck it," I said, "I'll fucking drive." Then I called Ed in Nova Scotia and affronted him as well.

With that promising beginning, I called Jeanne on the Cape and got no answer. It dawned on me that she had driven to Hyannis to pick me up. I asked my secretary to tell the answering service to page Jeanne at the airport and call her at the cottage until they reached her and delivered the message. My secretary, ordinarily the most cooperative of women, had plans to visit the Maryland Shore that weekend and was uncharacteristically snappish. But she made the calls. I was later to learn that the answering service did not and that Jeanne waited at the airport until after 10 P.M. for me to arrive by plane.

A lot of other people had the Maryland Shore and other leisure spots in mind that Friday night. I did not escape traffic until I was well into the stinking flatlands of New Jersey. In the New England dawn, east of Fairhaven on Route 28, I got pinched for speeding. The cop paternally advised me to slow down, or I would have eternity for a vacation. I did not bite clean through my lower lip and did not say anything, either, which justified the pain.

It was almost nine o'clock on Saturday morning when I pulled into the driveway of the cottage in Dennisport, shut off the engine, staggered into the kitchen, and confronted a haggard wife and two surly boys. They said: "Hi," which is

187

about as much as I have grown accustomed to expect. Never having received my message, she said: "Where the hell've you been? Don't you ever think of anybody else besides yourself?" Not knowing that she had never received my message, I said: "Fuck you," and went into the bedroom, where I collapsed. It was almost 5 P.M. when I woke up, nearly 6 when I emerged from the shower, and close to 7 when I had consumed enough coffee to feel prepared to undertake human conversation.

The boys, of course, did not. Terry just having turned eleven, and Frank nearly fourteen, they had long since entered the transition period between sunny childhood and loutish adolescence, Frank presumably because of developing hormonal changes, Terry in mimicry of Frank, as well as in competition with him. Terry's adolescence is likely to be the longest ever recorded, beginning at age nine, as it did, when his brother was twelve.

Gradually, over the course of a year or so, Frank had changed from an outgoing, cheerful, cooperative kid, whose marks at school were unexceptionable even by his mother's exacting standards, into a cranky, slothful, clumsy, acned, insulting, and generally repellent goddamned kid. Terry, laboring furiously, within another year had managed to equal Frank in every category but acne, but I had every confidence that he would overtake his older brother on that score as well, as soon as Mother Nature deemed it fit to approve his production of testosterone. Two more disagreeable human beings, so far as I knew, could not be found outside the investigative offices of the Internal Revenue Service, but those had the mitigating claim that they were adults, doing it for a living, while Frank and Terry were obnoxious on a purely volunteer basis.

They lay all over the living room of the cottage, that August evening, feet on ivory couches that I did not own and would in October find myself having cleaned, at considerable expense to my security deposit. Terry had four Coke cans on the floor next to him; one lay on its side, dripping soda—Edgar would have called it tonic—on the rug; he was engrossed in *The*

188

Flintstones, which was being rerun on television. Frank had two Fresca cans and one Miller's can next to him. He was looking at the pictures in *Penthouse.*

I will say this for Frank: he does not pretend he buys those magazines for their verbal content. He buys them to look at the pictures, and the only reason that I never accused him of jacking off over them is because I knew very well that he does, and I know he knows I know, and so on, far into the night.

Jeanne took me to task one evening at home, when both boys, mercifully, were out playing baseball or else getting into scrapes with the juvenile authorities, which we would hear about soon enough anyway, if they were. In her view, I had not done enough to instruct Frank on the mysteries of the sexual act. I confessed my sin of omission, at once. "No," I said, "I haven't talked to him at all. I have also failed and refused to enlighten the Pope on the correct interpretation of the Holy Scriptures. I have been equally remiss in my duty to guide George Allen and the Redskins to victory in the Super Bowl. As far as I know, Sinatra never had the benefit of my musical tutelage, Nixon got from me no coaching in prevarication, and I was no help whatsoever to Admiral Halsey in the naval battles of the Pacific. What Frank doesn't know about sex, Einstein didn't know about relativity, and in each case, the information lacking is quite minor. In Frank's case, it probably has to do with practices injurious to life and limb."

"You should've talked to him sooner then," Jeanne said in her practical fashion.

"Sooner?" I said. "When, sooner? One day he was reading *Ranger Rick* and tangling himself up trying to tie bowlines with his kite string. The next thing I came home from work, and he had fifteen copies of *Swank* and *Gallery* on the floor of his bedroom, and he was in the bathroom with a copy of *Playboy* in front of him and the door locked behind him. God knows what kind of knots he was tying in there or what he was tying them with."

"It's not good for him," she said.

"It's better'n having him displaying it to the fourth graders," I said.

"Are you sure he isn't doing that?" she said.

"What I am sure of," I said, "is this: either he is not doing it, or he has selected the more sophisticated of the fourth grade for his audience, and they are interested enough in the education not to be offended by it. If he is doing the first, he is showing good judgment, and I will not reprimand him for that. If he is doing the second, he is also exercising good judgment, along with available parts of his anatomy, and I'm not gonna rebuke him for that either. I've got trouble in adequate supply. I don't go looking for it."

"He's a bad influence on Terry," she said.

"Well," I said, "if you'd've had a girl, as I suggested, it probably would've been even worse. All teenaged boys beat their meat. For a while. The time to start worrying is when they either stop beating their meat and walk around with a smirk on their faces, which is probably going to mean that Mary Lou's daddy will be calling in a month or so, with stress evident in his voice, or stop beating their meat and start walking around looking guilty, which means that something unnatural is going on in the locker room. Let him get hair on his palms. It's better'n making bail for him on a rape charge or fronting him the cash to pay for the abortion out of what he earns mowing lawns."

"It's not a healthy situation, Peter," she said.

"Jeannie," I said, "if that's the case, the bees that pollinate the roses should be seen by competent physicians."

"I don't think you care about our children anymore," she said, pouting. Jeanne pouts very well. Her mother taught her that. Her mother does not pout—she sulks. But Jeanne has more class and accomplishes the same purpose with less effort.

"If you mean that I don't especially like them in their current revolting phase," I said, "you're right. I find them boorish, uncivil, lazy, and intractable. The way that they've been acting, the most charitable thing that I can think of to describe them is to call them little stinkers. If they were adults, and I had to deal with them every day to make the comfortable living which they don't appreciate at all and waste at every opportunity, I would quit the job and go on welfare in the Northeast Kingdom of Vermont. But since they are not adults, and since the SPCA doesn't run a shelter for deservedly unwanted, disagreeable, preadolescent children, and since I bear some responsibility for their toilet training and whether they are likely to eat soup with their fingers when there is company at the table, what I like doesn't matter.

"Their manners are revolting when not completely nonexistent. Somehow they manage to resemble orphans who spend the morning in a culvert stealing coal from the railroad, while wearing a hundred bucks' worth of Saks clothes, and look like they've got yaws and beri-beri after two straight weeks of sunlight, roast prime rib of beef, and milk enough to slake the thirst of the Eighty-first Airborne. They are perfectly disgusting creatures, dirty and unkempt and smelly."

"It's a wonder you even bother to come home as seldom as you do," she said. "I suppose I should be grateful. I was afraid it might be me."

"One fight at a time, please," I said. "In the first place, while I stand by my judgment that they are perfectly loathsome, I have talked to some friends of mine about this, and I'm satisfied that Frank and Terry are not *abnormally* loathsome. They are about as loathsome as most of their contemporaries are. Those less loathsome worry their parents, because they already seem to be quite delicate, are very interested in reading about people making public confessions of bisexuality, and have asked a couple piercing questions about sex-change operations. Those more loathsome are in trouble with the authorities, most of them for selling substances such as Angel Dust and cocaine to cops working undercover. If you want to put Frank's masturbation in its proper perspective, you should have a chat with Tommy Lee, whose seventeen-year-

191

old daughter discovered sex about three years ago and seems to have spent most weekend nights, ever since, lying supine and exhorting all young males within earshot to make the same discovery, with her enthusiastic assistance. Tommy is thinking about having her welded into a chastity belt. 'She'd pick a lock,' he told me. 'Or get some young stud to pick it for her, more likely.' "

"Well," Jeanne said, "all right. I guess I know where I stand. Somebody has got to do something about Frank."

"Look," I said, "short of an orchidectomy, which I think he would resist, there is nothing you *can* do about Frank. Right now, Frank is doing it all for himself, and he knows right where he stands, too. Right in front of the flush. If he gives himself bunions on it, leave the Vaseline Intensive Care Lotion out where he can see it. If he grows warts on his hands, we'll get him some mercuric oxide, and if he starts to get simple—which, considering his marks lately, may be what is happening—we'll put him in a special school where he can learn to make raffia mats and do weaving and fashion sterling silver jewelry to sell from a table on a corner of Wisconsin Avenue. The one next to the Riggs Bank, where the one-man band plays on Saturdays—that's a good location. Forget it, Jeanne—at least he's not sticking it into the night-light socket and frizzing his hair."

"What about Terry?" she said.

"I don't think the sap's flowing yet in Terry," I said. "It won't be much longer before it does, though, and when it does, he'll be the same way. We'll probably have to put in another bathroom."

"I wish that I could take things as casually as you do," she said.

That was an unkind cut. I do not take things casually. As a matter of fact, I tend to become enraged when frustrated. But for that very reason, I try to estimate accurately the probabilities of whether something is likely to frustrate me and to stay away from situations where I am likely to be thwarted.

I had troublesome gastric problems, when I worked as an associate with a three-hundred-member firm in New York, before I came to Washington, and I want no more of them. I do not tackle any problem unless I think that I can bring it down; I still get frustrated, because I infrequently misjudge the magnitude of a problem, but I never, never assault any obstacle which is clearly beyond human capacities.

So far as I know, no one has ever found a way to prevent an adolescent from becoming fascinated by sex. The truth to tell, I am not sure that I would have welcomed the invention of such a process before I received certain information. I do not envy adolescents the experience, and I would not willingly endure it again, but I survived it myself, and not without certain enjoyments either. Not as many as I fervently wished, but enough bare tit, and wrists nearly sprained in panty girdles, as to furnish as least a few fond memories. Nothing I accomplished in my feverish state approached Nelson's victory at Trafalgar, let alone fulfillment of my own far more extravagant ambitions, but disappointment is regular in the adult world, and it does no harm to learn about it early.

The thing of it was, Jeanne takes everything either far too seriously or else too casually, I have never been able to decide which. She was invariably lighthearted about the concerns that troubled me, so that I finally learned not to bother discussing my practice with her. But she was tenacious about every trivial aspect of raising the kids, until at last she had persuaded me to do something about whatever it was that had gotten her attention. I told her once that most of the men I knew left the office after completing their last appointments for the day, while I had to go home to finish mine, and she replied that I had responsibilities there, as well as at the office.

For that reason—more accurately, because of the experiences accumulated in the seventeen years that we had been married— I did not sincerely dislike her absence, and that of the boys, for the first half of August. I said I did, but I did not. And my principal motive for joining them on the Cape for the last half of the month was to get away from the office, the telephone, and the catastrophes committed by clients of my similarly absent partners. I would have preferred to go off by myself, but I had managed that in the winter, when I went to Majorca and Jeanne declined to go along, reciting the necessity that the boys stay in school and that there be some adult at home to care for them. In addition, presumably, to the maid, the governess, and the legions of the variously skilled for whom I seem to be a monetary life-support system. I did not want to jeopardize my chances of getting away by myself again, with Maggie, by attempting it too frequently. All I hoped was that everyone would leave me alone.

Unfortunately I went to the Cape in a filthy mood and found all three of them in equally filthy disposition. So that what would have been, at best, a fortnight's rustication from my work, in wretched company, became hard labor. It was not the same kind of heavy lifting that I did in the office, but it made my back hurt and my head ache to about the same degree.

That first Saturday evening I opened hostilities. I was tired, but I still should have known better. "Frank," I said, "you're drinking beer."

Frank somehow dragged his attention away from the beaver picture he was studying, granted me one disdainful look, glanced down at the Miller's can, favored me with another disdainful look, and said, voice overflowing with scorn: "Mum lets me."

"I don't," I said, "and I'm here now. Rid of it."

Frank executed a Nixon segue from aristocratic hauteur to whining innocent victim of dictatorial injustice. *"Mum,"* he sniveled, "Dad says I can't have my beer."

"He *always* has beer when you're not around," Terry said smugly, proving that he was still aware of his surroundings even though absorbed in watching idiotic cartoons, particularly when there seemed to be an opportunity to make a little trouble for his brother.

"Shut up," Francis said. "Just shut up, *little* Terry, and mind your own fucking business."

"He swears, too," Terry said, with satisfaction.

"Dad says it, too," Frank said.

"I'm older'n you are," I said.

"What's going on here?" Jeanne said, coming in from the sun deck with a gin and tonic in her hand.

"Nothing you need to get involved in," I said.

"Frank's drinking beer . . ." Terry said.

"Dad won't let me have my beer," Frank said. "Shut up Terry, you little bastard."

"Fuck you," Terry said.

"What's the matter with you?" Jeanne said to me.

"Up yours," Terry said to Frank.

"With me?" I said. "There's nothing the matter with me. I'm the kid's father. He's fourteen years old. He's drinking beer. He's too young to drink beer. I told him to stop drinking beer. What's the matter with *you?*"

"You little asshole, Terry," Frank said.

"Is that what Judy Lynch called you when you touched her bee-hind at the dance the other night?" Terry said.

"Look, Peter," Jeanne said, "I'm the one who takes care of these kids most of the time, and Frank said all his friends' parents let them have a can of beer if they want it."

"Judy Lynch is a cunt," Frank said.

"How do you know?" Terry said. "You haven't seen it."

Fred Flintstone said: "Yabba-dabba-do," on the television set.

I said: "Oh, grand. What're you gonna do next month, when he tells you all his friends' parents treat them to heroin once a month and marijuana every afternoon? Take up pushing for him?"

"That's what you think, *kid,*" Frank said.

"Yup," Terry said.

"Oh, for Christ sake, Peter," Jeanne said. "It's true. I checked around. Most people think it's a hell of a lot better to let the kids have a little beer or wine at home than have them getting stinking drunk in some park somewhere. Or using dope. If your friend Edgar'd been brought up to treat liquor as a beverage, he might be able to handle it better today."

"Leave Edgar out of this," I said.

"Well, Terry," Frank said, *"little* brother, I fucked Judy Lynch the other night, it so happens."

"*What?*" Jeanne said.

"He said he fucked Judy Lynch the other night," I said. "You wanna call his friends' parents and see if they approve of letting *their* young lads fuck Judy Lynch? Or maybe, call Judy Lynch's parents, and see if they approve of Judy fucking Francis Quinn, I dunno. Because, after all, it might be that kids who get a little pussy in the park somewhere'll grow up to know how to handle ginch better'n my friend Edgar."

"Didja eat her?" Terry said.

"Both of you," Jeanne said, I think to the boys, "go to your room."

"Right, Mummy," I said, "that'll keep the peace nicely, the two of them in one room. They had your help in Belfast, they'd be settling the difficulty by giving equal numbers of neutron bombs to the Ulster Defense League and the IRA."

"Shut up, Peter," she said.

"Dad," Frank said, pretty much satisfied that everyone had forgotten what started the whole thing, "can I have a Honda?"

"No," I said.

"Go to your room," Jeanne said.

"Just a trail bike," Frank said, whining again.

"No," I said.

"Go to your goddamned *room,*" Jeanne said.

"Why *not?*" Frank whined.

"Your *room,*" Jeanne said, pointing her finger.

"*Dad,*" Terry said, on the stairs, "how come I have to go to the room if Frank doesn't have to? Mum said. . . ."

Frank stooped and picked up the Miller's.

"Put the fucking beer down," I said.

"Go to your fucking room," Jeanne said. When they had gone, she said: *"Jesus."*

I shut off Fred Flintstone.

"Christ," Jeanne said, putting her drink on the end table and massaging her temples, "what a fucking insane asylum this is. I don't think I can stand it."

"Well," I said, "you're the one who evidently allowed the inmates to take it over. Would you mind telling me what the hell possessed you to let a fourteen-year-old kid drink beer? Have you lost your mind entirely?"

Jeanne sat down suddenly on the couch, on Frank's copy of *Penthouse*. She has this level, quiet voice that she uses to indicate that she is holding her temper under severe provocation, and she used it then. "Peter," she said, "you don't know half of what goes on, because you're never home. I can wait around airports for six hours for you. . . ."

"I had you called," I said. "I missed the plane because of business that I couldn't help, and I couldn't get another one. If you think I enjoy spending all night on the New Jersey Turnpike, getting here at dawn, and then getting this kind of crappy reception when I've finally gotten some sleep for myself, you've got another goddamned think coming."

"Well," she said, "nobody called me, Peter, no matter who it was that you called."

"Then they fucked up," I said. "I didn't expect them to fuck up, and I didn't know they fucked up, but apparently they fucked up."

"They certainly did," she said.

"Now," I said, "here's one for you. Did you by any chance call the office? Or did you just sit there in Hyannis, weaving your crown of thorns and practicing your martyr's expression?"

"I called," she said. "I called, and nobody answered. No answering service, no nothing."

"Shit," I said.

"I did," she said.

"I didn't mean you didn't call," I said. "I was just pissed off at the answering service."

"Oh, shit," she said, getting up, "I don't care. Let's just forget about it, all right?"

"No," I said, reaching over to touch her shoulder. "For the luvva Mike, sit down, and let's talk about this."

"You take your goddamned hands off me, Peter Quinn," she said. "From now on, you don't touch me unless I ask you to."

"Oh," I said.

"And you can believe this, too, my friend," she said. "I'm not liable to ask."

She went into the kitchen, and it was my turn to sit down on the couch.

We went from that delightful beginning into an evening made hideous by Frank's second-story stomping, brought on by my refusal to allow him to attend a disco night at a hall five miles away and egged on by Terry's taunts about who instead of Frank was consequently doing carnal things to Judy Lynch.

Since the boys had eaten before I woke up, and since I was not about to roust Jeanne from the porch in order to negotiate for cooking about which Edgar had been quite correct, I left around nine and drove down to the Polynesian restaurant at the traffic circle. There I had wretched spareribs, some vile concoction made of wild rice, two thimble-sized cups of weak tea, and five Heinekens. Then I went into the bar and drank gimlets until the late news and movie were over and the bar closed. Still alert, after sleeping all day, I drove to the beach and walked until the rain began around 3 A.M., hoping that this would enable me to sleep through most of Sunday.

It did, but the stratagem was nevertheless ineffective. The rain that began in the dawn's early light continued into Thursday morning, four full days of gloom, fog, easterly winds, and, inside the cottage, stalag atmosphere.

Lacking separate rooms to which they might retire from each other, along with separate television sets, the boys fought upstairs about who was disturbing whose concentration on whose book, and downstairs over which of them should choose among two situation comedies and a Robert Mitchum movie that each of them had seen at least three times before.

Jeanne retreated from the sun deck for the duration of the rain, taking over our bedroom. That left the kitchen to me, but the contemplation of the landlady's trivet collection did not divert me for long, and I found her sampler mottoes unenlightening ("Ve Are Too Soon Oldt, Undt Too Late Schmart." "New York World's Fair, 1964").

With the rain sheeting down, I got my golf clubs from the station wagon, threw them into my car, and headed for the Country Club to claim the guest membership and locker that Ben Bellow had arranged for me. I put the clubs in the locker. I went into the bar and gave thanks that the Red Sox were on the road that day, playing a doubleheader in sunny Chicago, while hoping desperately that I would recognize someone who showed up, who might be persuaded to have dinner with me. On Sunday, no one did. Neither did anyone on Monday or Tuesday, and I grew quite tired of lousy, phony Polynesian food at the restaurant at the rotary, though not bothering to explain my predicament to the bowing Polynesian proprietor, who had understandably concluded from my regular visits that I was absolutely gaga over his horrid cuisine, served to the background music of the goddamned Ray Conniff singers. If one did not give a man diabetes, the other one was likely to.

On Wednesday afternoon, Terry vented one of his grudges against Frank—which one, I do not know, but I am sure it was a minor one—by taking advantage of Frank's absence with his mother, on an expedition to purchase a surfboard, to fink on him. It seemed that Frank had been carted home a week ago Thursday by two auxiliary police, who had rounded up a passel of his new friends along with him, dead drunk and vomiting on the beach. Inasmuch as Frank had not been delivered until shortly after 2 A.M., Jeanne had apparently been concerned and had herself called the police to inquire after where she might view his remains, if they had been recovered from the ocean, where he had surely drowned. Addled as he was, Frank thought erroneously that there was a connection between Jeanne calling the police and the police quite unaware of Jeanne's call—and probably not the slightest bit interested in it—picking up him and his friends. From what Terry said, Frank was absolutely "bullshit," and Jeanne was totally "ripshit." Terry recounted their conversation with relish.

Childishly seeking to get even for my exclusion from the surfboard expedition—of which I had disapproved anyway, until it occurred to me that the effect of my dire predictions about the certainty of Francis' getting skulled by the goddamned thing would reduce my annoyances by a third—I invited Terry to dinner and a movie. I was sick of the Country Club in the rain and sicker still of eating counterfeit Polynesian food, particularly alone.

Terry accepted with alacrity, which for the merest instant made me think some vestige yet remained of at least one of the lovely children I had fathered. Then Terry demanded to see *The Goodbye Girl,* which I vetoed on the ground that it was either "R" or "PG," I forget which, and Terry was sullen until I agreed to let him pick the restaurant. He chose the Polynesian restaurant at the traffic circle. I chose *The Amazing Dobermans* as the evening's entertainment, although now that I think of it, we may have watched the Polynesians and eaten the Dobermans. It's hard to tell.

On Thursday, the fucking rain, as we had routinely come to call it around the cottage—it was the only subject that seemed safe for conversation by all—stopped. Jeanne took Frank to Nauset with his surfboard. Terry went to the beach with some of his friends, giving his solemn word that he would not be back until dinner. I went to the Country Club and found a threesome looking to become a foursome and thus to secure priority off the first tee. Joe—"I'm Joe, howya doin'?—Joe—"He's Joe, too." "Hiya, Joe. I'm Pete." "Hiya, Pete, howya doin'?"—and Bruce—"My name may be Bruthie, but I ain't queer, and I ain't no fuckin' hairdresser neither. You make any smart remarks, I'll hit you with my purse"— were modest about their skills, claiming handicaps ranging from five to nine. In fact, they were complete liars, each of them being a scratch golfer. I played nine holes with them while they discussed their common business in office furniture supply, and quit at the clubhouse, pleading too much sun.

I went home later, full of beer, bile, and a club sandwich, to a deserted house, planning to read the newspapers on the sun deck. Instead, I took a nap, awakening, chilled, around seven-thirty, to the doorbell. Terry, wrapped in a blanket which did not stop him from shivering terribly, stood under the protection of a very nice young fellow who identified himself as Ron, the lifeguard from the town beach, and informed me that Terry had somehow hurt himself. "What he did, Mister Quinn," Ron said, "he swam out further'n he should've, and the wave came in, and all of a sudden he had about two hundred Portuguese men-o'-war around him. Got stung pretty bad. We took him over the hospital, and he's okay, but you'll wanna watch him. Fever, chills, that kind of thing. Get enough of that poison in your system, you can *die*. Good night."

"Uh, thanks, uh, Ron," I said.

Jeanne got home with Murf the Surf around ten-thirty. She said that they had stopped for dinner. She looked flushed and sunburned herself. She had been surfing, too. On Friday, they were going back to the surfboard shop and then back to Nauset. They were going to take Terry, so I could be by myself, which she knew I enjoyed much more. Wishing that I had Ron's last name and phone number for Jeanne, I reported Terry's accident. She dashed upstairs to wake him up, in order to comfort him and thus cause him to repeat the achievement of going to sleep with a stinging pelt wrapped around him.

On the way upstairs, she allowed as how it was my fault. Frank took considerable satisfaction in his brother's discomfort, though not quite as much as he clearly did in having shown my wife a better time than I had. I kept my big mouth shut. I read *Oedipus Rex* in college, and if the little bastard wanted to go that route, he was welcome to it as far as I was concerned. I went to bed early and slept well.

On Friday morning, I got up in the sunlight before anyone in the house—or anyone in his right mind, for that matter— and opened the Country Club. I was first off the tee, somehow enduring the absence of Joe, Joe, and Bruthie, all by myself. I played an acceptable round, showered, took some steam, showered, swam ten laps in the pool, and had a second breakfast on the terrace. I read the papers and remarked that the Sox were home. I called for a telephone and reached Franklin Melcher at his office in Boston. I hinted around. I said: "Frank. I'm in Dennisport with the family, and I think I may have twenty-four hours at the outside before I lose my mind." I told him that I did not know what had gotten into Jeanne, but that it certainly wasn't me. "Now what I want from you," I said, "is this: I want your fucking tickets to the game tonight. Actually, that's wrong. I want one ticket. Just one. One ticket to the ball game, so I can go watch grown men try to hit round balls with round sticks. I need something sensible in my life for a change. If you tell me I can't have it, I will probably have to kill you."

Franklin told me that as a matter of fact, he did have an extra ticket. One extra ticket. Wendy's sister from Sarah Lawrence was in town. Wendy's sister's boyfriend, Hal, had unexpectedly drawn mandatory overtime from his supervisor with the Pennsylvania State Police. Wendy's sister, Kristin, had come to Boston in a snit, without Hal. "Now look," Franklin said, "I'll be candid with you, if that's all right." I assured him that it was all right. "Franklin," I said, "people've been candid with me for the better part of a week. Most of them seem to be related to me, if not by marriage, then by blood.

I'm used to it. I don't like it, but I'm used to it. I don't like them, either, a whole lot, but that's none of your jelly roll. Assuming that I won't dislike you, after you're candid with me, in which case it is. But fire away."

"Okay," Franklin said. "Wendy doesn't like you, and she's reasonably sure you don't like her. That's okay. I can live with that. I am reaonably sure that you can also."

"Look, Franklin," I said, "I am calling in a *Mayday*. I just wanna go to the ball game. I don't care who else is going to the ball game, as long as I am. They can get thirty-five, thirty-six thousand people into that little ball park. I don't care who gets invited. I'll behave myself. I'll drink a little beer and eat a hot dog and watch another pitching duel that winds up Sox eleven, Tigers nine. I won't care. I really will behave myself. Just let me come to the ball game. Please?"

"That isn't what I meant," Franklin said. "Just between you and me, Wendy and I've been having a few little tiffs now and then."

"Oh," I said.

"Which is one thing," Franklin said, "and none of your particular business. The other thing is this: if you don't like Wendy, you will find Kristin insufferable. I happen to like Wendy, although there are times when she is certainly a little dizzy. The night, the last time that we went to the ball game with you, I could quite cheerfully have strangled her. But that's all in the past. Kristin is in the present. Kristin is younger than Wendy, and Kristin is a theater major. Which means Wendy's father is supporting her while she learns about life in a loft in New York. And Pursues Her Career. She's a good-looking kid, but without lead weights on her shoes, she would float right off the ground. Do I make myself clear?"

"Abundantly," I said.

"Understand, now," Franklin said, "I do not dislike Kristin. The matter is much simpler than that. I can't *stand* Kristin. So if you would be good enough to drive all the way up to Boston this afternoon, and join us for dinner at the Harvard

Club, and come to the ball game with us, I will be eternally grateful to you, because that will mean that I will have somebody to talk to, while Wendy and Kristin, just the two of them, manage a creditable imitation of some damned rock group. If you are willing to put up with what Kristin will surely put you through, generations yet unborn will rise up and call thee blessed."

"Done," I said, and hung up. Being prudent and wanting a bed for the night, I then called Edgar, both at the paper and at his home. He was out at the paper, and he did not answer at home. I therefore reserved a room at the Parker House and went back to the empty cottage to change into a blazer.

It was a most enjoyable ball game. Rick Wise, still with the Sox then, managed to keep the ball down until the seventh inning, and by then he was so obviously exhausted in the still, green, well-lighted evening that even Don Zimmer knew enough to yank him and bring Bill Campbell on. The Tigers were still a very young club and could not manage to get enough runners on ahead of Jason Thompson to make full use of his two homers. Yaz hit one, Rice hit two, Scott doubled twice, and Hobson snapped one into the screen with indisputable authority. Sox won, 9–4.

Kristin, as matters turned out, was a little breathless for my taste initially, but a surprisingly good listener. She shared my fondness for Dennis Brain's renditions of the Mozart horn concerti, and when Franklin complained that the Sox somehow never got the sort of pitching that the Yankees had with Raschi, Reynolds, and "the other guy," she at once supplied the name of Eddie Lopat. We were arguing in friendly fashion, a few minutes before "The Star-Spangled Banner," about whether Campbell was the equal of Albert "Sparky" Lyle, when I glanced down from the skyview box to see Edgar escorting Maggie Capeless to the field box behind the first base.

That night I invited Kristin to have a nightcap with me in Parker's Bar. She did not plague Franklin with her chatter in the waterfront apartment the next morning, and I gained that night a new respect for the instructional abilities of the Pennsylvania State Police.

Not quite a week later, after the Red Sox left town and Kristin went back to New York and I had at last checked out of the Parker House, as I sat on the deck at Baxter's in the remainder of the evening, inspecting those appalling creatures with whom, for some reason or another, I was making my home, Jeanne said: "You know, kids, there's one thing that I can't understand."

"What's that, Mum?" Terry said, the little suck-ass.

"Nantucket," she said. "I can't understand why Daddy took us over to Nantucket."

"I liked it," Terry said, looking anxiously at me, playing both ends against the middle, as usual. Trimmer.

"Why," Jeanne said, "so do I. But Daddy always said he liked the Vineyard. How come we didn't go to the Vineyard this year, Daddy? We heard so much about it when you were up conferring with your client there. What was his name?"

"Damned if I know," I said. "That case was years ago."

"It was last year," Jeanne said. "But anyway, can we maybe go to the Vineyard tomorrow? Or sometime before we leave? You talked so much about it. I'd like to see it."

Strongly suspecting that I did not have a hell of a lot to lose, and pretty much uncaring if I lost what I had, I said: "Sure. Lemme know how you like it."

"What?" she said. "Aren't you coming?"

I yawned. I stretched. "Nope," I said, "I've seen the Vineyard."

"The boys and I haven't," Jeanne said.

"So," I said, "go and see it. When I saw it, it was years ago. Islands and other things change."

Eleven

I did not hear from Edgar until late in September, long after I had left Jeanne and the kids, a privation I was able to bear with fair equanimity, considering the number of other things I had on my mind. The first weeks back on the job are always a madhouse; when those happen to be the ones coming right after Labor Day, as agencies and offices dormant for the summer begin to get their wits about them once again, schedules hectic under ordinary circumstances become absolutely frantic.

I had by no means straightened out my tangled personal situation either; while I had secured an apartment for myself, in Foggy Bottom, it was filled with shabby rented furniture and virtually empty of such trivial supplies as extra light bulbs, toilet paper, soap, and toothpaste. Each morning, as I ate toast and drank bad coffee at the counter of the People's Drugstore, I made a mental note to stop on the way out and at least get a coffeepot; each afternoon, after I had forgotten and it became apparent that I would be working long after the stores closed, I considered asking my secretary to step out for the appliance. Each time I remembered that of course, I had no coffee, no cup to put it in, no sugar or cream to sweeten and lighten it, and no spoon with which to stir it, so I did not ask her. I had, in the refrigerator, four bottles remaining from the six-pack of Kronenburg which I had taken home from the office one night after I took tenancy of the place. That was in order that I might have some refreshment while I watched the late news on the small black and white TV that was part of the rented package. But the experience of drinking Alsatian beer from a plastic cup, left behind in the bathroom by the people who had sold me the five months remaining on their lease, was rather unsatisfying, and since I had not gotten around to purchasing any glassware either, I did not bother to repeat it.

By the first of the year, I kept telling myself, I would have something lined up in Georgetown, decorated and furnished according to my own preferences, if to some decorator's more refined tastes, and I would take care of such things as large, rough-textured bath towels, honest beer mugs, a blender, suitable cutlery, and dishes at the same time. The trouble was, of course, that nearly a month had gone by since the necessity had been raised, and working weekends as well as nights, I had done nothing about a new apartment or any of its equipment either. My steadfast refusal to call Maggie only bothered me at night, when I was alone.

What little time I did have free, I tried to spend with the boys. Terry seemed somewhat subdued by what had happened, but separation and divorce were developments familiar to most of his friends at school, and he seemed to be working it out pretty well. Frank, though he tried to conceal it, was plainly just as pleased to have me out as he had been to have me in: not very. It was a matter of no especial interest to him either way.

I was therefore candid with Edgar when he called. "Lousy," I said. "I'm working too hard, I'm tired, and I've consequently got the disposition of a scorpion with a hangover."

"So, what else is new?" he said. The son of a bitch, I thought, sounded indecently cheerful, in view of his secondary contribution to my woe. If it had not been for him, I would at least have had a place of refuge, comfort, hope, and light, as well as very good food, served on china of good quality, bought twenty years before by Vernon Capeless for his young bride. Instead, I had been left to do a creditable imitation of a Bedouin, in a run-down apartment filled with chairs and couches last let out to the penurious company touring *Death of a Salesman* through the smaller cities of the Midwest. I resolved to tell Edgar nothing, denying him at least the satisfaction of hearing me whine about my problems.

"Nothing much," I said. "If there was anything new, I probably wouldn't know about it. Unless it involved one of my clients being put out of business by some idealistic little shithead from the Cornell Law School, with a GS Thirteen rating in the Occupational Safety and Health Administration, who thinks no human hand should ever be permitted to come within a mile and six furlongs of a casting mold, because some drunken asshole got his paw caught in a similar device three years ago in a small plant outside Fort Worth. I suppose you're in town for no more'n forty-eight hours, and you want me to remake my entire schedule so as to buy you a Lucullan lunch with money that I haven't got, at a place I don't like, with more booze than I can drink without losing the rest of the day to intermittent dozing and poor judgments."

"Actually," Edgar said, "you're right, but you're wrong. I *am* in town for about forty-eight hours, but the town I'm in is Boston. The town I'm leaving for is Washington, and I'll be in that one off and on for the next month or six weeks. And then almost entirely on."

Consciously carrying a very serviceable grudge against Edgar, dwarfed but by no means unnoticed in my extensive collection of much larger grudges against Jeanne, Terry, Frank, Maggie, my partners of senior rank who had left me, low man on the totem pole, with the shortest vacation and the obligation to take it so that I would return at the busiest season of the year, I was surprised to find that I was pleased by Edgar's news. It is hard, when hungry, fatigued, lonely, and mildly depressed, to maintain a schedule of adequate cultivation of more than three or four good grudges. Like a litigious client, spitting brimstone and demanding retributive lawsuits in 1973, distracted four years later with fresher annoyances supplanting the old affront in his affection, I was prepared to settle my grudge with Edgar at a price favorable to him, just to be rid of it, in order to concentrate my limited firepower on more pressing matters. Such as whether I could juggle personal and professional demands upon my time with skill sufficient to prevent the government from beggaring my clients—by which event, of course, I too would be beggared and shortly eased out of my partnership. While at the same time thwarting Jeanne's full-time campaign to reduce me to alimony beggary no matter what happened to my carreer.

Then there was the matter of Torbert Lynch. Torbert was a gentleman whom I had never met, but whose employment as a middle-level supervisor in the Massachusetts Department of Corporations and Taxation had apparently furnished to him whatever evidence of his moral superiority to his fellowman as had been needed after his election to the presidency of the Holy Name Society of the Church of the Holy Sepulchre in Weston, Massachusetts. Mr. Lynch became rather officious with my secretary when I was Out to his repeated calls (though, in fact, I was out when he called, and failed to return his courtesies because he refused to state his business to her. Anyway, I had more than enough calls to return, from people whose names I did recognize and whose business was perfectly—and pressingly—well known to me).

On his fourth inquiry, Torbert obtained the deference he appeared to feel to be his natural right, or else his proper entitlement by reason of his high religious and secular attainments, by telling my secretary that he was calling in reference to my "goddamned kid." I still did not know what he wanted, but he and I obviously had at least one opinion in common, and I called to determine what had brought him to the same conclusion.

That was when I learned that Torbert's daughter, Judy, had tearfully corroborated Frank's claim of sexual congress, made in August, doing so after a tony gynecologist in Wellesley had diagnosed with certainty, in September, that Judy Lynch had certainly been fucking somebody, and without effective precautions, too. Grilled by her father, an interlude which must have been extremely disagreeable, Miss Lynch had impliedly rebutted Terry's allegation that in Frank's absence from the disco on the Cape, while he was under house arrest for conduct insubordinate to his father, she had committed intimacy with another gentleman. At thirteen, Judith believed in true love, according to her father, and had limited her passionate embraces to the arms of my bestial son. This, Torbert seemed unshakably convinced, was the sole cause of her pending eligibility for the honor of Catholic Mother of the Year. For such recognition, he deemed her much too immature. He was, by her condition, stimulated to regard with concern his own otherwise-superb qualifications for further personal recognitions, both sacred and profane.

Torbert, using the Commonwealth's Wide Area Toll Telephone System, made and returned protracted calls to me at no expense to himself whatsoever, muttering into the receiver like a man negotiating a substantial bribe, lest "somebody in my office hear about this." He demanded, first, that I execute Francis; then that I execute certain documents permitting Francis to enter into holy wedlock with Judith, at the age of fourteen; and finally, that I "think of something, wise guy. Smart-ass Washington lawyer that can't even control his own kid." Momentarily bemused by Torbert's first proposal—shooting Frank, which I rejected promptly upon realizing that no matter where or how I did it, or had it done, the act would be considered a felony, and a rather serious one at that, perhaps resulting in my disbarment and certainly my incarceration— I instantly and correctly denominated Torbert's second proposal—Frank and Judy's marriage—the output of a fevered brain, irrational in the extreme. I therefore accepted both the third invitation, and the compliments that he then extended, and informed him that I would give the matter my earnest attention.

Torbert snarled something to the effect that the situation was one of urgency: "What she's got in the oven, there, smart guy, you know, isn't gonna stay in there till Flag Day, I don't think. And if it does, it's not gonna be too hard for somebody lookin' at her tell what it is that's in there. You gonna think of somethin', you better do it goddamned fast, is all I got to say. That kid hasn't got all that much time, which means that you and your wild-ass kid haven't either."

I then lost patience with Torbert. I pointed out to Torbert, not gently at all, that my wild-ass kid had not been wearing the dainty panties that Judith Lynch had evidently removed from her wild ass, before admitting the Quinn organ which had evidently contributed to the creation of the problem. Torbert said something stupid about statutory rape. This I jeered at and recommended that he research the statute: while it would have been a criminal offense if I had done the dirty deed, it was nothing whatsoever when performed by a fourteen-year-old. Then, with no more justification in my threat than Torbert had had, I suggested that he check the statute also on contributing to the delinquency of a minor. Which Judith, at her age, could not have done either. But it silenced Torbert, and that—not a lawsuit vindicating Frank's purity—was my principal objective.

Thus abundantly supplied with entertainment and diversion, both on and off the job, I was gentler by far with Edgar than I otherwise would have been. "What're you coming back down here for?" I said. "Thinking of reconciling with your wife, I suppose." I was determined to make the son of a bitch tell me himself about Maggie. But after he did so and had been acceptably sheepish, I was fully prepared to be magnanimous.

"Sure," Edgar said. "How'd you know?"

I was stunned, and I fell for it. I should know better than to attempt to maneuver Edgar, or anyone else, for that matter, when my attention is otherwise fully occupied. "Jesus, Edgar," I said, "I didn't. That, that's wonderful . . . news."

"I knew you'd think so," Edgar said warmly. "If you'd been sitting in the Oval Office, instead of FDR, the day the news came in from Pearl, you would've gone up to the Hill and made a speech telling Congress the Japanese attack was the fruition of all our hopes and dreams, making it a day that would be celebrated with thanksgiving until the end of history."

"You bastard," I said.

"Did Samson put up a rose-covered temple for Delilah when he had the choice?" Edgar said. "Did Adam Clayton Powell thank his wife for wrecking him in the House? Sure they did. And following their grand example, I am going back to finish out my days with Mary Claire, no longer forgetful of my vows, repentant of my transgressions, and humbly bent upon the making of contrite amends for all the heartache I have visited upon her. What's the matter with you, Peter? Have you lost your fucking grip?"

Since he had done it to me once again, and since I obviously lacked the resources to do it then to him, I at once forgot about revenge. Rather desperately, I guess, I began scrambling for a friend. I was running a little short that month. "I may be starting to," I said. "The bastards're coming at me from all sides, it seems like, and my sword arm's getting weary. None of them's big enough to do me in all by himself, but there seems to be a whole bunch of them. When I wound one, he goes off and recuperates, and the rest gang up on me. When I get one of them, the one I stabbed the last time is all better and cutting me up pretty good. There's so many of them, I never get the chance to finish any of them off."

"Better start at the beginning," Edgar said, and I did.

"Not in any particular order of importance," I said, and began with the separation from Jeanne. "We had a truly shitty vacation," I said. "Rained the first week on the Cape."

"Jeez," Edgar said, "I'm surprised to hear that. I didn't hear anything about Jeanne's vacation on the Cape, but I heard you had one a Sultan would've envied, at the Parker House."

"Jesus Christ," I said. "You fucking amaze me." My secretary came in as I said that. "Wait a minute, Edgar. Pauline, hold my calls." She told me a six-figure account of mine was calling, greatly agitated, from Chicago. I told her to switch the call to Bradley and tell him this was what he owed me for what I went through with his client who acted out whipping fantasies with whores who didn't go for that sort of thing. "And I mean it, Pauline," I said, "I'm talking to a friend of mine, for a change, and I will not take no goddamned calls. Clear?" "Great," she said. "I'm glad to hear it. Will 'He's-tied-up-on-long-distance-on-a-very-impor-tant-matter-and-cannot-be-disturbed' do it?" "Perfect," I said. "Edgar," I said, "back again. How the hell did you know about that?"

"Simple," Edgar said. "You know everybody you're ever gonna meet. There're only ninety-six people in the world, and every one of them knows all the others. I just ran into one of the ones that knows you, and the rest of it was easy."

"Who was that?" I said.

"Up here in the Athens of America," Edgar said, "we have got a sportsman-philanthropist by the name of Cosmo."

"I don't know a soul named Cosmo," I said.

"Bear with me," Edgar said. "Very few guys know Cosmo. Very few guys in your exalted circles, I mean. They think Cosmo has something to do with a private club down there in Washington that don't allow ladies to use the front door. And the ones that do know Cosmo deny it, except when some-body gets a hold an FBI transcript under the Freedom of Information Act.

"That," Edgar said, "is when it turns out that somebody in your circle does know Cosmo. Some Cosmo or another. A Johnny, a Carlo, a Vito, a Sam: all Cosmos, except those

Cosmos run operations someplace other than in Boston.

"It turns out," Edgar said, "because a good Cosmo or two can be a very helpful sort, if you are running the government, and the government is getting a good hook on his private parts at the Department of Justice, but the government would like to see something drastic done about some troublesome Latin American dictator. Something drastic. Because your basic Cosmo is a man who has contacts and can get things done, as folks in your line of work are fond of saying. And he is also a man who is willing to haggle a bit with the opposition, if the opposition might be willing to call off some U.S. Attorney in Nevada who's getting close to a nifty little skimming operation in Las Vegas. You follow me?"

"The Mob," I said. "As far as I know, I don't know a soul in the Mob." If Kristin was tied up with the Mob, I had a potential problem, though—that I did know.

"I'm glad you put that preface on it," Edgar said. "I would bet you a vacation in a garden spot of your choosing, with a companion of your designation, guaranteed to be complaisant, that you do, if you had said that you did not, flat-out. You know some Mob, but the Mob you know is the Mob guys that the Mob guys put on the payroll to know guys like you, and part of their job specs is: 'Get to know Peter Quinn, but for Christ sake, don't let Peter Quinn know you know us.' All right?"

"All right," I said.

"Now," Edgar said, "if I have the floor once again, Cosmo is definitely one of the Mob guys that you do not know. In fact, Cosmo is one of the Mob guys that even many guys in the Mob do not know, although they all know who Cosmo is and would account it a very large step upwards in their careers if they could get to know Cosmo. Because the only guys in the Mob that know Cosmo are other dons that now and then call him in to mediate tedious disputes about who can operate where those people who don't know Cosmo, but would like to, are shooting each other about and putting each other in the trunks of stolen cars that're very soon thereafter fed into car crushers. Do I make myself clear?"

"Yes," I said.

"Cosmo takes no active part in none of this," Edgar said. "Or at least, if Cosmo does, he does it very discreetly, so that for some time even people who were under the strong impression that Cosmo knew of, and approved of, what they were doing to guys and stolen cars did not know Cosmo. Cosmo runs this here kind of Clean-and-Reasonable motel, which in the summertime you would expect to see a lot of lower-middle-class folks staying in with their families. And if you went there, you would. He also has a small cleaning business that does towels and nappy-kins and tablecloths for restaurants—every restaurant within a hundred miles which likes the idea of staying in business much better'n the idea of getting fire-bombed some night around three inna morning, and having to blame it on a Fry-o-later accident. He also operates a modest liquor-distributing business, which supplies to a lot of bars that feel the same way about electrical fires as the restaurants feel about the deep fryer fires. He sits on the porch of the office of his motel, and he's a friend to man.

"That's what Cosmo is," Edgar said. "Just an old man that the papers keep calling a Mafia Kingpin and won't leave him alone.

"This is partly because," Edgar said, "guys that talk on the telephones that the FBI and the State Police from time to time choose to tap also keep calling Cosmo a Mafia Kingpin. That is not the word they use. But that is what the words they use mean. And when those guys get caught, their dumb lawyers keep demanding transcripts of the taps. The government keeps handing the tapes over, into the court records that we scribblers've got the right to see. And we keep printing how all these ginzoes keep calling Cosmo a Mafia Kingpin. Or Chieftain. Sometimes it is Chieftain. Or Boss.

"We have it on reliable authority," Edgar said, "that Cosmo is not all that enthusiastic about this celebrity he gets, while

215

sitting on the porch of his motel in his redwood chair, smoking an occasional cigarette, and having a cup of coffee and a little anisette now and then. Cosmo don't talk on the phone a whole lot himself. Indeed, I have heard it said that Cosmo not only practices, but invented, the maxim popular in Massachusetts and national political circles, which is: 'If you can say it, don't write it. If you can whisper it, don't say it. And if you can nod, don't whisper.'

"Cosmo, I understand, nods a lot, and he cannot understand why a man does so much nodding of his head and shaking of his head should be having all this goddamned trouble with guys he doesn't even know. Who talk onna telephone all the time and keep taking his name in vain and calling him the Boss of the Mafia. I understand Cosmo has sometimes broken into speech on the subject, he has become so upset. Though to be sure it was speech conducted wholly in Sicilian dialect, on a terrace above breaking surf, with a radio playing loudly, so far away from a building or natural cover that not even a parabolic microphone could pick it up. And that as a result, guys have turned up dead afterwards. But that, of course, is rumor. Rumor and hearsay, as you lawyers say.

"For years," Edgar said, "the result of this is that while every sentient human being above the age of seven, north of Providence and south of Quebec City, has for the last thirty years been convinced that Cosmo is the head of the Mafia, and in that capacity is reported to have commissioned many nefarious deeds, nobody has been able to catch him at it. Until, it is alleged, now.

"About fourteen months ago," Edgar said, "the *federales* and the State Police became interested in a gentleman named Samuel, the cops apparently having an ambition to persuade a gentleman named Willie that he was going to go away forever did he not see fit to trade his miserable pelt for the scalp of larger game. Such as Cosmo.

"Willie had taken umbrage at the tardiness of a car salesman in repaying certain gambling debts, and the car salesman had

216

apparently taken Willie's distress quite seriously. Along with Willie's remarks about some big fellows who would meet the saleman after work and rearrange his skeleton for him, while it was still covered by his too, too solid flesh.

"The salesman called the police. Said gendarmes did wire said salesman until he was getting UHF reception on the top of his bifocals and three channels, VHF, on the bottom. Except for Providence, because the antenna running up his tailbone was apparently too short. Or else his tailbone was.

"Then they recorded, but did not transcribe, marine weather advisories that the salesman pulled in with his sophisticated electronic gear, last employed to detect jungle infiltration by the Vietcong, as well as most of *I Love Lucy* and several memorable interviews in which the newly confident salesman inveigled stupid suburbanites into giving away their Oldsmobile sedans and paying extortionate rates of interest as financing on new Chevrolets. They did not have those gems written up neither.

"What they did write up," Edgar said, "with loving care, was certain dire predictions made by Samuel, acting in behalf of old Willie, about what was about to happen to the car salesman did he persist in his refusal to pay Willie. Some of what Samuel had to say applied to the salesman personally. Some of it concerned the health and well-being of his children; some more consisted of what was about to happen to the salesman's wife. Samuel was also specific about what was going to happen to the salesman's house, while he and his wife and children were in it, sleeping, and perhaps to the salesman's car, while the salesman and his family were in that.

"Samuel was very confident that his predictions were trustworthy," Edgar said. "Because, as Samuel said, he was the fellow who was going to carry them out. Samuel suggested that the salesman abscond with certain funds belonging to his employer, lest any or all of those dreadful things happen to the salesman, his wife, family, realty, or car. When I say they wrote it up," Edgar said, "I mean they wrote it up real good. Then the federal grand jury wrote a few comments down, after hearing it all, and those were called indictments. For racketeering.

"Now," Edgar said, "this seriously complicated Samuel's business life. Regular customers of his services rather abruptly stopped calling him. That was the only trade he had, breaking people's legs and doing other mean things to them. Losing it diminished his cash flow. It diminished his cash flow down to about zero, as a matter of fact. In the meantime, Samuel's lawyer, having his own cash flow to worry about, began to lose interest in working for Samuel, because those diverse and sundry other folks had lost interest in having Samuel work for them.

"Samuel, taking stock of the situation, recollected that he had done a little time before. He was a four-time loser even if the trial jury took complete leave of their senses and let him go on the car salesman. Which seemed unlikely that the jury would tell Samuel to go forth and sin no more, him being without a lawyer and all—you guys're really no damned good at all, are you, Peter? Leaving a guy in the lurch like that. And besides that, there was more: two of the previous four falls were for breaking the hind legs of people who had been delinquent in paying their debts. Samuel decided he was going away for all day, unless somebody did something, and that since there seemed to be a shortage of volunteers, he would do something himself.

"So," Edgar said, "he did. The feds did not have Willie. They also did not have three other guys, in lines of business similar to Willie's, who had also encountered collection problems with their customers and had called upon Samuel to resolve them in the past. A number of those debtors had some difficulty getting around, long after Samuel had performed his usual efficient service, and harbored grudges about the summary fashion in which they had been treated. Two were dead, which added an interesting dimension to the negotiations and

218

brought the state authorities into the discussion. But the feds did have Samuel.

"Samuel warmed to his role, imitating Enrico Caruso before several grand juries. Pretty soon Willie and his fellow tradesmen were themselves in urgent need of counsel. All of a sudden people were looking down the barrel of Murder One charges. There is a noticeable difference between what will happen to you if you get nailed for registering bets, or even having the bettor beat up if he don't pay, and what will happen to you if you get hauled in on Murder One because the guy didn't pay and wound up floating around with the broken pallets and the Bud cans just off Pier Four.

"Willie became quite alarmed," Edgar said. "What he did, in point of fact, was shit his personal knickers. Having been forthcoming from that end, he became forthcoming from the other. He called up the feds, to see if they would like to chat.

"Those guys," Edgar said, "those guys're better listeners'n most monsignori. They were more'n happy to hold Willie's hand, while he confessed not only to a misspent youth but also to an adult life of practices prohibited by the statutes. And they were patient, too; they had started off with Samuel, who had given them Willie and three other guys considerably higher up, and now they had Willie, who had gotten his betting lines and layoff information from somebody still higher up from him, and who had gotten Samuel, and other people lower down, to deal with his deadbeats by asking somebody, also higher up, who clearly knew what it was that Samuel was best at doing. Samuel was a good grab, but Willie was a gift from God. They were very nice to Willie and quite patient with him, too. They met with him in out-of-the-way places and did not publicize his recitations. They especially did not see fit to divulge what Willie had to say about one Guido."

"Edgar," I said, "who the fuck is Guido?"

"Another ginzo that you lofty types don't know about," he said. "Nothing but a hard guy. A very hard guy. Next to

Cosmo, the hardest guy, is what they say. And considerably younger, too. Very mean temper. Knows a lot of things which would explain a lot of things that certain cops already know the explanations to but cannot prove. Never done a minute in the can. And doesn't plan to either. Which is probably the explanation for why he is so well wired in and how he knew what Willie was saying about the time that Willie paused for breath. Guido took offense.

"Making Guido mad is not a good idea apparently," Edgar said. "Because while Cosmo is the very soul of circumspection, there is some obscure reason why he would prefer that Guido did not get his cock caught in his zipper. Like, perhaps, that Guido knows a thing or two about a couple projects that Cosmo has needed handled. Whatever Guido wants, Guido gets. At least from Cosmo.

"What Guido wanted," Edgar said, "if the government's evidence is to be believed—and considering that it is mostly from live witnesses who are clearly scared shitless, and tapes of people who seem to be defendants in the matter, maybe that evidence should be believed—was for Willie to be unavailable for testimony, first of all. And secondly, for Willie to provide accurate details on who else might be unavailable, lest some Designated Hitter take his place. This Cosmo is alleged to have okayed, and Willie is said to have provided."

"Why would Willie do that?" I said.

"Willie hasn't said," Edgar said. "Willie is no longer with us."

"Willie's dead," I said.

"Willie's dead now," Edgar said.

"A case of premature cardiac arrest, no doubt," I said.

"If what they did to Willie, they did to me," Edgar said, "the answer would be Yes. But Willie lacked our common sense. Have you ever been in a deli?"

"Sure," I said.

"I have, too," Edgar said. "So, apparently, had Willie, but either he was not impressed, or else he didn't believe what they were gonna do to him, or else he had something wrong with his skull."

"What the hell did they do?" I said.

"The guy that owned the deli," Edgar said, "who is now, by the way, in a fair hod of shit of his own for being so hospitable to Guido and his deputies, apparently was known to book a horse and a Red Sox game or two on his own hook now and again. And to need a Samuel from time to time, when some cheater didn't pay up. So he wrapped the corned beef and the macaroni salad in the tinfoil, unplugged the coffee brewer, and let the chaps in, telling them to shut the lights out when they left."

"I presume they did that," I said. "What difference does it make, they beat up a guy in a deli?"

"You ever have a nice thin salami sandwich in a deli?" Edgar said. "A little corned beef? A little roast beef? Maybe some ham?"

"Sure," I said. "Dinner last night, matter of fact. Had the office gofer pick me up a roast beef sub before he left. Took it home in the waxed paper. Ate it around midnight. Soggy piece of shit."

"See how they make it?" Edgar said.

"Put the roast beef between the halves of the roll," I said. "Fold it in, add tomatoes, little oil. . . ."

"Right," Edgar said, "and they get those lovely thin slices of roast beef by slapping the roast beef down on a circular knife on a white motor housing, and setting the gauge of the cut, thin or thick, and whirring the animal through there until they get about enough meat for the sandwich that you ordered."

"Holy Jesus," I said.

"Exactly what they did to Willie," Edgar said. "When the cops found their star witness, it took them three days to make sure, 'cause Willie didn't have no face, and Willie didn't have no fingerprints, and it was only luck he had enough teeth left, the Bureau had a dental fix on him. Apparently, whenever

Willie was a bit too taciturn for them, they put his hand on the circular knife and took off another layer. And when they got down to the bone on the left one, they started in on the right one. They also touched up his right foot a little bit. Then they crushed his face with the tenderizing mallets, and just in case he was still alive, they shot him several times with large-caliber handguns. Then they put Willie in a stolen Chevrolet and left it in the parking lot at the State House. By then, I would imagine, Willie was grateful for the respite. Dead, but grateful."

"Good Lord," I said.

"However good," Edgar said, "the Lord, from Willie's point of view, was inattentive."

"I don't quite see how this has anything to do with me . . ." I began.

"Patience, patience," Edgar said. "That was the way the Bureau and the Staties felt. Very impatient. They didn't see quite how old Willie'd decided to skip his usual meetings and ignore them, like he was doing. So they sent out an APB on him, and when this skinned cat with no paws and damned little face showed up in the car trunk, they had a strong suspicion it was Willie. And when them guys've got a strong suspicion, there ain't no stops whatsoever that they don't pull out. Three days was *lightning,* considering what was left of Willie that they had to work with."

"I still don't see," I began again.

"Lemme finish, and you will," Edgar said. "See, I am covering this because our regular court-and-Mafia-type reporter is languishing over to the Peter Bent Brigham, where he repaired with a transparently feigned heart attack. Except considering what he smokes, the amounts, I mean, and how much he drinks, generally finishing a quart, Old Forester, a day—and that is *before* he gets off work—it is possible that he is not faking it at all, and he may actually have one.

"Anyway, there is nothing that pisses the Bureau and the Staties off like losing a canary, you know what I mean? Damned

222

right. For one thing, they went to a lot of work, get this canary. For another thing, his untimely demise is not gonna improve the sales pitch when they go out again, looking for new song-birds. And for the last thing, the Staties think it was the Bureau's fault, and the Bureau thinks it was the Staties' fault, and it really wasn't neither of their fault at all. Willie was *always* wandering off, and taking rides with strangers, and doing other things he shouldn't've, so that he got turned into a roast beef sandwich and, later, dead. So the Staties're gonna catch the guys what did it and show the Bureau up for the bunch of assholes that they are, and the Bureau's already jumpy on account of all their fellows getting themselves indicted for doing things that Richard Nixon said he thought they should, and I'm telling you, Peter, it was like martial law around here for a while.

"Well," Edgar said. "one thing and another, pretty soon the Bureau finds a guy that works for Guido and has maybe got a thing or two to say. Particularly after he hears some of the tapes that Willie made for the Bureau, which mention his name now and then, and not in any flattering context either. As his lawyer shortly finds out, those tapes're now admissible against this particular gentleman, on account of as how Willie is so completely dead. In federal court, that is. To be sure, cross-examining a tape is gonna be fairly difficult for this Guido's lawyer. He is thinking about Murder One if he doesn't win and a whole mess of other unpleasant stuff.

"With Johnny," Edgar said, "the guy that worked for Guido, the authorities were more careful'n they'd been with Willie. Johnny stayed in protective custody and had his wife brought in to see him, diaphragm already in place. Johnny sang like Snooky Lanson on his best day wished he could've, and what Johnny did to Guido was not pleasant.

"The interesting part," Edgar said, "was that Johnny claimed that Cosmo took an active part in all the things that Guido did, to give the whole matter a gloss that it probably does not deserve."

223

"Whaddaya mean?" I said. "Hoods."

"Exactly," Edgar said. "Hoods. Cosmo is an old hood. He did not get to be an old hood, without serving one instant of time in no jail whatsoever, by sitting in at conferences where the likes of Guido set about to save their asses, turning their enemies into roast beef sandwiches. But according to Johnny, who said he ran the slicer, where there was Guido, there was Cosmo, and he had some rather colorful dialogue for Cosmo, too. It was mostly grunts and stuff, but in the situation, where the question is whether you put the guy's paw in the slicer again, it was colorful."

"Didn't Cosmo know about it?" I said.

"Cosmo didn't know about it only if Queen Isabella didn't know about what Chris Columbus wanted the boats for," Edgar said. "The question is whether anybody could prove that Cosmo wanted it, and Johnny took care of that. Guido, who goes down the drain with Cosmo or without him, can't do very much for Cosmo, no matter what he does. Because if Guido says Cosmo didn't know shit about serving Willie up with a little horseradish and mustard, everybody will know that Guido did and that he's lying about Cosmo to save Cosmo. And they will use that against Cosmo. You talk about the rock and the hard place; those two guys were in it. They're maybe no good, but Cosmo, I felt sorry for. He's not too charitable to have prevented Guido from doing what he did to Willie, but he's way too smart to have gotten involved in it like that."

"Apparently," I said, "he did."

"So," Edgar said, "the jury found. And that was what convinced me."

"To do what?" I said.

"Come back," he said. "I'm not used to people who leave bodies around. The people that I'm used to—politicians, people such as that—they accomplish the same thing, without a lot of tiresome cadavers turning up in cubes of steel that used to be Ford coupes. They get rid of the competition, but they usually leave the guy alive. I'm more interested in somebody like the Most Reverend Paul Doherty, Auxiliary Bishop of the Archdiocese of Boston."

"I saw your piece on him the first Sunday I was on the Cape," I said. "You never did tell me you were in Washington here to cover him. God, what a puff piece. You in bed with him or something?"

"You never asked me," Edgar said. "Paul Doherty is a piece of work. Known him for years, and he knows everybody. On a dry day, I always call Paul and come up roses. That guy knows how to be neat. There he sits, out at Holy Sepulchre in Weston, doing the Lord's work and beating the shit out of the abortionists. . . ."

"What?" I said.

"Doing the Lord's work," Edgar said. "What Paul does seldom leads to gaudy anecdotes. Paul is careful. Like all the guys I'm used to dealing with. To hell with these guys that resort to guns. Give me the dangerous kind that knifes you with a ballpoint pen. Or a neat little telephone call. That guy Don Bolles, the reporter out in Arizona, got blown up? Not me. Paul Doherty does it with novenas."

By now the buttons on my phone were flashing like a pinball machine. "Edgar," I said, "when're you coming down here?"

"Friday night," he said. "Friday afternoon, actually. I've got. . . ."

"You've got a flight," I said. "I don't care about your goddamned flight. Are you staying with Maggie?"

There was a long pause. "Edgar," I said, "I asked you a question. I asked you because I want to know where to reach you, not because I want to have you killed. I need some help. If you and Maggie're happy, I'm delighted for you. What I want to do is talk to you. Not complicate your life."

"Yes," he said.

"Call me," I said, "when you hit the deck."

That night I drank all four remaining Kronenburgs, from the plastic cup.

Twelve

Late on Friday afternoon, I let the lights start flashing on my phone once more, cracked two Kronenburgs, handed Edgar one of them, and leaned back in my chair. "So," I said.

"What's this help you say you need?" Edgar said.

"In good time," I said. "You never did tell me how you found out about the little frolic and detour I had on my vacation. As opposed to the vacation that I had with my family. My former family. Which was, by the way, awful, and not improved one bit by seeing you and Maggie at the ball game or watching you get on the Martha's Vineyard ferry."

"Where the hell were you?" Edgar said.

"I was in the skyviews at the ball game," I said, "with the young lady about whom you apparently know so much, and I was sitting on the deck at Baxter's Landing, eating fried clams with my devoted offspring and my bride the night you went to the island."

"I'm impressed," Edgar said. "Although I must say, from what I hear about your week with Kristin, I owe you a few hundred words for all the guff that you gave me about old Linda Morse."

"Thank you," I said. "I take that considering the source, and consider it high praise. How'd you find out?"

"Same way I find everything out," Edgar said. "I was covering Cosmo's crucifixion. . . ."

"I assume he got convicted," I said.

"Certainly did," Edgar said. "Conspiracy to do a whole lot of terrible things, accessory before, accessory after, and doing the wicked deeds as well. Got thirty years, the feds invoking this statute which about triples the punishment for anything they catch you doing if they can prove you were doing it as a ginzo moving in interstate commerce. Cosmo ain't young, and he ain't well neither. I think somebody else's gonna have to make sure the linen's changed at the Nifty View Motel, or whatever he calls it. I doubt Cosmo's gonna drink much more anisette before he checks out.

"Anyway," Edgar said, "like I said, Cosmo is smart. They hooked him, but I got some doubts about the way they hooked him. By implication, they also convicted him of being stupid, and that Cosmo is not.

"Cosmo does not go to court with guys that never go to court unless they got a guinea in the gravy that they're representing. Cosmo only goes to court with guys that only go to court when some goddamned public asshole sues General Motors for being a corporation, or something, and wants treble damages because he caught GM making Cadillacs as well as Pontiacs. Cosmo hired this big Boston firm that I think got an old friend of yours in it, and the guy that was trying the case with two pair of clean socks, calf-length, in his mouth, brought along a whole entourage of associates and spear carriers and other aspirants to financially secure futures, who are already walking around practicing looking worried.

"One of them," Edgar said, "the only one that I could talk to, was this young lady by the name of Wendy, who apparently has got a rather strong thing going with this friend of yours. Name of Franklin. She mostly works in antitrust, I gather, but she was in on this one. And since the only way that I could get any handle on what was going on at all in this trial I am supposed to be covering was to ask somebody who knew what was going on, who would tell me without going through a lot of rigamarole first, I had quite a lot of coffee with old Wendy. Who found me, by her own voluntary admission, quite charming. By which I think she meant to say that she likes men who remind her of her father, and that led to me saying that I was old enough to qualify and to her saying that she wished her sister, Kristin, would shape up and get herself a boyfriend with some ballast.

"This," Edgar said, "Wendy had high hopes Kristin might be doing when she took up with this Washington lawyer that was in town in August. But it didn't work. Wendy said. Out, that is. And she babbled on and on, and I in my usual fashion listened on and on, because you never know when somebody will tell you something that will be useful, and pretty soon I had a fairly thick book on your little interlude at the Parker House. Simple, huh? Just like I told you it was."

"Good," I said. "I hope things always stay as simple for you. Particularly, one or two of the things that're bothering me. I have got a little problem."

"As the captain of the *Titanic* said to the steward when he was asked if he wanted milk or sugar," Edgar said.

"Damned right," I said.

"Fire away," Edgar said.

"I plan to," I said. "I have got a kid. Actually, I have got two kids, but it's the oldest that concerns me, inasmuch as the youngest isn't producing enough semen yet to create further amusements for me."

"Frankie knock somebody's daughter up?" Edgar said.

"The lady's father seems to think so," I said. "The lady's doctor says that she's knocked up. The lady says Francis stood to stud for the happy event, and Francis long since took to boasting about having wet his end in her—'fucked her,' was the gentle term he used. So I am inclined to think that the lady is *enceinte* and that Francis is probably the proud father."

"Congratulations," Edgar said. "Myself, now that I've loped my pony for the doctor about eight times and come up the last two, so to speak, as sterile as an instrument that ever emerged untouched by human hands from the autoclave, I am inclined to think all males should be gelded at eleven. This would save everybody a lot of trouble, particularly the males."

"You're all right then?" I said. "It didn't fall off, after all?"

"Nope," Edgar said, "right as rain. Recovered nicely from the shock and indignity of it all, and the nice healthy pink look as well. Of course I may grow gill slits or something in a few years, but in the meantime, I can fuck my brains out, without so much as a by-your-leave."

"So I gathered," I said.

"That was tactless of me," Edgar said.

"Forget it," I said. "You've been fixed, and apparently you've fixed up a few more things as well. Including me. Now. I need something fixed, and apparently it's too late to make useful repairs on Francis, who has already done his dirty work."

"Look at it this way," Edgar said, "it could be worse. Could be fuckin' hard drugs, you know. You get a kid on those things, welcome to watching your own flesh and blood succumb to hepatitis from a dirty needle, or getting lobbed into one home after another while he screams about big snakes with feathers, and giant birds with teeth, in the room with him. Give me a traditional shotgun wedding. . . ."

"That's out," I said, "and stop trying to make me feel cheerful about this. The kid's far too young to get himself married. He's still eligible for Little League, for Christ sake. I'm not gonna have him raising babies while I'm still trying to get him to stop picking his nose at the dinner table. Jesus, it was all right with me if Mother Nature decided to mature them faster, but if she was gonna do it, she should've done it all at once, so they'd be ready for PTA meetings by the time they produced something to parent."

"It's improved nutrition," Edgar said. "They gobble up the milk and nourishing groceries, and they eat so many Twinkies at the same time you don't even notice all the chops and green beans that're also going down those traps they've got built into their heads. The boys're bigger now, at twelve, than our grandfathers were when they were carrying hod for the thieving Protestant contractors at twenty-one. Every time I see one of my daughter's little friends, the kid's increased another cup size."

"Yeah," I said, "well, if I'd've known that, I would've induced yaws or something a long time ago to hold the kid's build back until his brain got large enough to make him sensible enough to change a light bulb without shorting out the whole Potomac power system."

"Speaking of shorting out," Edgar said, "how about treating the young lady to a salting out? They run them in and out like greyhounds now, you know. Take their clothes off, spread their legs, sluice 'em down, and send 'em home. Safe, secure, and fairly cheap. Not like when the most prosperous families sent their errant females off for short vacations down in old San Juan, at inconvenient times, and the little flirts came back and gave the whole damned thing away by speaking fluent Spanish and playing with maracas."

"Edgar," I said, "did I not know you to be a devout Catholic, ardent in your fidelity to the principles of the Church as laid down by the Holy Father, I would take you seriously. And agree at once, I might add."

"Just for a minute," Edgar said, "pretend that you don't know and sort of roll the idea around in your mind, like a throat lozenge made from single-malt scotch whiskey. Because the laying down that you're concerned about right now was not done by the Holy Father, but by your little boy. In whom, I gather, you are not well pleased at all."

"Edgar," I said, "I am not only displeased—I am thoroughly pissed off. Things being what they are, I figured that sooner or later, if things went badly, I would need the name of a reliable bail bondsman to get the kid home for Easter dinner on time. If things went pretty well, as I hoped, I was resigned to a pot bust or two. I had my arguments already for the night when he came home in an orange bathrobe, his hair shaved down to one pigtail, with a fistful of brochures about Krishna, a new name swiped off a package of herbal tea, a concert of zither music, and unrealistic ideas of financing ten years of meditation in a cave in Nepal, out of my Keogh Plan.

"I have already beaten back four assaults on the Honda, Kawasaki, and Harley-Davidson fronts; established, I thought, once and for all, that I refuse to buy him a Corvette for his sixteenth birthday, no matter how much his marks might improve; seen to his more-or-less regular attendance at school, though to what purpose I am not entirely sure; and prevented him from housing a collection of poisonous serpents in the basement with such tact and delicacy, I believe, as to leave unscathed his zest for herpetological knowledge. I was prepared for trouble, and I had met successfully, I thought, those troubles that have come already. I was not prepared for him to get himself into a scrape that an eighteenth-century tenant farmer would've found familiar."

"The bogtrotters lacked the excellent medical services available to you and your offspring," Edgar said. "There's a difference between the local witch brewing up a potion of wormwood in a big iron pot last used to boil the goat for dinner and an MD in a New York clinic giving orders to a registered nurse. About the little bitch."

"It won't go, Edgar," I said. "If it would go, I would go for it. But Prominent Catholic Layman and I've agreed already that the choices're: marry them off, or she goes for a few months' visit with her nonexistent aunt in Florida."

"Well," Edgar said, "those're pretty much the alternatives. You're gonna have to pick one, I think."

"I am prepared to choose," I said. "Francis is also prepared to choose. In fact, Francis is so prepared to choose that he's waived his right to choose and has for once agreed to do whatever I say. If I tell him to wash his face and comb his hair and see if he can find a clean T-shirt, preferably one that does not have something rude painted on the front because he's about to go and get married, he will go obediently and get married. If I tell him to carry with him always the guilt of knowing that he connived in the murder of his unborn child, he would do that—although the prospective maternal grandfather won't—and perhaps look hangdog for two or three days. If I inform him that he is never to inquire after the location and happiness of his firstborn in the care and love of its adoptive parents, he will quite cheerfully do that. Very cheerfully, in fact, because Francis has the attention span of a flashbulb, and forgetting about one of his mistakes is a talent he enjoys in enormous measure."

"How about Jeanne?" Edgar said. "What does she think about this?"

"Jeanne has quite a lot on her plate right now," I said. "Or else she has very little on her plate at all. One or the other. I left her, as you know."

"I should say I'm sorry?" Edgar said. "She's a bitch."

"Oh, yeah," I said. "Well, you're the only one who thinks so. I'm a rat everywhere else. Ye gods, I thought divorce was like a small salad before lunch these days. If you didn't have one, it was probably because you were in the mood for soup. If you did, and you looked around you, just about everyone else was having one, too.

"Isn't so, I find. Women still married that I scarcely know look at me like the fellows at the Yorktown and Valley Forge reunion catching a glimpse of General Benedict Arnold. Women that aren't married right now 've got a different expression, which is just as unsettling, in its own way. Married men think I'm going to hell if they're happy, and going to heaven if they're not. I feel like a scab that isn't quite ripe on the body of somebody with no willpower."

"I know it," Edgar said. "Divorce is the middle-aged form of influenza of the emotions. The ones that've had it are morbidly curious to see if you'll survive, like they did or did not, and they plan to watch you carefully, in case you know something that they don't and somehow come through it with all banners flying. The ones that haven't had it wonder if it's contagious and whether there's some symptoms that you've got that they should be on the lookout for, in their beloved spouses. Or themselves."

"I almost feel like I've got a moral obligation to go all to pieces," I said. "Like people'll be disappointed if I don't drink myself into a stupor before ten each morning or take to chasing blondes with huge tits naked through the halls of Congress."

"Otherwise, you're taking it too lightly," Edgar said. " 'Abandoning his wife and family like that.' 'Best years of her life.' 'Those lovely children.' "

" 'That beautiful home,' " I said.

"Right," Edgar said.

"Who the fuck do they think bought that beautiful goddamned home that he's not allowed to live in anymore?" I said. "Just out of curiosity, I mean."

"You're getting the hang of it," Edgar said. "Give you a week or so, you'll be just as bitter and nasty as the rest of us. How's Jeanne taking it?"

"Like she'd been preparing all her life for the part," I said. "Carrying on bravely in the aftermath of the slap in the face that I gave her, after all those years. Keeping the family together. Spending every fucking dime that she can get her hands on. Having root canals and caps and. . . ."

"They all do that," Edgar said. "They all get their teeth fixed the minute there's no more of your shirts in the bureau of the master bedroom. Honest to God, you'd think it was a horse auction, and the first thing a new man was gonna do was fold their lips back and look at their choppers."

"Then there's the other variety of medicals," I said.

"Right," Edgar said, "the gynecologist. They go every fifteen minutes. That's another thing they all do. I dunno whether Goldfinger's better'n what they were getting—although, in Mary Claire's case, it has to be, beause she goes for it a lot more often—or it's that they think they better have the running gear in order, case some studly golf pro takes a fancy to them. But they all do that, too. I think there's probably a cassette course that they sell through the mail in the women's magazines, on What to Do Next, After You've Finally Driven the Bastard Out, and Have to Settle for Making His Life Miserable at Long Range."

"I'm beginning to sound like a recording myself," I said.

"Sure you are," Edgar said. "There're things we always do, too. Got your pots and pans yet?"

"No," I said, "as a matter fact, I haven't. Now that you mention it."

"Didn't think so," Edgar said. "This is because you don't really have time to go shopping for kitchenware. Partly because you've got to work. And partly because there's a part of your brain that will stay married for several months and believes that you *have* pots and pans, because they came with her, from some goddamned bridal shower, when you got married. That happens to be the part of the brain that is responsible for man seeing to the purchase of a pot in which to cook his dinner. It took care of that matter years ago. It does not wish to be bothered at this late date about pots, because it is thinking about how soon it will have to replace the air-conditioner filters, and get an estimate on a new roof, and whether there is any merit in the lady's claim that the carpet sweeper has seen better days and needs to be replaced.

"The purchasing agent of the brain," Edgar said, "does not like to think that it has to start out from scratch, assembling a whole new inventory of spoons and can openers and knives, and something to sharpen them with. It does not like its job

234

very much anyway and will do almost anything it can to put it off.

"What happens, what will happen, is this: some morning you will get so goddamned pissed off at having no pot in which to heat water for instant coffee, because you have also no machine that makes regular coffee, that you get through to the purchasing agent. The purchasing agent happens to need its coffee in the morning. 'Now look,' you will say, 'facts is facts: you are not getting any coffee this morning, because you have been avoiding reality and pretending that you did your blasted job and got a pot for us.'

"And that afternoon," Edgar said, "you will cancel two appointments, and go to the drugstore, and buy a whole mess of junk in a box labeled 'Pots and Pans.' Also a pretty good coffeemaker and some cheap kitchenware that'll bend if you get the forks in the dishwasher, tines down, and a couple knives that the handles'll fall off the third time you use them. You will lug all that shoddy merchandise home, feeling very self-sufficient and very triumphant over her. You will pile it all in the kitchen and go out to the goddamned Safeway in your suit. You will march up and down the aisles with your cart, with all the ladies in curlers around you, buying toilet paper and paper napkins, and awful-looking crockery that's on sale, and plastic dinner dishes that're guaranteed never to break, but Jesus God, will they scratch every time you cut a piece of meat on them. You will get some coffee, and dry cream, and sugar, and chops, and tomatoes, and steaks. And go home."

"I will," I said.

"You will," Edgar said. "You will cook just about the worst dinner that you ever had in your life—well, maybe *you* won't, considering the cooking Jeanne did—and you will eat it in a grouchy mood because you forgot to get butter for the frozen green beans, dressing for the salad, salt for the meat and ketchup for the quickie fries that you made on a sheet of tinfoil in your nifty oven, on account of how you forgot to get a broiler pan."

"I thought you said I just bought a whole set of pots and pans," I said. "At the drugstore."

"You did," Edgar said. "And you thought there was a broiler pan in that sixty-three piece set, not knowing they were counting the covers to the pots, and the little black knobs on the tops of the pots, to get that number of pieces, and because you were in too much of a hurry, cutting classes as you were, to read what was in the box. Which, of course, was why you went to the drugstore to get the pots, instead of to a department store or a pot shop, where if you bought a set of pots, it would've cost you twice as much, but would've been about four times better. You don't know anything about pots. You haven't had any reason to learn anything about pots. That's why you went to the drugstore to get pots, you flaming asshole. Would you go to the pot shop to get something for your bronchial asthma? Nope. But you went to the drugstore to get pots, because you've been going to the drugstore to get coffee ever since you found yourself living in a place with no coffeemaker, and you've seen the big boxes of cheap pots on display in the drugstore every morning ever since."

"I see," I said.

"Someday," Edgar said, "you will get yourself a decent place to live, and you will throw those pots out the goddamned window. You will buy the most beautiful pots and pans and knives and stuff that you can find. Paul Bocuse of Lyons would be content with the pots and pans and soufflé dishes that he would find in the kitchens of divorced men who have finally gotten themselves resettled, because us guys know about pots now, boy, and we will never forget.

"In the meantime," Edgar said, "you will get one hell of a lot of mileage out of that drugstore cookery stuff. Because every time you use it, which will not be very often, you will get mad at her again and cut another thirty bucks a month off of what you are prepared to give to her in alimony. Cheap utensils keep the teeth nicely filed. Lastly, you will learn much about good restaurants, or else you will starve to death and not have to pay any alimony anyway."

"Can't I short-circuit any of this?" I said.

"It's permitted," Edgar said. "It's just not done very often. Guys in your situation're very concerned that people in the shop will think they're Going All to Pieces, like you said. So guys that were perfectly confident about taking a couple days off to set up housekeeping when they first got married never even consider taking a day or two off to set up housekeeping for themselves when they first get unmarried. And you feel foolish doing it anyway, putting together a fucking trousseau for yourself."

"I may just break the pattern," I said. "I was depressed enough before you started talking. Jesus, from the way Jeanne acts, you'd think my name just turned up as *Gauleiter* at Dachau."

"What set her off?" Edgar said. "I thought you folks got along together pretty well, no screaming fits or walking out that I ever heard about. No scenes at dinner parties. Always the charming pictures in what used to be Washington *Dossier,* big white smiles and well-coiffed hair, the suave one-liners in the gossip columns, all that high-calorie shit. Ducks on a pond in the springtime sun. What happened?"

"Piecing things together, as best I have been able," I said, "Jeanne apparently decided to react to my platonic friendship with your new sidekick, Mistress Capeless."

"Bit late in the day, I should think," Edgar said. "What I heard, that'd been going on since right after MacArthur had his ticker-tape parade, and Jeanne seldom had much trouble finding out what was going on in this town, if the cutting remarks she made to me were any indication."

"I did something stupid," I said. "When Jeanne had the kids up visiting her folks in Poughkeepsie, I spent about as much time in that house as I had to, and it doesn't take me long to resupply with shirts and leave the suits off for the maid to have cleaned. I probably averaged a good forty-five minutes to an hour every week. Paid the kid that cuts the lawn, patted the dog, had a drink, and wrote a check out to the maid.

"Now," I said, "Rita's a nice lady, and even if she didn't want to keep her mouth shut, it wouldn't make much difference because Jeanne doesn't speak much Jamaican. The difficulty evidently came up when Jeanne called one afternoon to tell Rita to save the papers from that day, because there was something in the *Post* that Sally Quinn'd done that Jeanne had heard about, and it left one of her most cherished enemies for dead. Jeanne apparently wanted to make sure I hadn't taken the thing to work with me or thrown it out. Rita blabbed: 'No, Miz Quinn. Mister got all the papers right on the dining table where I put them.'

"Now," I said, "I've got this thing about accumulating junk. Particularly old newspapers. You read 'em, you throw 'em out."

"Thanks a lot," Edgar said.

I ignored him. "I've made speeches on that point. So Jeanne's suspicions were aroused, and she kept after Rita, who of course thought Miz Quinn was just talking about newspapers, and pretty soon she has the poor black lady so bedazzled she was hearing about beds that didn't need to be made very often, and bathrooms that didn't need any cleaning, and all the rest of it. From which she concluded that very few people were actually living in that beautiful home, and with which she was able to extract a whole barrelful of information from people who would otherwise have volunteered nothing but who were not one whit reluctant to have information pried out of them. By the time I got to the Cape, in August, I had a telephone credit card bill for calls made from Poughkeepsie to Washington that staggered me when I received it. But that was after I got back to Washington, and by then I knew what Jeanne had obtained by using the credit card. Apparently I overstepped the bounds of a harmless little affair that she could tolerate."

"She got somebody else?" Edgar said.

"Doubt it," I said. "Other than a network of leaks that the FBI would envy, I doubt it."

"Too bad," Edgar said.

"Well," I said, "she does have me, of course. On those inevitable occasions when I simply have to talk to her, she gets it into me pretty good at every opportunity, and that probably distracts her. This thing with Francis, for example, is, I will have you know, entirely my fault, apparently because I neglected shamefully to instruct him in the rules of the Church about premarital sex, and she has declared the matter to be exclusively within my jurisdiction. Pontius Pilate would be proud of her position."

"I assume you said that to her," Edgar said.

"Afraid I did," I said.

"Right," Edgar said. "Well, I can't blame you. I got the credit when the middle kid flunked math, and she was responsible for the astonishing improvement that resulted from the special tutoring that cost me four-hundred-fifty bucks. Heads, she wins; tails, I lose."

"Right," I said. "Another beer?"

"Yup," Edgar said. The beers were brought. "So I gather," Edgar said, "that as far as Jeanne's concerned, you can do anything you want about Frank's early flowering. Or deflowering, depending on how you look at it. Except that she retains the right and obligation, later, to disapprove of whatever it is that you choose to do, and use it as the explanation for any further shit the kid may decide to wade in."

"I think that would be a fair statement," I said.

"This leaves the young lady and her daddy," Edgar said. "What are their respective views on this unfortunate situation?"

"The young lady," I said, "I have not spoken to. I have

not asked to speak to the young lady, but I see no point in it. I don't believe the lady has any views, and I'm not sure she should be allowed to, if she is dumb enough to let Frank Quinn get into her pants. Daddy is a vastly different matter."

"Who is Daddy?" Edgar said.

"Daddy is one Torbert Lynch," I said. "Employed as some sort of factotum for the Department of Corporations and Taxation in the Commonwealth of Massachusetts."

"You know," Edgar said, "so far as I know, I never heard the guy's name before. I probably never laid eyes on him, and I was certainly never introduced to him. But you've already told me enough. He's about forty-two. Red face. Five-ten. Overweight. Not much overweight, but overweight. Red face, partly from sun he got down at Green Harbor. . . ."

"Dennis," I said, "The Lynch family had a cottage at Dennis this summer, which is what put Judith within fucking distance of young Francis Quinn, whose family had a cottage in Dennisport."

"Dennis," Edgar said, "I stand corrected. Good war record, which he got without ever leaving the United States, and Veteran's Preference on the Civil Service thing when he got out. Graduated Holy Cross, majored in business administration, accounting. Weekly communicant. Four lovely children. Lives in a nice suburb that he can't afford, and worries about that all the time. Along with everything else."

"Weston," I said.

"Ahhh," Edgar said, "the Church of the Holy Sepulchre. The plot begins to thicken, and it was roughly the viscosity of me sainted mother's terrible beef stew as it was. Is Torbert, perhaps, one Prominent Catholic Layman, aforementioned, in that particular church?"

"According to what Torbert tells me," I said, "when he isn't screaming into the handset, that is a rather understated way of putting it."

"Papal Knight?" Edgar said.

"Not as yet," I said. "I think he would've mentioned it if

he was. But he's certainly got ambitions in that direction."

"I see," Edgar said. "Well, not that I need to ask, but what does Torbert think should be done to resolve this little difficulty, aside from a decree making his daughter retroactively virginal and a postulant in the Convent of the Sisters of Charity?"

"Torbert seems to be a little short in the Ideas Department," I said.

"I'm sure he always has been," Edgar said. "Probably never crossed Torbert's mind that his nubile little daughter was entertaining impure thoughts and consorting with horny little boys of similar outlook. Not till recently, at least. I bet he's got the idea now, though."

"He seems to have gotten the hang of it pretty well, actually," I said. "The trouble is, I don't know how to make it happen that Francis and Judith never rolled around in the dark with no clothes on, making lascivious noises, lubricious sounds, and, horror of horrors, babies. I tried the abortion route on Torbert, and it was like I shoved a blowtorch up his respectable Catholic arse. I tried adoption on Torbert, and he was nearly as scandalized by the potential damage to *his* reputation that would happen if his daughter didn't start parochial school in the fall as he had been by the casual violence to the doctrine which would have been occasioned by a harmless operation. Which operation would have let her sail through school as though nothing happened. He more or less agreed with me about the marriage thing, more because I think he hates Francis than because he disapproves of teenage marriage."

"And how do you feel?" Edgar said. "Considering that you seem to be the only player on the roster not currently on the mentally disabled list, and somebody obviously needs to do something?"

"Look," I said, "I don't even know how I feel about abortion. I never needed one myself, and I guess, having no daughters, and a wife with ligatures in the necessary places, I assumed I never would be forced to get it sorted out. Stupid of me."

"Stupid of you," Edgar said.

"Still," I said, "I don't particularly want to cram my lack of conviction down anybody else's throat. I don't care if Judy has the baby. I don't care if Judy doesn't have the baby. I won't submit to Judy marrying Frank, unless one of Baby Doc Duvalier's Tontons Macoutes gets ahold of me and starts removing my fingernails with a pliers, but otherwise, I'm flexible."

"So," Edgar said, "Torbert should bite the bullet and put Judy in some home where all the young ladies have big bellies, in order that some good Catholic family, childless, should be able to afford a lovely infant a good home."

"I think so," I said.

"And somebody should talk to Torbert about this," Edgar said. "Somebody whom Torbert would respect."

"I wouldn't mind," I said. "I'm spending more time on the phone with Torbert'n I am with the people on the Hill, who are responsible for much of the living that I make."

"Peter," Edgar said, "I am beginning to see how you make such an excellent living for yourself. You are a consummate diplomat. If I asked Bishop Doherty to flog old Torbert into an abortion parlor, he would rend his cassock and eject me from the room. But if I ask Bishop Doherty to counsel Torbert on what Holy Mother Church believes to be the only acceptable answer to unwanted pregnancy, he will be more than happy to summon the goddamned prelate fucker into chambers, allow him to kiss his ring, and make damned sure that Torbert Does the Right Thing. Particularly if you agree to pay for the confinement."

"I will, I will," I said. "It'll save me hundreds over the cost of returning Torbert's calls."

"Peter," Edgar said, "consider it done. Get me a phone, and if you are free for dinner, I will be pleased to buy."

I got Pauline on the intercom. "Get us," I said, "a table for two at the Jockey Club, and tell them to have two bottles of the Nuits-Saint-Georges breathing now. Eight o'clock."

"It's only six, Mister Quinn," Pauline said.

"And find me an empty office for Mister Lannin," I said. "Edgar's got a couple calls to make before we leave."

Thirteen

And so, commencing that evening, late in September, and continuing not only through quite late that evening in September, but well into January of the following year, I saw quite a lot of Edgar. Sometimes I saw him for lunch, and sometimes I saw him for drinks. Other times I saw him for dinner. Often I joined him and Maggie for dinner at Executive Towers. The first time was a trifle awkward, for about the first split second, until Maggie embraced me. Maggie is a good cook and also a fine lady. And I was hungry. There is much to be said for all of those things.

"Edgar," I said, over the steak au poivre at the Jockey Club that September night, exhaling the residue of peppercorns and fine wine across the otherwise-unsullied table, "your turn."

"My night in the barrel," he said, equally noisome.

"As you say," I said. "How come? You hate this place. You got out of it. I didn't say that you were wrong, notice. I said that you hated it, and you got out. Now you're telling me you're coming back. If you hated it, and it was killing you, and you got out, how come you're coming back?"

"Well," Edgar said, his mouth full of prime beef, "the first thing is certain obligations."

"Your family," I said.

He shook his head. "Nope," he said. He said it very firmly. "Those obligations I have not done bad on. I have not done well on them either. But I have not done bad. I have done the best I was permitted to do, whether by external forces or the lamentable limitations of my own deficient character."

"So," I said, "why come back?"

He chewed. "Good question," he said. "First, I have other obligations. I have not thought a hell of a lot about them in the past three hundred years, but I have them, and the fact that I have gotten away with not thinking about them does not mean that I don't have them." I was going to say something, but he munched and continued.

"I have obligations to myself," Edgar said. "If I don't keep my lily-white nostrils clear of the shit, when the Devil comes through Saturday, water-skiing behind the speedboat and leaving six-foot wakes behind him, I will probably drown. I have to keep myself alive. If I die, this will not help the kids, which will be a matter of comparative insignificance to me if I am dead. But it also will not help me, if I am dead. Let alone them. Because me being dead is not a matter of comparative insignificance to me. It is a matter of central importance.

"Then," Edgar said, "there is the matter of my obligation to the paper."

"Oh, come on," I said.

Edgar had his mouth full again, this time with wine and baked potato. I was grateful that he swallowed before answering. "Don't be cynical," he said. "Them fellows've made bail for me more years I care to count. They're no good, mean, and vicious, but they carried me when I was tipsy and looked out for me when I was hurt. And when there was not very much going on between my ears, they still published what I wrote and paid me an honest wage. I've pissed off Senators, annoyed Vice Presidents, gone to the mat with Presidents, and been quite disrespectful in the direction of august personages confirmed to serve as Secretaries in the Cabinet to the President of the United States. What I have not done in person, I have done in print. Their print."

"That was what you were supposed to do," I said.

"It was," Edgar said, "but they took quite a lot of flak from publishing the words I wrote, because I was supposed to write those words. You think Paul Doherty likes the pranging that I give him when he gets up to promulgate the latest received wisdom on some doctrinal point that the Cardinal wants him to present before a Senate committee?"

"If he doesn't," I said, "he's got a weird way of getting even. Doing favors for your freinds."

"Nope," Edgar said. "Wrong again. Just like you, the Bishop has a good idea of what is possible. And that is all. No, I'm wrong. What is right, given what is possible. Same thing with the guys that run the paper and the guys that run the desk. They know all the crappy things I've done when I was off the reservation, and it seems that they don't give a shit.

"The trouble is," Edgar said, "I know very damned right well that they do give a shit. And furthermore, that the things that I was doing, then, created a considerable amount of furor for those folks. Which, somehow, they handled without bothering me about it. Without ever mentioning it, in fact.

"Now," Edgar said, "this is better treatment'n I've generally gotten from people near and dear to me. So, it occurs to me, if they're losing the chief of the Washington bureau to the Stanford version of the Nieman Fellowships for somewhere near a year, and if I have gotten some small smidgen of my equilibrium back, or maybe a whole lot of it, maybe it is time for me to resume behaving like an adult and get some other adults off a hot seat. Go back to work."

I drank some more wine. I gagged somewhat on the question, but asked it anyway, and got the answer that I had expected.

"Edgar," I said, sounding like a man gargling turpentine, "are you in love?"

Edgar drank some more wine, too. "Yup," he said. "Wanna make something out of it?"

As a matter of fact, I did. And since I was in a self-indulgent mood, I did make something of it, on fairly frequent occasions from week to week thereafter. They still go on.

"So," I said, "you're coming back down here."

"Yup," Edgar said.

"And you're gonna live with Maggie," I said.

"Already am," Edgar said.

"And you're probably gonna get married," I said.

"Yup," Edgar said. "Soon's I can talk her into it."

"And you're gonna finish your book," I said.

"Yup," Edgar said. "Soon as I can talk me into it."

"About how long do you think that is gonna take?" I said.

"About a week," Edgar said. "Give or take a day or so."

"The book or Maggie?" I said.

"Maggie," Edgar said. "The book isn't due until next year. But I want Maggie now. And this, Peter," he said, "is the end of my tutorial with you. This is the last lecture, and I've called off the final. From now on we will meet again as equals, and I will offer you instructions in the art of life only upon your express request.

"I waltzed into your office, with my little marital problem, a few short months ago at Maggie's request."

"Holy Jesus," I said, "were you people hanging out then, too?"

"Holy Jesus was one of the phrases that I used, as I recall," Edgar said. "I hadn't heard from Maggie in months. Years even. I knew she was divorced, and I'd been in love with her for years, but I was up in Boston, and she was down here in Washington. And she was doing well while I was turning into one of those dog-eared, functioning alcoholics of which my line of work's got more'n yours, or maybe it's the other way around. What'd she need a bum like me for? I did the

Bogart part in *Casablanca:* I loved her enough to send her away with the other man. I let her go to you. You lost her. Dummy.

"I asked her what she wanted, and she said she was worried about you. She said she knew how I must feel, having her ask me to help the guy who got her when I didn't, but she knew that you and I were old friends, and she didn't know anybody else to call. She said you had a rotten marriage, no fun, and that although she'd tried to get you straightened out and away from that bitch, whether you went with Maggie or with somebody else, she couldn't manage it by herself. And so, would I help? And so, because I cherish you both, I screwed up my courage and said that I would."

"It must've been hard as hell for you," I said, feeling the wine and the sentiment wash over me.

"Snap out of it, my friend," Edgar said. "It was the best thing that ever happened to me. Because you see, I did screw up my courage. It was the first time in a long time that I had done that. Thinking about somebody besides myself. And I began to plot and scheme, extraordinary skills of mine left long neglected. As soon as Mary Claire began to raise hell with the alimony, I had my excuse, and I started in.

"Did you think, Peter, that I expected to win that case? I did not. But there was no way I was going to let her get that Cost of Living increase without a fight, and I couldn't fight it myself—I needed a lawyer. And that was how I got my hook into you."

"And all the while, you fucker," I said, "you were plotting how to get your hook into Maggie."

"No," Edgar said, "as a matter of fact, I was not. Wistfulness was most of it. Until July, when I began to see that you weren't doing her any good, and you weren't doing you any good either, because you were just gonna end up making your life miserable with Jeanne and being unfair to Maggie, who deserves full-time attention. Then wistfulness changed to determination, and if you'd thought about it, Counselor, you would've reflected that July day on how it was I knew so much about how you could probably have a nice cookout on the beach at her house on the Vineyard."

"You son of a bitch," I said. "You're both sons of bitches."

"Thank you," Edgar said. "As a matter of fact, we're pretty proud of ourselves. And you, too. Because you're a son of a bitch yourself, but now you've stopped pretending that you aren't. That is our accomplishment."

I called for Rémy Martin, Very Special Old Pale Champagne Cognac, and we drank to Maggie.

That, by the end of the year, was more or less the way things stood. Judy Lynch, according to her father, reflected on her situation, made a good examination of conscience, decided on fidelity to Christian doctrine, and spent the fall and early winter visiting some nonexistent aunt in the Southland. Torbert was not elevated to the Papacy, but he came close. Francis was somewhat subdued by his experience—not as subdued as I would have liked, but somewhat. Terry remained a little prick, but seemed unlikely to attempt anything with the equipment that he had. Jeanne grew tired of maligning me and gave it up. She did not give up cheaply, but she gave up.

I shared, and that is the right word, Christmas Eve with Edgar and Maggie. We had Dom Pérignon, turkey stuffed with oysters and truffles, Château Mouton Rothschild, which Edgar had come close to stealing, fresh strawberries that Maggie had somehow obtained, with *crème fraîche,* espresso, and Bras Arme cognac. When we opened presents, theirs was field box seats to twenty Red Sox games at Fenway Park, which Franklin had gored his whole firm to obtain. And mine was equally as good: twenty Yankee games, four seats each, at the Stadium. "Two for us," Maggie said, "one for you, and a player to be named later." After diligent questioning, it turned out that Edgar had done several mean things to somebody on the *Times,* who owed him a favor, to accomplish that.

"You talk about Washington lawyers," I said to Edgar. "You guys talk less'n we do."

"Of course," Edgar said. "Nobody prints what we say. Not if they're careful."

" 'God rest ye merry, gentlemen,' " Maggie began. Edgar and I joined her in the sentiments about dismay. And so began at least another year or so, the thirty-second, with Edgar.

That winter, the Sox got Torrez, Eckersley, and Remy. But the Yankees came from fourteen back and won the pennant at Fenway in the play-off, while Edgar sobbed. Edgar is not a bad fellow, and he is a loyal friend, but nobody can have everything.

6-7-79
(1)